Take My Hand

Kathy Szymanski

Copyright © 2013 Kathy Szymanski
All rights reserved. No part of this publication may be reproduced, distributed, or transmitted in any form or by any means, including photocopying, recording, or other electronic or mechanical methods, without the prior written permission of the publisher, except in the case of brief quotations embodied in reviews. For permission requests, you may contact the publisher via KathySzymanski@bevcomm.net

Publishing and Imprint by Change The World Books
A division of Szymanski's S. I., Inc.
www.ChangeTheWorldBooks.com

ISBN: 0615774849
ISBN-13: 978-0615774848 (Change The World Books)

DEDICATION

This, my first novel, is dedicated to my dad. An amazing man, he helped form me into the person I am today. Dad always encouraged me to follow the path I wanted, regardless of what others around me were doing. That principle has served me well in life. Thanks, Dad.

ACKNOWLEDGEMENTS

My first and most important thanks goes to my Lord and Savior who has blessed me with a talent for writing, and the Holy Spirit for inspiration. Thanks also to the 6th grade nun (sorry, Sister, I don't recall your name). Sister "made" me enter a writing contest and I won statewide, a seed was planted.

Thanks to Lisa, my friend, to whom I first submitted my very raw, unpolished story. She encouraged me to turn it into a novel.

My editor, Deb, provided me with helpful feedback and suggestions.

And of course, my beloved husband of 36 years, who never complained (well, not much) about the endless paper spewing out of his laser printer, or my smiling request to please insert (again) a new toner cartridge. His support and confidence in me has been invaluable.

Chapter 1
The Beginning

Steve took the office stairs two at a time on this early, bright Hawaiian morning. As usual, he was first to arrive, and as he went about the task of preparing the coffee, he mentally planned his day: paperwork, running down leads on a few cases, following up on some interviews.

Dazzling sunlight from one of a half dozen floor-to-ceiling windows played across his face as he strode to his teakwood desk. A gold Cross pen in a holder, a gift from the governor, was centered at the front. The blotter held a small pile of files, corners aligned perfectly. Crossing the fifteen feet from his door to his desk, his attention was captured by a boy curled up on the couch, his face to the wall as he nestled on his arm, the thin chest rising and falling in rhythmic sleep, and Steve tripped a step in shock. The logic and order drilled into the former Commander at the Naval Academy in Annapolis then kicked in. Glancing at the windows and doors, he noticed they were untouched, with no evidence of breaking and entering. Scanning the room, he was sure that all appeared as it had been left the night before. *How did that kid get in here? Who was he? Why was he here?*

With steel blue eyes drawn back to the child, Steve cocked his head to the side. The boy's sandy hair was shaggy, definitely in need of a haircut, but not greasy or stringy. Dark circles under his eyes and a slender, gaunt face painted an uncomfortable picture. The old and shabby but clean clothes had splatters of faded stains; some rips had been patched with crude repair jobs. *Well, he's not a rich kid, nor properly taken care of. Scrawny, thin.*

Steve moved to the sofa and bent over the boy, about to shake him awake, when the shoes caught his eye. His hand returned to his side. The boy's worn sneakers were placed neatly, side by side, on the floor near the couch. The lad had the courtesy to remove them before settling himself onto the sofa. Not just kicking them off, but precisely lining them up. Impressed by this tiny detail- perhaps that was the subconscious motivation that made Steve change his mind. He stood up straight, deciding to let the small intruder sleep instead of rousing him to get answers to questions. As he backed away, Steve noticed holes worn in the heels of threadbare socks.

Moving on auto-pilot to his desk chair, his mind worked on this puzzle. A shudder ran through his entire body, as he struggled to identify the emotions and feelings surging through him. There was something, in his subconscious, a fleeting, not-uncomfortable sensation which didn't annoy Steve, nor upset him; it just was. *Could the boy be related to someone I know? One of the staff? The child of a friend or acquaintance?*

He shook his head as memories of his own childhood began to bubble to the surface; his stomach growled, surprising him. *Was that true hunger, or a memory of hunger? I'm not hungry — I just ate an hour ago.*

Knees drawn to chest, his free arm hugging himself, the boy was scrunched up. A shiver gripped Steve. *My office is warm, why am I chilled?* He pushed down the thought that the cold was a memory.

From the closet, Steve retrieved a blanket he kept handy for the occasional long nights when he worked 'til the wee hours and slept there instead of heading home. He gently draped the coverlet over his uninvited guest.

This boy, whom he had never seen before, had gotten into his locked office. *I'm not upset or angry. Why not?* At each window and door, he ran his long fingers along the surfaces, checking the locks for scratches or any sign of illegal entry. Nothing. He moved out onto the second floor balcony — everything was as it should be — no dirt on the tiles, no broken vines where someone might have climbed up. He clenched his jaw and furrowed his eyebrows. A small boy sleeping on his office couch at 6:30 a.m. didn't fit in his ordered world. *What am I supposed to do now? Why does all this remind me of my childhood? Nah....it doesn't, really. Or does it?*

Unable to contain his curiosity, he got up and walked over to the couch again, intending to awaken and question the boy. As he reached to jostle him awake he stopped, hand in midair. A memory of himself as a child came unbidden into his consciousness. He had been woken harshly from a sound slumber, startled and terrified, by a drunken father. Steve studied the small peaceful face in front of him; no wrinkled brow or tension visible. *No, I'll let him sleep.*

After sitting five minutes with his fingers templed to form a triangle, Steve blocked out the word QUIET on a simple sign and taped the sheet of paper to the outside of his office door. At his secretary's desk, he put a similar one, telling Lisa no calls, no paging, and he didn't want his phone to ring.

Something about this child was touching him deeply, bringing up emotions foreign to Steve — protectiveness, sympathy, paternal concern, and ones he had trouble identifying. The paperwork he had intended to tackle remained untouched. His gaze kept heading back to the couch to study the lad. A pale complexion, protruding cheek bones, stick-thin arms indicated he hadn't been well fed. *I'll have to get some food into him.* What else was there? Aloneness?

The hairs on the back of Steve's neck stood on end. For a second an image flashed through his mind. A small boy lying scared and alone on a thin mattress in a shabby farmhouse, late — well past midnight— tired and trying to sleep, but with ears perked, listening and waiting for the father to come home. He would hope and pray the man wouldn't be drunk, but rather exhausted and wanting to fall into bed. Or else too boozed up to be aware of anything and pass out. Steve pushed the image away.

The outer office door creaked open and the cheerful whistle of Marco reached his ears as his second-in-command entered; Steve smiled. He had met Marco in Korea during the war and recruited the man seven years his junior shortly after he opened his business. Hawaiians would call their relationship a kaikaina/ aikane bond. Big brother/ little brother. Steve and Marco, along with the rest of the office staff, were ohana — family. A strong connection existed amongst them all, though in particular between these two. More than once they had saved each other's lives. With no wife and his only sister living far away in California, Marco was the sole person whom Steve trusted without reserve. No secrets from him.

The tune Marco whistled reminded Steve of a day years earlier when he sat in the audience as Marco got his master's degree. The younger man, holding his magna cum laude award, at 5' 8", was the shortest of the group posing for pictures. The woman sitting in front of Steve elbowed her companion, "Who is that kid? He looks all of about fourteen."

"Oh, he's Marco Atkins. Actually, he's twenty-two, really smart. I think he won third place at the North Shore Sunset Beach Semi-Annual Surfing Competition for amateurs last month. He dated Annie Hopkins — you know how finicky she is about guys."

That was Marco — intelligent, athletic, popular with the ladies. Steve grinned as he figured Marco was probably thinking of his date the night before and imagined the stunned expression that would be on his face as he would spot the unusual sign taped to the office door. Sure enough, a head appeared around the heavy koa wood frame. Steve motioned him in, a finger to his lips indicating silence. Marco saw the sleeping boy and, with a slight tilt of his chin, turned his gaze towards his friend and boss, who shrugged and quietly apprised Marco of what little he knew. Surprised that Steve hadn't done much, in a low voice he said, "Steve, why don't you just wake him up and ask him?"

"No, Marco, let him rest. Look at him, he's beat. He needs to sleep." Steve pointed to the phone. "Order in a couple of big breakfasts; milk, eggs, toast — the works."

A half hour later the child began to murmur and awaken. Steve went to the couch, crouched down, smiling, and stayed a few feet away so as to not appear threatening in any way.

The boy bolted upright, eyes wide open and focused, going in an instant from the disorientation of slumber to instant alertness.

"Good morning, sleepyhead."

As he relaxed his rigid posture slightly, the boy said, "Good morning, sir. Mr. O'Shaughnessy?"

Alerted by the voices, Marco entered and stood by the office door.

"Yes. And you are?" Steve asked in a kind voice.

The boy hesitated. "Tommy."

"Tommy, are you hungry? Marco got two big breakfasts. Usually we share, but he didn't realize I had already eaten this morning. You take mine; the food will go to waste otherwise."

Marco's wondering about me, why I'm not laying into him about breaking into my office. About why I'm giving him breakfast. Steve nodded, and the associate brought the trays in and set them on the coffee table. Another slight nod from Steve indicated to Marco to chow down. Willingly, he complied.

"Mr. O'Shaughnessy, I need to tell you something. It's important!"

Steve shook his head. "No, Tommy, breakfast first. Whatever it is can wait."

Tommy surveyed the tray of food, his gaze going from the huge meal to Steve and back again.

His lip quivered slightly as his teeth bit the inside flesh. He sighed and fidgeted. Steve's mouth was closed in a thin line, and his arms were crossed over his chest as he sensed the internal battle warring within the boy's mind.

A few tears pooled in the Tommy's eyes as he mumbled, "Mr. O'Shaughnessy, I have no money to buy this."

Steve's heart practically broke. "No one asked you to, Tommy." *Why does he think he has to pay for this?*

Tommy maintained eye contact, those tears almost brimming over.

"Eat, Tommy."

And the boy obeyed. He didn't exactly devour the food, which would have been impolite, but ate heartily. Steve smiled as Marco, deducing some of the underlying story, rubbed his stomach. "Here, Tommy, I'm done, finish mine, too."

The two adults made small talk as the child ate. They asked nothing of Tommy, and he didn't offer any comments. And Steve watched him, observing, the feeling in the center of his soul was getting stronger. A kind of electricity was spreading out from his core, zipping through every nerve ending, heightening his senses and intuition. Almost like some sort of connection — bond — something way beyond an ordinary association. Just floating on the edge of his consciousness, but powerfully strong in his subconscious.

The penetrating scrutiny from Marco's ocean blue eyes reached deep into Steve's. "Steve, you okay?"

"Hmmmm... yeah, Marco... there's something... I don't know what... but yeah... I'm fine."

Tommy finished his feast and wiped his mouth. "Thank you."

Sitting up straight, Steve considered how best to get the answers he needed. In a gentle tone, he began. "Tommy, how'd you get in here?"

"The vent window on the lanai was open. I climbed up the outside to the veranda and came in that way. Popped the screen off and squeezed in."

That opening measured about eight by ten inches. *Geez, could he actually have wedged himself through such a small hole?* "Where are your parents?"

For a long minute Tommy stared down at the floor. Then he met Steve's eyes directly. "I don't have any."

Steve studied him. This boy had courage. The tall man knew from experience that many people found him intimidating with his powerful eyes, piercing gaze, and hard chiseled jaw, although he often didn't intend to be. Tommy looked at him frankly, without fear. The lad's movements — and words — were slow and deliberate. There was an economy of movement in his motions and a simple directness in his statements. The child, who in many ways seemed more like an adult, saw through wary eyes that picked up everything. All this impressed the detective.

Steve let the answer pass. "Why are you here?"

"That's what I tried to tell you earlier, Mr. O'Shaughnessy. There is something you *need* to be aware of, it's extremely important. This afternoon at two pm a series of six bombs will go off in the basement of the governor's office to assassinate him. He has a meeting then, so they know he will be in the building. They don't care who gets killed."

Steve interrupted, "Whoa, wait a minute. ... Who is going to do this, how did you get this information?"

As Tommy supplied answers, he reported verbatim. "Last night at two am I overheard four men in an alley behind Anders Street, near the Emporium. Tony Alika and another man were making the arrangements with two others, a Sanderson and someone else. They detailed their plan to Alika. I think the other guy with Alika was a bodyguard; he didn't say anything. They are going to go into the government office building this morning at nine am, into the basement, disguised as electrical repairmen and plant six plastic explosive bombs, one on each steel support column, set to go off simultaneously, bringing the whole building down."

Steve's mind spun. *This is way too far-fetched. How does he know Alika? Six bombs? Kid's got to be lying.* He ran through all the reasons he could think of why a small boy would be in an alley at two am. None of them good. *The way this kid talks is all wrong — way too advanced and mature for someone of his age.* Pinning him down with one thing at a time, Steve asked, "Tommy, what were you doing in an alley at two am?"

"Mr. O'Shaughnessy, why I was there isn't important. I was behind a dumpster."

"Did they notice you? Were you hiding?"

"No, they did not spot me. When I heard them I made sure I stayed quiet and out of sight. But I was close enough to listen and hear everything."

Tommy relayed things with minute detail. He got the color of Alika's and Sanderson's cars, their makes, models, license numbers, and the fact that one had a cracked taillight all correct. He described each man including complete descriptions of facial features and clothing. *It's like he's an adult in a child's body. Maybe he's some kind of midget or dwarf.*

"Tommy, you seem to remember lots of things here. I don't understand." *The kid has to be making some or all of this up, a nice story.* Yet many pieces fit. Alika did have a scar across his neck. Alika did go around with a bodyguard who fit Tommy's description. But it was almost as if Tommy had been "programmed" and was replaying some movie.

Steve could tell Tommy was exasperated as he shook his head. The boy sighed, got up from the couch and walked around the large office, looked at things, and returned to the sofa. Steve and Marco regarded each other, questions in their eyes. Tommy limped slightly. He sat down, shut his eyes and proceeded to describe in exact minute detail Steve's office. All the way to, "And your associate is wearing a tan suit with a yellow and blue print tie. His left coat pocket flap is tucked in instead of out. He has a one-inch scuff mark on the outside of his right shoe by the heel. On his left hand, middle finger, there's a gold class ring, with a ruby-red stone on it."

Steve was aware his own wide eyes and stunned expression mirrored Marco's perplexed countenance as they followed the descriptions, ascertaining the accuracy of Tommy's recital.

Even with his eyes closed, Tommy knew what their reaction was he had experienced it before in people when he remembered things so clearly. "Test me."

"What's on the wall to the left of the door, a framed item, third from the bottom?"

"An award from Hawaii Police Department: To Steven O'Shaughnessy of O'Shaughnessy Investigations in recognition of duty and service above and beyond the ordinary. Marcoh 1, 1963."

"How many masts and sails on the ship on the shelf?"

"Three, a tall one in the center, and two smaller ones. Plus a crow's nest at the top of each and coat-of-arms insignias on the sails."

Three more rounds of this, then Tommy opened his eyes. "Mr. O'Shaughnessy, I never figured out why, but I can remember almost perfectly things I see. Like a picture is painted in my head, a snapshot in my mind and I can recall all the details. Over 99 %

of what I see. The same with what I hear. That's not quite as good, but I still can remember perfectly over 95 %. That is why I can tell you all this stuff about Alika and the bombs."

Steve believed him — he had to — the kid had just demonstrated his amazing ability. Knowledge about people with photographic memories was not new to him, but he'd never met anyone in person who had one. *I'll bet this boy has tested himself somehow, knows how good he is at this.*

Steve asked, "Tommy, why didn't you find a police officer and tell him?"

Tommy sat, hands in his lap, chin resting on his chest, eyes downcast, looking very much like a lost little ten year old boy. "C'mon, Mr. O'Shaughnessy. You think they'd listen to me, a dirty street kid? With that kind of story? If I could finally convince them my report was true, by then, the assassination attempt would be done and over. History. I read in the newspaper that your company provides security for the governor, and decided you'd be the one who most needed to be informed. I hoped I could convince you. I'm sorry I broke into your office, but I didn't take anything, didn't steal anything, and didn't touch anything."

This kid is smart.

Steve started his private investigation firm, O'Shaughnessy Investigations, after his military service, about the same time Hawaii became a state in 1959. In the five years he had been operating, he had expanded to both consulting as well as providing security for people, companies and events. The company was highly successful and Steve intentionally kept the business small and family-like, choosing the cases he wanted — one of which was a contract to provide personal protection for the governor.

As Steve grabbed his jacket and stepped toward the door to investigate this crime in the making, he stopped suddenly and glanced over his shoulder. *What about Tommy?*

"Tommy, will you stay here, in my office, until we get back?" He didn't want this kid getting away.

Tommy shrugged, "Okay."

Several hours later, after Hawaii Police Department—HPD— had found and defused the bombs, and reports had been filled out, Steve and Marco headed back to the office.

On the way he voiced his confused thoughts aloud to his aikane. "What is it about that kid? Who is he? What is it with him??? Is it just me, or do you 'sense' something, too?"

"Steve, I don't know what it is, but there is something between you two. I don't feel anything myself, but I can through you, in you. And I think Tommy does, too."

Shaking his head, seeking hard and pat answers, Steve wasn't going to let this puzzle lie. He liked his world black and white. "What is it? It's like some connection. What? Marco, I've never felt anything like this before. You and I, we're like brothers, we're close. This is not the same; something different from what we have, but something just as powerful."

Looking sideways at his friend, he added, "Almost supernatural."

Chapter 2
Is He Still There?

Steve rushed back into his office, half afraid Tommy would be gone. He took the stairs two at a time and whooshed through the outer office. Whipping open his door, his eyes darted to all corners of the room. Then he saw the boy outside on the lanai sitting on the floor.

"Hey, you okay?"

As he stood up, he answered, "Yeah."

Stumped, Steve didn't know what to say or do next.

Marco noticed and picked up the slack. "Hey, Steve, I'm going to order in some lunch. Why don't you guys chat until I get back?"

"Sounds good, Marco." *More food into the boy's stomach is a good idea.*

"Let's sit inside, Tommy. Come on in." Steve had a couple of upholstered chairs in his office that he often used for interviews. They sat side by side in them, Steve on the edge of his. With no real idea where to start or what to ask first, he prioritized in his mind. *Okay, first thing was to make sure Tommy is okay, safe, and that his needs were met.*

"Tommy, where do you live?" *Stupid question! He's homeless, a street kid. And I'll bet he knows I know that.*

He answered evenly, "It doesn't make any difference, Mr. O'Shaughnessy."

Running his hand through his hair, he asked, "Who takes care of you?" *Another brainless question, O'Shaughnessy. You're batting a thousand here!*

"I get by okay." Tommy wasn't making eye contact, just looking at his feet and shuffling them a bit.

Yeah, sure. That's why you're starving, have something wrong with your leg, need a haircut and are wearing shabby clothes.

Steve stared at him. That feeling was there again, growing with each passing minute. Protectiveness, solidarity, more he couldn't articulate. Tommy eyes no longer seemed uneasy, wary. They were clear and direct. *He feels okay with this, too. Even though I don't know exactly what's going on. Neither does he. I bet he's surprised with what he's feeling, my guess is this is all new to him. And his past history has taught him not to trust.*

Steve jumped up and began his not uncommon pacing. "Tommy, ... I .... you... I want to help you...."

Tommy looked steadily at O'Shaughnessy. "Mr. O'Shaughnessy.... sometimes ... 'help' ..... doesn't work out... sometimes.... adults.... end up making you do things you don't want to do... things don't work out the way they expected....even though they meant well.... Please.... don't do that to me.....I don't need that kind of help...."

In that last bit, Steve detected a twinge of fear, pain, and hesitation in Tommy's voice, and saw the same in his eyes. *What has happened to him? I need to do something here. The wrong thing and he'll bolt. Be out of here before I can turn around. I want him to begin to trust me.*

He moved off his chair, got closer to Tommy, down on one knee, at his eye level, and looked into his wet teary eyes. He vowed, "Tommy, I will NEVER make you do anything you don't want to do. I promise."

It seemed as if Tommy's gaze penetrated all the way to the center of Steve's soul. "Do you really mean that, Mr. O'Shaughnessy? Really?"

The way he asked the question so solemnly made Steve nervous, but he didn't know exactly why. A lesson drilled into Steve by Doc Burns, the man who had raised him for a few years after his father had died, and become his friend/mentor/ foster father, was that you didn't say something if you didn't really mean it. "Yes, I really mean that." He repeated himself, "I will never make you do anything you don't want to do. I promise." *My God, where in the world did that come from? How can I make a promise like that? But I think he needed to hear it. I suppose if it comes down to it I'll just have to win him over to my way of thinking. I know forcing is not the answer with him.*

"Thank you." They maintained eye contact in silence another moment. Energy flowed between them …. giving and taking for both of them.

Marco returned with lunch. It was assumed that Tommy would eat with them. This was all understood without comment or explanation. But as the food was laid out, Tommy looked at Steve again, biting that quivering lip, eyes filling with tears, "Thank you." He stole several long looks at Steve before he ate.

My God! What is it? It's just a meal, some food. I mean, I know he's hungry. It's more than a meal to him, more than food, way more, apparently. What? He also noticed again (he had first seen it when Tommy ate breakfast) that he didn't use his left arm to eat, or do anything with it. *What's wrong with that arm? A birth defect? Whatever. Doesn't seem to be hurting him any.*

Lunch finished, Tommy said, "Mr. O'Shaughnessy, there's more about Alika…. He was planning on meeting at three p.m. this afternoon with Sanderson and the other guy at the same alley for the rest of the payoff."

Chapter 3
The Bust and The Injury

A quick call was made to Steve's good friend, the chief of HPD. Arrangements to apprehend the criminals were set in motion.

"Captain Daniels, this is terrific. We've been after this guy a long time; he's caused us considerable trouble. But it must be handled right, so he's not tipped off."

"Gotcha, O'Shaughnessy. We'll get him. Join us?"

The detective again asked Tommy to stay in his office while he was out.

This time, Tommy refused. "No, I'm coming along with you. I can show you the exact spot where things are going to happen."

Steve would have nothing to do with the boy's idea. Falling back on his usual methods, expecting his authority to be obeyed without question, he pulled himself tall and stood erect. "Young man, you will wait here in my office until I return."

"No."

A definite determination was set in Tommy's face and stance, but Steve detected no defiance in him. It flashed through his mind that he didn't want to alienate Tommy, and he had promised not to force him. But no way did he want the boy exposed to the dangers of the bust. Steve took a minute to try to reason, "Tommy, this will be dangerous. I don't want you getting hurt."

"Mr. O'Shaughnessy, I'm not planning on getting hurt. But I am coming. If I can't go with you, I'll get to the alley myself somehow."

Hard to believe he's only a kid. How old is he? I never even asked him. This is no place for a kid, but if I say no, he'll show up anyway, I'm sure of it. Geez!

Steve grabbed his coat and turned abruptly. "C'mon." They left with Marco.

At the scene, he turned and faced Tommy in the backseat. "Tommy, this is dangerous. Let me repeat, I don't want you to get hurt. Please stay in the car." Tommy met his eyes, but said nothing. Steve shook his head in frustration and left.

Tommy did, indeed, leave Steve's car. Being familiar with this alley and its nooks and crannies, hiding out of sight in a tiny spot behind a small ell in a wall, high up, about 8' on a ledge, was easy. His intention was to simply observe, and help if needed, and if he could — maybe warn the officers with a shout if he saw something they were missing. His plan was not a question of their competence or anything — not at all — just that he had been around this turf in a way they hadn't, which might prove helpful.

So he waited, eyes scanning the scene in front of him. Alika was driven up in a new Cadillac. Right behind him was his second-in-command and a few bodyguards. Unbeknownst to Steve and HPD, Alika had another man hidden in the location, who had arrived about an hour earlier. The criminals were completely surprised at the police presence. Out in the open, unarmed, Alika had his hands up and was talking with the private investigator. His bodyguards were with him, guns drawn. Alika's other man was still in the background, in the shadows, watching, waiting. O'Shaughnessy's bullhorn amplified his voice to a boom. "Alika, tell your guys to give it up. You're surrounded. No one is getting out of here!"

From his vantage point, Tommy spied one hoodlum with a pistol in hand creeping stealthily towards O'Shaughnessy, who was totally unaware of the man's presence. If he kept going, not too much farther, the gunman would have a free and clear shot at Steve. The 6' 4" O'Shaughnessy seemed even taller because of his perfect posture — he made an easy target for a gunman close by. Tommy had seen scoundrels like him before — the gangster would have no qualms about killing Steve. One possibility would be to holler an alert, but by the time Steve turned and realized the danger, a half dozen shots would be fired before he could get clear.

It stunned Tommy to realize in that moment he truly cared for O'Shaughnessy; he really didn't want him hurt or killed. Quickly going over his options, he decided the best course of action, and moved on it. With the advantage of the height of his perch, he launched himself in a flying tackle onto the gunman, screaming a warning as he went. Chaos broke loose and a firefight ensued, lasting less than a minute.

The sound of Tommy's shout caused Steve to turn, and he witnessed the boy leap towards an attacker, just as the turmoil started. After a few minutes of chaos and bedlam, all the assailants were under control, and Steve rushed to Tommy. He was sitting on the ground, and bloody. As he got a few steps closer, Steve realized he was cradling a bleeding arm — his "good" arm— he noted absently.

Not quite in a panic, but definitely agitated, Steve queried, "Tommy, are you okay? You're hurt."

The injured lad allowed Steve to examine his arm. A deep gash from a bullet creased his forearm. Relief flooded through Steve as he realized the wound was not life threatening. His initial reaction was to chew Tommy out for not staying in the car.

Pulse still racing, breathing rapidly, Steve's adrenaline was pumping since Tommy had jumped into the middle of all this. For a moment his heart had stopped. He didn't want this boy hurt!

"Keo, call an ambulance. NOW!" Keo (Keolani) was the third man on Steve's team, a husky young Hawaiian with about a thousand contacts, which came in quite handy at times. Steve believed he was related to every native on the island.

Dirty, with blood on his face from wiping his brow with his stained hand, Tommy was adamant. "No. No, Mr. O'Shaughnessy, no ambulance."

Steve jerked his head up, moving his attention from the wound to the boy's face. "What do you mean, NO ambulance? You're going to the hospital. You've been SHOT!"

"No, Mr. O'Shaughnessy, no ambulance, no hospital. I'll be okay." The boy took a deep breath and sat as tall as he could, squaring his shoulders back.

Steve inhaled, held it a bit, then exhaled calmly. "Tommy do you realize you've got a bullet wound? You've hurt your arm pretty badly, you need to be seen by a doctor and get stitched up. I've got a good friend, Doc Epstein; he'll fix you up. Okay, no ambulance, I'll take you in my car."

"No, Mr. O'Shaughnessy. I'm not going to any hospital. I'll be okay. My arm hurts, but I'll be okay. All I need is a bandage." Pain-filled eyes implored the man.

I'm not going to settle for this. He needs medical attention. Go! dang. There's that feeling again I've been having off and on all day. I want to take care of this boy somehow. I'm compelled to act. If I force him, which I can do, I'll lose him the first chance he gets, and he'll be gone for good. He'd slip away somehow; easy for him to do, I'll bet. He knows how to hide. Force won't work. Even if I hadn't made that promise.

His voice so quiet no one else could hear, Tommy reminded, "Mr. O'Shaughnessy, you promised you wouldn't make me do anything I didn't want to do."

"But, Tommy, you've been shot!"

Face impassive, Tommy said nothing, just looked at him; Steve got the message loud and clear. *Geez! He's holding me to that stupid promise I made — testing me to see if I truly meant what I said. Or if I'm going to turn out like the other adults he's encountered.*

Marco had been watching this, and was aware of Steve's dilemma. Pain, agony — almost. He could see Steve was deeply drawn to Tommy. He knew Steve hated seeing Tommy hurting. He knew he wanted to scoop him up and take him to the hospital for care. He knew this was an important moment for the two of them.

On the ground on one knee next to Tommy, the knuckles of Steve's clenched fist knocked against his forehead; he had screwed his eyes shut tight in thought, trying to decide what to do. *Okay, maybe this.*

"Tommy, can I please take you to my house, and have Doc come and patch you up there?" Steve had seen the wound, pressed his clean white handkerchief on the injury, and secured the cloth. *This laceration is serious, but not life threatening. A house call ought to do it. Doc might not think so, but he'll come around. Please be reasonable. Say yes.*

Tommy considered the proposal for a moment. "Okay."

Steve helped him up and to the car. A surge of emotion overtook him. *What I want to do is bundle him up and carry him, hold him and care for him. Keep him safe, protect him.* As Tommy allowed Steve to help him, he sensed the taut muscles relax under his hand, indicating the boy felt safe and secure. Their eyes met, Tommy's blinking a bit from tears, and Steve's feelings deepened. Steve knew this was a good thing.

He got Tommy into the Mercury and carefully surveyed his young passenger. "You okay?"

"Yeah."

Before driving off, Steve motioned Keo over. "Keo, call Epstein to ask him to meet us at my house."

It didn't escape the detective's notice that Tommy had a painful wound, yet he didn't make much of a fuss over it. No tears, no crying. Even in his face he didn't show discomfort, except maybe some slight twitching of a few muscles around his eyes. Steve could read the signs of hurt. The trick of not showing pain was one Steve himself had learned as a young boy, and again in Korea. *His arm's got to hurt, yet no tears. He's an expert at keeping silent. What has happened to this boy?*

Steve parked in the carport and again he helped steady Tommy, who by now looked a little pale. After settling him on the couch, he went to get some supplies. With a soft damp cloth he wiped his face, cleaning off the blood, and also washed the uninjured arm. Recalling that Tommy didn't really use that left hand or arm, as he wiped he noticed a distinct lack of strength, no muscle tone. Comments were kept to himself.

Doc came bursting in, toting the proverbial black doctor's bag. He surveyed Tommy and Steve, and moved right over to the couch. Before the quick introductions were finished, Doc barked, "Steve, Keo says he's been shot. Why didn't you take him to the hospital?"

He began to examine the boy's arm.

Steve was leaning against the door frame, arms crossed loosely, presenting a quiet and serene image. "Doc, just patch him up here, please."

Small grateful eyes focused on Steve.

"And why here and not at the hospital?"

He probed the wound carefully, and spoke in a much gentler voice. "That hurt, son?"

The answer was a non-committal shrug, but Steve noticed the boy just barely biting the inside of his lip.

The physician rummaged in his bag. "Stitches, antibiotics, pain meds, some IV fluids wouldn't hurt at all. I want him in the hospital, Steve."

Steve had not moved at all. "No, Doc."

Doc Epstein jumped up and spun around to face Steve. "No?? What do you mean, 'NO'? What's gotten into you, Steve???"

Standing straight now, instead of leaning against door, he didn't raise his voice, but in its quietness it carried authority. "Doc, I told him he doesn't have to do anything he doesn't want to do. I don't have any idea why, and I have no knowledge if his reasons are valid or not, but Tommy doesn't want to go to the hospital and I won't force him, and neither will you or anyone else."

Tommy exhaled at this statement; his shoulders relaxed.

"You're telling me he's not going to the hospital because he doesn't want to? And you're going to let him get away with that? To accept that? You're nuts!"

Glancing at Tommy, Steve smiled. "Yep."

After studying the pair a minute, Doc realized more was going on here. He decided to agree to the situation without delving into the details. He expected at some time, Steve would clue him in. If not, he'd pry it out of him. So he set about his task of treating the boy. Tommy eyed him carefully, tensely. Aware of the scrutiny and fear, Doc tried to put him at ease. He came to realize it wasn't the particular treatment things he was doing (injecting Novocain, cleaning the wound) that unnerved Tommy. Something else, something underlying was at work. Procedures like the suturing seemed to faze him barely at all. The boy's muscles were tight, his movements tense, his eyes tracking everything and taking in every detail.

Doc finished, studied his patient a bit longer, and rechecked his vital signs. "You know, Steve, I'd really like to do an IV. He's dehydrated, needs some fluids... Let's set it up in the bedroom."

Not having thought that far ahead, Steve considered Tommy. He moved to kneel next to him, and took his hand.

"Would you be willing to stay, spend the night, and let Doc hook up some fluids? Be a good idea, I think."

With a long look back, eyes pooling with tears yet again, the boy nodded his assent. Doc regarded this interchange with intense curiosity.

"Doc, before you start an IV, let him get out of that dirty shirt. Tommy, you can wear one of mine. The size is too big, but it's better than your soiled one. I'll help you get into it."

"No, I can change myself." He went alone into the bathroom and put the oversized garment on.

They got Tommy settled, the IV in and rigged up with a makeshift stand.

"Steve, I want to give him a mild sedative. When the Novocain wears off he'll be uncomfortable, the medication will help him rest."

Tommy looked at Steve questioningly.

"It's a good idea, Tommy. But first, Doc, can we get something to eat? We haven't had anything since lunch. Some sandwiches and fruit will be quick and easy."

As they ate, Tommy used his newly injured arm to hold his sandwich and fork. *Apparently that was easier for him than using his other one. That left arm seems to be of no use to him at all. I wonder why.* The sedation was administered; they stayed with him in silence a few more minutes until he dropped off. And Doc headed out of the bedroom, expecting Steve to follow. Something held the tall man back; he lingered just contemplating the child.

Doc waited patiently. Finally Steve came out and they went out onto the lanai. Marco had returned as well.

Steve asked, "He gonna be okay, Doc?"

"He should be fine. Watch the arm, change the bandages tomorrow, keep on the antibiotics. I'll check him in a day or so. But there shouldn't be any problems."

After a few minutes of silence, Doc faced his friend. "Steve, what?" The one-word question meant, what is going on here? Who is he? Why are you acting the way you are?

Steve pondered the inquiry silently, then answered, "I don't know, Doc. I really don't know."

Continuing to think out loud, Steve spoke slowly, "There's something about him that reaches deeply into me. I don't know what it is or why. Doc, Marco, I've never felt this way before. It's not bad, it's good. It feels very, very good. You now, when I helped him to my car… I felt so… what, I don't know what… happy, fulfilled, protective… all that, but more. When I saw him leap out onto that guy, my heart stopped. I didn't want anything to happen to him….. This goes deep…. Very deep… where inside of me, to what, I don't know…. I can't wrap my mind around it. This morning, fourteen hours ago, I had never seen nor heard of this kid, yet now, I am profoundly affected by him. Linked. Bonded. Connected. Why? How? I have no idea."

Steve stared off at the ocean — his mind churning, captivated by all this. *I'm not upset. This is not a bad thing, not a threatening thing. How will this unfold? Into what?*

Looking at the two friends, Steve said, "It's okay. It'll all be okay."

After some time, the pair of them left, Doc first checking in one last time on Tommy. Steve continued to sit on the lanai, thinking. Ideas came unbidden into his consciousness. *Doc Burns also taught me about being aware of opportunities and gifts God sends your way. Tomorrow I'm slated to appear in court. I hate testifying. Dull, boring, dragging on much longer than I'd like. Starts at 9 am. I want Tommy to stay here. I hope he will. I really hope he will.*

Chapter 4
Steve, Not Mr. O'Shaughnessy

Tommy woke early, just as the clock in the hallway chimed six a.m.. Steve had been up since five. Seeing Tommy awake, he disconnected the now-empty IV, and gave him some of the pain meds Doc had left. It occurred to him Tommy was still in the same clothes as yesterday, except for the shirt; he had nothing else to change into.

Steve grabbed the phone and called his friend. "Marco, it's early, but you get up with the birds anyway. I need a favor. Can you stop and pick up a few items — some clothes — for Tommy and bring them out? With court at nine a.m., a shopping trip won't work for me."

"Sure, Steve. Happy to help out. How are things?"

"Good. Talk to you later, Marco."

A small head appeared around the corner.

"C'mon into the kitchen, Tommy."

The boy sat on a stool at the counter as Steve went about preparing breakfast. Soon two attractive plates of cheese omelets with juicy pineapple, toast, and fresh squeezed orange juice were set out. Steve sat across from Tommy. Tommy gazed at the food, then at Steve, back and forth a few times, reminiscent of similar actions the day before.

The big brown eyes couldn't hold the tears anymore; this time they spilled out. Steve moved over next to Tommy, and took his face in his hands. The man pulled the small head to his chest, his own cheeks wet. *What's with me? Why am I upset? Tommy's upset, and that bothers me. A lot. He's been hurt. A lot.* The two connected in silence for a while.

Finally, in a sobbing hiccup, Tommy started to speak, "Mr. O'Shaughnessy..."

"No, Tommy. Call me Steve."

Absorbing the significance of the invitation to closeness and intimacy, the lad's tears flowed once more.

He tried again, "Steve, no one has ever done anything like this for me."

What? I haven't done anything, really.

Tommy appeared surprised with himself with his openness as he confessed, "I mean, you've been so generous and kind to me... You gave me something to eat. Nobody's ever given me something to eat before, that I can remember. I've been able to take things, but no one has ever given me anything. And not only did you give me food, you made the meals yourself— for me. Yesterday, and again, now."

Overwhelmed by that act of charity he cried more. Steve eyes moistened — such small things meant so much to this lad. Yet one more time, the question nagged at Steve. *What has happened to him?*

Tommy continued, "And then you listened to me. You made a promise and kept it, even though I know it was hard for you to do stick to what you said, especially after I got hurt. You took me into your house, you had a doctor come to help me, and you gave me a bed to sleep in. Last night was the first time I can ever remember sleeping without being afraid. And it wasn't from the doctor's drugs…. It was from knowing you were here, I was safe….Steve… I….. don't know what to say…."

The tall man held back from the great bear hug he wanted to give the poor child, suspecting an embrace would be too much and upset him more. Instead he gently put his arm around the boy's shoulders and squeezed.

Tommy let himself be close to Steve for a long time. The man's mind drifted as he held him. Thoughts wandered to another little eleven year old boy he knew once, who needed help and didn't get it. Who was afraid, scared, alone, hungry, hurting. Who had no one to hug him, to hold him, to protect him. And being here for Tommy was healing, in one way he was holding that other little boy.

When the intensity had subsided, Steve leaned back a bit and smiled gently. "Tommy, let's eat."

Marco came in before they had finished breakfast. No need to hide the red eyes from him. He didn't ask any questions — he was content just to be present for his friend. No— his friends — he realized, now including Tommy in that inner circle.

"Hey, Tommy, I've got a present for you." Young eyes widened as Marco pulled out clothes, socks, underwear, shoes, everything necessary.

"This is for me?"

Steve held a new shirt up against the boy's frame. "Yes, you needed some things. Good job with sizing, Marco."

Marco questioned, "You need help showering or getting dressed?"

Tommy shook his head no, and headed to the bedroom.

"Wait a second. Let me come with you and remove the bandage then clean your arm." Checking the injury as he washed it under warm running water at the sink, Steve observed that it had developed some redness and swelling, to be expected, but appeared okay.

"We'll put fresh gauze on after you shower."

Tommy finished in the bathroom and came out in his new clothes.

"Tommy, tell me about yourself," Steve requested as the boy took a seat on the sofa across from him.

The boy shrugged. "Not much to tell."

Steve let the non-answer pass. *Too overwhelming a question, probably.*

Steve explained to Tommy, "Tommy, I've got to be in court today. And most likely tomorrow as well. I'd like it if you stayed here. When I'm done testifying we can talk and get to spend some time together." Looking carefully at Tommy, he added, "Figure out where to go...."

"Court usually lets out early, judges don't like long hours, so I should be back late afternoon. Okay with you?"

Watching the boy consider this, Steve sensed Tommy wasn't sure. A big part of him probably really liked the idea. And another warring part was understandably wary.

"Okay. I can stay here for now."

Steve smiled revealing his relief. "Good, go ahead and make yourself at home. Read, walk on the beach, anything you want to eat you can have. Expect me back about four or five. You going to be okay? Any questions?"

Tommy had none. Steve reluctantly left, "See you later." As Marco and Steve walked out together, the older man groused about court and testifying, "Court's the last place I want to be today. And it's Judge Adams. He is so slow."

Marco nodded in agreement, "Nothing you can do about it, Steve. Tommy'll be fine."

"I know. I'd just rather spend the day with Tommy."

During the preliminaries of the case being presented in the courtroom, Steve's mind wandered. *I wonder what he's doing right now? Who is he? Where's he from?* Steve had a thousand questions. He didn't need to concentrate on routine testimony being given at this point.

Court had been back in session after the lunch recess for about twenty minutes when one of the jurors, a middle aged woman, fainted. The building air conditioning was out yielding a quite warm courtroom. Judge Adams adjourned court until the following morning. This pleased Steve on the one hand, as he could get back to his place and Tommy. On the other, the delay meant probably yet another day of the trial for him.

Chapter 5
The Greatest Adventure
Is What Lies Ahead

Steve drove back to the house in a quick, direct route. *What now with him? I like Tommy. I admire the kid. He's got savvy and courage. And I'll bet a long nasty history of some sort. I intend to help him, seriously help him. Doc Burns helped me; I am going to help Tommy. Not as any kind of "payback"— helping is the right thing to do, and I'm able. Being young, scared, and alone is no picnic. I don't want him to suffer those kinds of feelings anymore. I've got to be real careful. Tommy's wary. I am amazed at how much he trusts me. Some anyways. God is working here. I push too hard, or too fast, he'll bolt. But he belongs with me. My heart's got no question about us being together. I think he senses the same thing. Don't blow it, O'Shaughnessy!*

Arriving home, Steve smiled as he discovered Tommy was asleep in a hammock on the lanai. A treasured book — *The Hobbit*— lay open on his lap. The man studied him in his sleep a few moments. *Tough as nails on the one hand, vulnerable as a newborn baby on the other.*

Steve went into his bedroom and changed clothes. He found Tommy awake when he returned a minute later. "Hi, how are you?"

"Fine. I thought you wouldn't be back until around suppertime. Good day for you?"

Steve told him what had happened. Tommy turned attention away from himself by asking Steve about himself, his work and so on. Conversation flowed, Steve was more than happy to answer, filling Tommy in.

He learned some about Tommy from the questions the boy asked him. Steve was a good detective, but a genius IQ wasn't required to figure out the lad was quite intelligent. Steve tossed a few inquiries Tommy's way. Replies consisted of vague non-commital answers, no surprise to Steve. He accepted Tommy where he was, and allowed the child to figure out his own comfort level without pressure.

Steve debated how to spend the rest of the day. *We could go out someplace. Nah, that's not what I want. We could just sit and talk, or try to talk. That won't work, I don't think— it'd be awkward. Maybe I'll just putter around the house, and let things happen as they will. God, direct me— us— here.*

Thinking about the book Tommy had been reading, Steve chose to organize his bookshelf.

"*The Hobbit* is one of my favorite books. Is this the first time you've read it?"

Tommy nodded.

"How far are you? Does it interest you so far?"

"Yeah, it's pretty good. I'm at the part where Bilbo is hiding in the cave."

"Little Bilbo Baggins is a fellow full of wisdom. Want to listen to a story? There's some substantial history behind how I came to have this book. Did you spot the autograph inside?"

Tommy checked the inside cover of the book. "No, I didn't. Sure, I'd like to hear your story."

Steve smiled— Tommy seemed more animated than he'd seen him yet. "I'd been at Doc's about a year. I'll tell you more about Doc later— but I lived with him for a couple of years when I was in high school. One night he went to a lecture by Tolkien. Came home with a signed book he'd bought. Tolkien had written the chronicle maybe ten years earlier. Doc read it, told me it was a first-class novel and I'd enjoy it. Not too many days later I read the volume through. A darn good book. I liked it. A lot."

Steve stopped his organizing and sat back, staring into space, reminiscing. "Doc always tried to let me figure things out. He asked what part I liked best. I hadn't thought about it, said it was all wonderful. Doc told me to think about my favorite scene and we'd talk later. The next day I leafed through the book to see what I did like best. I ended up reading the whole thing all the way through again."

Steve took the leather bound tome from Tommy and lovingly caressed the burgundy cover. "We talked — long into the night that evening. We discussed Bilbo and things that happened to him, his journey, what he learned along the way. Doc showed me how the hobbit's insights might apply to my life. Three chimes on the clock — three a.m. — before I went to bed."

The man tousled Tommy's hair. *God, he's just like I was — eager, anxious, scared, uncertain.* "I memorized part of the book, a section that moved me. The lessons Bilbo shares have been guiding principles for me. I discovered tremendous meaning and wisdom in his words."

Intentionally Steve paused here, baiting Tommy to ask for more, and he went back to shelving. *Let him hang for a minute. Get him interacting more with me. I know he wants to know, let him ask.*

Finally, Tommy asked. "Well, what part?"

Again Steve stopped with the books. He stood erect, cleared his throat and began in a musical sing-song voice:

The greatest adventure, Is what lies ahead,
Today and tomorrow, Are yet to be said,
The chances the changes, Are all yours to make,
The mold of your life, Is in your hands to break.

The greatest adventure, Is there if you're bold,
Let go of the mood, That life makes you old,
To measure the meaning, Can make you delay,
It's time you stop thinking, And wasting the day.

The man who's a dreamer, And never takes leave,
Who thinks of a world that is Just make believe,
Will never know passion, Will never know pain,
One who sits by the window, Will one day see rain.

After a short silence Steve looked intently at the boy. "Tommy, Doc showed me breaking the mold of my life can be done. I could make my life whatever I wanted. The future — my future — genuinely was in my hands. Ahh,... Tommy, my boy, the exact same is true for you. The very same. Take your life, you can make it be what you want. God, Tommy, go for it! I want to infuse into you what Doc gave me. Hope, and more. You can accomplish anything."

"Live your dreams. Sure pain is a part of life, but also passion. Don't just sit and watch life pass you by. Don't think too long about things. Act. Move. Decide. Go for it."

Steve paused, took a deep breath and chuckled. "Geez, I'm sounding preachy. But so much has happened to me, and letting life slide by would be easy. You know the commercial? 'Go for the gusto!'"

The man stared off into the distance a while. He finishing shelving the few last books then moved to the task of preparing supper. Tommy followed him. The pair spent the rest of the day discussing dear Bilbo Baggins, often looking something up in the book. They chatted about Bilbo's feelings and thoughts. Steve was pleased when Tommy argued a bit with him over a difference of opinion. *Ahhh, this is good. He not just agreeing with me, he's standing up for what he thinks. He seems considerably more comfortable talking now, about the book and Bilbo. Much more than about himself. But I also think that underneath his comments he's referring to himself. He probably doesn't even realize it! We'll have to do more of this kind of thing.*

The grandfather clock in the hallway chimed nine pm. Steve went to Tommy. "Will you stay?" He had been going to ask, "Will you stay tonight?" and changed his wording. The question he asked, and the tone of voice he used, gave Tommy clues to its meaning. Their eyes communicated wordlessly. After a minute, Tommy nodded yes.

Steve smiled, put his hand on Tommy's shoulder. "Good."

"Can I check your arm, clean your wound, and change the bandage?" Another nod and the pair headed to the bathroom.

Slowly and gently Steve did the nursing duties, talking as he did. "We've had a heck of a time the last two days, haven't we?" Tommy nodded. He hadn't been saying much, but Steve intended to get him chatting. Having a pretty good idea of what might be on the boy's mind, he wanted to bring the thoughts out into the open. Naturally and without thinking he began to use a technique of asking open-ended questions. First he hoped to make Tommy unwind a bit, so he talked about his own thoughts and feelings.

"I have no idea about you, but I've got a hundred different things running through me. A psychiatrist friend taught me the value of trying to figure out what you're experiencing. So, for me, I'd start with shock, I suppose. When I saw you in the office the other morning I admit being startled and astonished. And surprised at myself for not immediately waking you and asking why you were sleeping on my couch. I had some sense of protectiveness towards you. I wanted to let you sleep. I admit to not understanding my thoughts and emotions."

He moved Tommy's arm under the faucet and ran a thin stream of warm water over the injury, cleaning the somewhat red and sore, but not infected gash. "And then I guess more shock, and astonishment when you did your little demonstration. You talent, or gift, or whatever, still amazes me. Next I was preoccupied with the crime and all. When I saw you flying off your perch on the wall in the alley, my heart froze. Tommy, that minute went by in slow motion for me. My affection for you— yes, affection— became prominently evident. I'd care about anyone, I wouldn't want anyone to get hurt, but somehow especially not you. This runs deep, Tommy. Again, I'm not sure how or why, but we're connected, bonded, almost."

All the while Steve was talking and working he observed Tommy, overtly gauging his reaction. The boy seemed to be accepting the care and taking it all in. After patting the arm dry Steve began bandaging. "Last night, after you went to sleep, Doc and Marco and I talked a long while. They asked what was up. Those two understand me as much as anyone can understand another, Tommy. Apart from them, I'm pretty private— few people know me intimately. I told them, honestly I had no idea what was up; why you — this — is affecting me so strongly. I still am unsure. Today I did something I haven't done in a long time and don't do often. I thought about God. I'm getting the feeling that God put us in each other's lives for a reason, it wasn't merely chance." Steve chuckled, "I don't think much about how God might be working in my life, but I have learned not to try to figure Him out, just go with the flow."

Steve was quiet a minute, hoping Tommy might say something. He didn't.

Steve sighed and gazed at the ceiling while he thought, "Tommy, I think there are things … that have….. happened … to you. Sometime I think — I hope — you'll be able to share them. Getting things out into the open is good."

Tommy remained silent. Steve went back to his litany. "Relief is another reaction I have. I am relieved you are staying. Like I said, I care about you a great deal, having you stay and being able to help you— on your terms— eases some of my concerns."

The man's eyes focused on the boy again. "Tommy, I am also hesitant. I like being in control, having all the facts, knowing and understanding details. With this, I'm not in command, maybe God is. I have no idea how things will work out for you, or for us. They will, I'm sure. But one thing I'm apprehensive about is you. There is a lot inside of you, bottled up. My experience— and Samuel, my psychiatrist friend, would agree, I'm sure—is the more of that you can get out, the better. The longer negative emotions stay inside you, unexpressed, the more they eat at you. I know, Tommy, I've been there. You might think you're okay, but in reality, you're not."

The pair was quiet for a few minutes. "So, what are your feelings, your thoughts?"

Tommy shrugged. "I dunno." Then following Steve's example, he too went through sort of a chronological list.

"I was pretty scared when I went into your office. Afraid you might be furious. But you needed to be informed, so I snuck in. Getting breakfast was a surprise bonus. I hadn't expected a meal. I had figured I'd tell you and leave. I was also uneasy that you wanted me to stay."

They had finished with the arm and moved to the living room. Steve's face remained passive, warm, non-judgmental. "You guys came back, all excited. When you were gone, I thought about leaving, but I had promised you I'd stay. Honesty is important to me — if I say I'm going to do something, I do."

Steve stopped his pacing and spun around on his heel. "I totally agree with you on that, Tommy. Being a man of your word is imperative."

Tommy continued, "Anyway, I didn't like you giving me orders in regards to going to the bust." A crooked smile appeared on his face. "You got my message. I went along."

"I hadn't thought I'd be hurt, Steve. I spied that guy creeping towards you, and you didn't spot him. I knew he probably wanted to kill you."

He stopped here, his gaze moved to the ceiling, the floor, and eventually to Steve, "You know what you said about realizing you cared deeply about me? Well, that's the same thing, I think, I realized when I saw him going in your direction. Like you said, some sort of link between us. I don't know why. I don't ever remember feeling like that before. I didn't want you to be hurt."

He continued, "Then I got grazed by the bullet. What I was most scared about was you making me go to the hospital." As the boy sat in the wingtip chair, he shuffled his feet. "Thank you for not forcing me to."

Steve smiled and mussed his hair gently, "Man of my word, and all that. Tricky how you made me promise earlier."

Tommy's head jerked up, startled. "I didn't expect to get shot!"

Steve smiled, "I know, Tommy, it's fine."

The quiet was not uncomfortable. Steve encouraged, "Tell me more."

Tommy grinned, "Well, when you told Doc Epstein, 'No' the way you did, I realized you did care and I kind of felt warmed inside. You did what you said you would. I was relieved. Watching you stand up to Doc was fascinating, too. He seems like a pretty demanding fellow."

Steve explained, "Well, he is, or can be. He's a good man. He cares. I trust him, Tommy."

The lad thought and continued, "Another thing, another feeling is gratitude. You've done things for me no one has, given me food and stuff. The way you act makes me believe I'm safe, comfortable. Thank you."

The hesitancy in his speech indicated to Steve that Tommy had a hard time putting words to the emotions and sentiments he experienced. The tall man smiled and mussed his hair again. "Thanks for sharing, Tommy. Good for me to hear how you are thinking."

Tommy filed Steve's comments away in his mind. While he didn't trust Steve yet, a beginning was developing. *This might be okay…*

"Okay, buddy, I'm going to bed. I like getting up early and jogging. You need anything, holler. You can stay up or sleep, whatever you want."

Slowly, deliberately, words carefully chosen, Steve said, "Make yourself at home, Tommy."

Chapter 6
Steve and Doc Burns

Steve rose early the next morning and went for his jog. He came back, got cleaned up and visited some with Tommy while he made coffee and fixed breakfast for the two of them. He had Tommy help him with the toast, a job fairly easily done with one hand, Steve figured.

"I'll be gone today, as I said. Most likely all day. My testimony is crucial, I'm planning on being precise and articulate, hoping the District Attorney won't need to grill me extensively. If he does want to, I won't be finished today. I'm anxious for this trial to be done."

As Steve sat in the courtroom, the day dragged on. Eventually he presented his statement, working hard to be markedly clear and succinct.

It didn't work. He was informed he would have to be back again for additional cross examination tomorrow. With court cases, you can't argue with a judge or attorney, saying you had other things you wanted to do. You were stuck with what they said. So another day.

On his way out of the municipal building he spotted his photo on the front page of a newspaper lying on a bench. The picture accompanied an article about the case and his testimony. He hated publicity, but sometimes it came with his job/profession. *I don't look too bad. My angular, square jaw makes me appear firm but not mean. My hair's windblown— needs its monthly cut.*

Fresh sea breezes blew in through his open windows as he drove. *Doc seemed to weave me into his life pretty effortlessly after my old man died. I wonder if it really was easy, or he just made it seem that way? I think it wasn't that hard for him....*

Steve decided to make a detour before heading home and stopped at work — he needed to talk with Marco.

He checked his mail and messages. He ducked his head into Marco's side office. "Got time to take a walk with me?"

They sauntered along the deserted boardwalk not far from the office. "So, Steve, what's up?"

Steve had no hesitation. "Tommy. God, Marco, I have no idea what, yet, but I think that boy has been through hell. And somehow, by helping him, I am helping myself. Providing for him, protecting him... it feels like I am the one receiving all that. Things I never got when I needed them."

Marco knew he was referring to times when Steve was a child. His friend had shared the story with him years ago.

His mother died when he was eight, and his little sister, Betty Jean, barely two, in a tragic car accident. A neighbor a mile up the road took the child in. She would have taken Steve as well, but his father forbade it. The man, never an especially nice person, became an abusive drunk.

They lived in a rural area, and at a time when others didn't interfere in families. Steve pretty much was on his own, having to fend for himself. His father hit him, sporadic beatings, a couple of times a month, maybe. The situation seemed to get worse with each passing year. Steve never knew when he'd get hit, there was no real reason attached. They were always when his father was drunk, and for some imagined offense— Steve hadn't swept the floor properly, or Steve hadn't bought the right groceries with the money his father gave him, or Steve hadn't bought enough cigarettes (never mind that he hadn't given him enough money). Almost as if beating Steve was a way of letting off steam for his father. Sometimes it was just a few lashes with the belt behind the woodshed. More often it was many blows, sometimes until the man passed out from drunkenness. It wasn't uncommon for Steve to pass out, either.

Steve did have one friend, the elderly local doctor in their small town. There were times, the morning after a beating, when Steve would make his way the two miles to see Doc Burns. The retired physician operated his tiny practice from the front rooms of his large colonial manor in the small community. He had no nurse or receptionist. Steve would come in, Doc would know right away what had happened. He'd bring him back into the office, shoot him up with pain killer and start working on the lacerations. Often the boy spent the day and night there after this. Doc had gone and talked with his father, tried to reason with him, anything to stop the beatings. The man was angered by his interference, and Doc had to be careful not to cause more trouble for Steve. Steve's father knew that he sometimes visited Doc. The man didn't care, so long as Doc stayed out of his way.

He'd punch his finger in the physician's face and holler, "Look, you jerk, my kid is my concern, not yours. He's a shitty little bastard who needs to be put in his place now and then. So stay out of it."

Doc was powerless, there was nothing he could do, other than offer medical care and support for the poor kid when he needed it, a refuge, a safe haven, at times. He did once suggest Steve "leave"; the twelve-year-old boy couldn't envision that possibility.

Betty Jean had a good life with the grandmotherly Miss Delores. Her five children were grown and gone, and all but one had moved to the mainland. She didn't see them often, so caring for the young girl filled her hours with pleasure as she doted on Betty Jean. Steve was able to stop by occasionally and enjoy their company. Mr. Bill, Delores' husband, was also kind. Some nights Steve listened as Miss Delores sang lullabies to his little sister as she went to sleep for the night. The melodic voice lulled Steve into relaxing. These memories imprinted in his mind, ones he would replay many years later. The elderly couple was aware of the abuse going on, but felt incapable to stop it.

Mr. Bill had a heart attack and passed away a few years after the child had gone to live with them. Miss Delores moved to town and became Doc's live-in housekeeper. Betty Jean was welcomed into Doc's home, as well.

The whole sad scenario with his violent father came to an end just after Steve's fourteenth birthday. He had received a pretty intense whipping; and had slipped into unconsciousness early on. Usually when he passed out, his father quit and slunk off with his bottle. But this time he kept going at the unconscious child, flailing away, finally passing out. He never woke up again. They suspected a heart attack.

For some reason, Doc had been worried about Steve that day. He headed out to their farm the morning after the fateful night, found the father dead, and Steve still out cold, with the worst beating he had yet seen. He loaded him into his car, went back to town and mended the boy as best he could. It was very hard for Doc to see the wounds that one man had inflicted on a young innocent soul. Steve floated in and out of consciousness the next few days. Doc tenderly nursed him. When the patient improved, he relayed the news that his father was dead. The boy's face was stoic, revealing no emotion. Inside, he was elated. No more beatings. That made him almost giddy. His only nagging concern was what he would do now. He was capable of taking care of himself, sort of. He could get a job.

Doc Burns had other ideas, much better ones. Steve stayed with Doc, his sister and Miss Delores. There was never any spoken agreement, Steve just remained, moving in his few belongings. He'd help Doc with things now and then in the home, office and yard. Doc made sure Steve got enrolled in school full time. The boy had been in school off and on, but there were frequent absences due to the beatings and demands his father had placed on him. The man didn't value formal education and was not at all supportive of Steve's attendance.

Doc realized Steve was quite intelligent, and tutored him to catch up to his age-mates. He supplied the boy with everything he needed to excel in school. Steve liked learning and did well. Life was so much better now. But the long hard years of pain and suffering were forever etched in his memory; that would not be wiped away or erased.

Steve and his little sister became closer living under the same roof. They loved their surrogate parents.

Steve was seventeen the year Doc's health failed. The man had done so much for him — it was hard to see him dying. He didn't linger; it was only about a month from the first signs of ill health until his death. The old man and soon-to-be-adult teen had many long talks late into the evenings in the days before he died. Doc was so wise and had much to pass on to Steve, a young person very willing and eager to absorb the wisdom. Many of the things Doc told him stayed with him.

"Steve, you can do anything you want. You are very gifted in many ways. I want— I expect— you to achieve great things in your life. You've had some challenges; you never got the love you deserved as a younger child. Terrible things have happened to you, Steve. What you do with that is your choice. You can allow those memories to taint you, to stifle you, to inhibit you, or you can put them behind you and move boldly forward." The old eyes twinkled. "Steve, I know you'll do well."

Steve had no idea how he'd continue without Doc. Doc had literally been his lifesaver — his body, but more importantly, his mind, and though he didn't know it, his faith— "a" faith. Doc helped him slowly overcome his tortuous past. Not to ignore or forget it, but to move past it. But they also both knew that the history was enormous, a key part of Steve, who he was, why and how he had built walls around himself. Doc was always able to fill Steve's needs, without being gushy or condescending. He seemed to easily sense what was best to help him.

The parish priest had come earlier and given Doc the Last Rites. Steve watched the ritual with the awe of religious mystery. Doc had been a faithful Catholic his whole life. The years Steve lived with him, he learned a lot about the faith, and joined Doc for Mass on Sundays by his own choice. Steve had been baptized Catholic as an infant, but that was as far as things went for him. He never had any sort of faith formation, nor did he go to Church after his mother died.

It wasn't just the trappings; Doc had faith, deep internal faith in God and His goodness. The father-figure never pushed his beliefs on Steve, but always welcomed his participation and inquiries. The idea of a loving God was foreign to Steve. Doc could understand that. Unbeknownst to Steve, he daily prayed mightily that the young man would someday come to know God closely. He especially asked the Holy Ghost to guide and protect him.

Steve was with Doc, just the two of them, that last day together. It was almost as if Doc was infusing into Steve his strength, his energy, his life, his faith. Doc's optimism with him was a tremendous asset and a voice of confidence which Steve carried in his heart his whole life, helping him to succeed. Steve felt it, and was grateful beyond expression.

One of the lessons Doc transfused to Steve was about opportunities. He said God would present various opportunities and gifts to you in your life. And often you would not recognize them as such. You had the choice to accept them, or reject them. Doc shared how when he was young, probably only about eleven, he wanted to be a priest. At the time he had an opportunity to go to a minor seminary, for young boys like him. You left home, and moved to the institution. While not abandoning your family, you ended up being with them very little. And it was a challenge — the life, the academics, the strict discipline. People around him told him not to do it. He could become a priest later, he needed to experience life, he was too young to do something that radical. He was told that he'd miss his brothers and sisters and parents too much. People came up with a thousand reasons for him not to do it. His mother and father were neutral— they allowed him to make his own decision and said they'd support him either way. He chose not to listen to the small voice inside of him encouraging the priesthood. He easily rationalized that he could always do it "later".

What happened, what he explained to Steve, was that he "lost" the calling. It was a gift God had presented to him at a given time. He had assumed that it would be there later if he wanted it. It wasn't. He told Steve sometimes God presents us with opportunities only once. If we miss it, we miss it. That particular opportunity may not ever be there again. Sometimes He gives us more chances with the same gifts/ opportunities, but often not.

The corollary to this lesson Doc taught was to not to fear doing something. If you make a mistake, you make a mistake. You pick up the pieces and go from there. It doesn't mean you will be forever handicapped, or unhappy, or your life will be miserable. Again he used his own experience as an example. He said how he believed, in a small corner of the deepest part of his soul, that he made a mistake not becoming a priest. He shared how once in a great while he thought about it — usually at Holy Mass, during the Consecration when the priest changes the bread and wine into the Body and Blood of Jesus Christ. Thinking that could have been him at the altar, and wondering how many souls he might have saved. Though he didn't accept that gift from God of pursuing the priesthood, he wasn't abandoned by his Creator. He was presented with other gifts, and ended up with a happy and fruitful life. But there was a twinge of regret over what could have been. So mistakes can happen in life, but Doc warned Steve not to "not act" on something because of fear, or being unsure, or uncertain.

He counseled him to learn all he could about some potential opportunity/gift, study it, examine it, pray about it, and then act boldly. This lesson stuck with Steve; he learned it well and took it to heart. Looking over his life, he recognized missed opportunities because he didn't act — not many, but a few. And the times he didn't act was because he was afraid, or he didn't like the opportunity. Steve realized it was easy for him to rationalize away a lack of action, or make an easier choice. Most people did this all the time. Doc was adamant that life was for living— even if there were mistakes. And of course there would be mistakes, no one is perfect. He said mistakes are just opportunities to learn and grow.

Doc was sick, and dying; but not in need of nursing care, nor in pain. Simply a case of failing health. They both knew the end was near. Steve helped Doc get ready for bed as usual that last night. He sat with him, they talked quietly. Doc took his rosary from the nightstand. "Steve, will you pray it with me tonight?"

The teenager knew that Doc prayed the rosary every night. He knew the formula for saying it, but rarely did himself. He would when there was reason, like before Mass during Lent, but not on his own. Steve was happy to comply with the request; he'd do anything for Doc.

Doc smiled at him, took Steve's hands in his, the rosary between them. He spoke solemnly, but not sadly, and with a smile on his face, "Steve, when I'm gone, you keep this. You will use it someday."

A chill ran up Steve's spine; hairs stood up on the back of his neck. He simply nodded. Then Doc asked tiredly, "Will you lead and keep track tonight?"

Again Steve nodded. He looked carefully at Doc, their eyes met. "I love you, Steve."

Steve swallowed the lump in his throat. His voice was husky. "I love you too, Doc."

Doc indicated he should begin. "In the name of the Father, and of the Son, and of the Holy Ghost. I believe…"

Before the end of the first decade of ten Hail Marys Doc had drifted off to a peaceful sleep. Steve continued the recitation. Before the end of the next decade, Steve realized Doc had stopped breathing and died. He had a moment of panic before an inner voice told him to be calm and finish the rosary. And so he did. There was something soothing about the rote repeating of the same words over and over. He thought a bit about those words as he prayed them. Especially the end of the Hail Mary: "Holy Mary, Mother of God, pray for us sinners now and *at the hour of our death*. Amen."

Steve never understood this whole thing about Mary as the "Blessed Mother". He knew Doc prayed a lot, but it was never ostentatious. His prayers were always quiet, often silent. Steve knew he prayed prayers asking for things, but also a great many in thanksgiving for blessings. And he knew Doc thought of Mary as his own mother, but Steve couldn't relate to it. Doc tried to explain when he asked, but the idea didn't click for Steve. But now— here — it did make some sense to him. Some. In the Hail Mary, in that last sentence, he was asking "her" to pray for Doc. And maybe he felt her "presence" just a bit. Maybe the prayers that he was asking for were helping him, as well.

Regardless, by the end of the rosary, said with tears streaming down his cheeks, he was fairly peaceful and collected. He put the black-beaded rosary in his pocket.

There was the funeral. Doc was older, almost ninety, so it was not an untimely death. Steve was sad, but appreciated he had been given a tremendous gift in this man over the last three years. Doc had given him life. He would make him proud. Steve finished high school with high honors and went on from there, choosing the Navy as a springboard for his adult life.

Steve had shared all this with Marco long ago, it wasn't news to his younger friend. They stopped walking and sat on a bench facing the ocean.

"Marco, I never would have made it without him. Doc was my lifesaver. But Doc wasn't there for a lot of those years when I needed someone, and even when he did come into my life, my father wouldn't allow much. Doc did everything he could, but he was so limited while my old man was still living... Not Doc's fault at all….."

"It was just… day to day… no one made meals for me… no one talked to me much…. I had to wash my own clothes… I did have a bed to sleep in… Marco, I was always afraid at night... I never knew when he'd come home drunk and start in on me…. That was the worst, not knowing…. lying in bed listening for the sound of the old car… then listening carefully to see if he was stumbling up the steps or if he was sober… pretending sleep if he was drunk, hoping beyond hope that he'd leave me alone. Once I hid, thinking I'd avoid a beating. That was a big mistake. He found me and pounded the daylights out of me for hiding… never did that again…. Marco, I can still feel the rapid throbbing of my heart in terror…"

After a pause he continued, "There really was nothing Doc could do, Marco. My old man had pretty much shagged him out of my life. He knew I'd see Doc sometimes after a nasty beating, but he never wanted to see Doc around, and I knew better than to be gone more than a day."

His face was a somber mask. "Marco, it was no way for a kid to have to live."

More thinking. More silence.

"I don't know what kind of history Tommy has. I do know that he's been lacking some simple, basic things; my helping to meet them is overwhelming for him. That means no one has been meeting those needs. And no one met mine, those same ones when I was his age. Somehow, by my being there for him, I'm helping myself. Does that make any sense?"

"Yes, Steve, it does."

"And Marco, it's not the food and the bed… it's not the material things… it's the emotional, the mental, that's what's really matters here. Somebody to listen to him, to pay attention to him, to consider his feelings. To know he's not alone, he has help, he has someone who cares about him, will look out for him, will help him…. not being alone anymore…. not being alone, Marco…."

"Until my father died, I was mostly alone. Doc was there, but not much. I really was alone. And that, my friend, was far and away the hardest thing. Much worse than the belt. Not having anyone to turn to, not just for help, but to listen, to lean on. Tommy is younger than I was when Doc rescued me. I hope that helps him… I have no idea how long he's been suffering… nor exactly how. It makes no difference; I can feel it in him. He's been alone, now he's not. And he knows it and I know it, and it's good."

A smile appeared on his face as Steve turned his gaze from the ocean to his friend. "I'm okay, Marco, this is good. Painful, but good. We'll work through it. I'm lucky to have you for a friend." And the thought of gift/ opportunity again ran through his mind.

Placing a hand on his friend's shoulder in support, Marco asked, "You're okay, Steve?"

Steve answered sincerely and with conviction, "Yes, Marco, I'm fine. Thanks. You're a good friend. I'm heading home."

Tommy was there, as Steve had hoped/expected, his nose in a book. Steve asked him about his day which had been quiet and uneventful. Steve made supper for the two of them. He was getting to know Tommy and his likes and dislikes. They had chili rellenos, along with a big salad. That evening Steve took him grocery shopping and made him pick out foods he liked, a task hard for Tommy. Partly because he was happy with any food, partly because having someone buy something just for him was a foreign concept, something he had never experienced. Steve picked up on his unease and would suggest things. The shopping trip was awkward.

That night, Steve went through the ritual of nursing duties on Tommy's arm, as usual talking and sharing as he did so. The arm was much better, this routine wasn't necessary anymore— both realized that— yet they continued with it. Steve asked questions. And once more, it seemed as if Tommy was fairly closed; he divulged little about himself.

After putting the last piece of tape on the forearm to secure the fresh bandage, Steve began to get up to leave the room. Tommy stayed seated on edge of the tub. The tall man stopped and leaned against the counter, eyes questioning. A chill came over him. It seemed as if the child could read into his very soul.

Finally, Tommy voiced his question. "Where are we going?"

He doesn't mean are we leaving the house to go someplace, he means where is this relationship going, he and I as two people in this world. One loaded question. Steve paused thoughtfully before answering. "I don't know, Tommy. But I like the direction. It's good."

No additional comments were forthcoming from the boy, so Steve pushed on. "I think maybe God is in charge here, He'll lead us if we let Him."

Tommy changed the course of the conversation. "You like being outside, right? Like on the lanai, or the beach? I see you out there a lot. You're more... at ease, comfortable... outside, right?"

Whoa. That's a pretty astute observation. He picks up everything. Steve gave a guarded answer. "Yes, I like being outside. Why?"

Tommy shrugged and left the bathroom to go out onto the lanai. He stood at the railing looking at the ocean. Steve followed.

After a while, the boy said, "Would it shock you if I said I'm not sure if I believe in God?"

The conversation that ensued was slow, laden with reflective pauses.

"No, I suppose that wouldn't really shock me. Why might you not believe in God?"

Tommy became animated. "Well, God is supposed to be this all-powerful, almighty Supreme Being who can do anything. So why are there so many bad things in the world? Why doesn't He just make everything good? Get rid of all the bad?"

Steve carefully watched Tommy's reaction as he explained. "Well... God made man with free will. God doesn't make bad or evil things, but He does allow man to make his own free choices. And sometimes those choices result in evil. It's not God's doing."

Tommy spun around to face Steve. "Oh, please! Don't toss platitudes at me. I've heard that drivel before. If God really was so omnipotent and cared about people, he wouldn't allow horrible things to happen to someone who has no control over it. I mean, how would He explain something like ..."

The boy had become intense in his tirade, and suddenly realized it.

Tommy sighed. "I'm sorry, Steve. I'm babbling. I guess I'm just tired. I think I'll go to bed."

He's opening up some, this is good. I want him to stay and keep talking, but I've got to be careful not to push. "No, Tommy, I like hearing what you have to say, what you're thinking. It's okay to have different views on things."

Tommy remained, but again faced the Pacific, saying nothing. Five minutes passed. Steve sensed energy pulsing. *Okay, I'm going to try. Speak softly, O'Shaughnessy.*

"Tommy, tell me about yourself."

In the next two minutes, the pair made extended eye contact, neither breaking it. Without words, something was communicated between them, a deep and profound bonding— or a beginning of a deep and profound bonding. The energy gradually dissipated like steam off a mug of hot coffee.

Tommy sighed. "Like I said the other day, not much to tell."

He turned to leave. "G'night, Steve."

The boy paused before walking back into the house. He again made eye contact. Tentatively he reached out and touched Steve's arm. "Thanks." And with that, in a flash he was back in the house and in his room.

Whoa again! This was significant. He shared, vehemently, about God. Lots of anger there. Rage. Hatred, maybe? Like I figured, something bad has happened to him. He's the one who something horrible has happened to, that he had no control over. Yet he stayed when I asked him to, he didn't run out right away. And he touched me. He initiated that touch. Hesitantly, but he did. We've made one baby step forward, I think. We're connected. This is good.

Steve sat in the moonlight a longtime, mind whirling. And he made a decision.

Chapter 7
Calling in Help

"International operator, please. Person-to-person to Singapore."

As Steve waited, he wanted to pace, but couldn't go farther than a few steps — that's all the phone cord would allow. At last, the connection was made and a familiar voice spoke on the other end of the line.

"Goldberg."

"Samuel? Steve. I think I need you."

"Next plane, Stevie." He asked no questions.

I'm a lucky man to have such loyal friends.

Samuel Goldberg was an old contact of his, whom he knew from his days in Korea. He had first met him at a M.A.S.H. unit, along with a couple of cornball doctors. The man, a skilled psychiatrist who often used unusual tactics, and had been there for Steve in a way and at a time when Steve desperately needed help. Samuel was able to give it, to help him pull the pieces of his life back together after torture and captivity as a POW. Things also came up from Steve's childhood. Steve didn't go in at all for shrinks, but Samuel didn't fit the mold of any psychiatrists he was acquainted with. Samuel knew him in an intimate way few others did. Marco did, and Doc, to some degree, but no one else… there was a deeply private part of himself that he kept locked away from others.

A smaller man, maybe 5' 7" or 8", with a slender, slight build, in his forties, Samuel had wiry hair and liked his cigars. He had seen a lot of mental trauma in Korea and had learned a lot during the war about helping people who were hurting — how to really help them. The bulk of the formal education he had been taught was useless. But Samuel discovered what worked well. He acquired a way of reading people and situations and had become quite skilled at leading them out of pain and despair. Steve believed his friend had a natural gift for this.

Time differences made the call at that hour reasonable. Samuel had chosen to settle in Singapore after the war, making the Asian country his home.

Steve got a few hours of rest. His mind worked overtime thinking about Tommy. He called Marco at six a.m. "Marco, I asked Samuel to come. Can you call the airlines and find out when he'll be in and pick him up? He hoped to be on the next plane. Tell him anything you want about all this, Marco. You can talk freely. I hope to be done in court by noon. Bring Sam to the office, my house, whatever works. I'll touch base with you when I'm done in court."

Marco first met Samuel years ago when Andrea, Steve's fiancée, died. He saw how Samuel had helped Steve through that. And he knew there was much more between them from Korea that he didn't know about, nor needed to know. All he needed to know was that Samuel was a good friend and competent professional. And that Steve had called him for help. This was good, Marco thought. Samuel would help figure it out.

Steve was both excited and terrified about seeing Samuel. More excited than terrified. But he also recalled that "therapy" with Samuel was not usually painless and sometimes downright petrifying.

    That morning over breakfast, he told Tommy about his friend. "I've mentioned him before to you— my psychiatrist friend. Tommy, normally I think psychiatrists are a waste of time. But Samuel's good, very good. I think he may be able to help us both sort things out. Think about it. He's one of my few close friends. Samuel's good; he has helped me understand many things. He's more than good, he's outstanding. There is no one but him that I trust to 'get inside my head' and help me sort things out. He's been a lifesaver for me in the past. I knew him when I was in the Navy in Korea. I spent some time in a POW camp as a prisoner, not a pleasant time. He helped me work through that."

    Steve could tell Tommy was wary about the whole idea of talking to a stranger. Reassuringly, he added, "Tommy, I repeat, I'm not going to make you do anything you don't want to." The lines of worry in the boy's face eased somewhat; he believed Steve but this was unmapped territory for him.

    "I'm leaving now for court. I hope to be back around lunchtime. Any questions? About Samuel, or anything?"

    "No. Good luck in court."

    Court went well; Steve was done by eleven a.m., and dismissed— finally! He called Marco to find Samuel's flight was delayed and he wasn't yet in.

    "It's supposed to arrive within the hour. I'll pick him up and bring him to the house. You go on home."

    Steve did. He visited with Tommy as he fixed lunch — typical Hawaiian fare of lomi lomi, a salmon dish, and a fresh green salad. He had Tommy helping him.

    The boy stared at him curiously. Steve hadn't been looking at him, then turned and did when he felt the boy's gaze on him. He jerked in shock. For a split second he didn't see Tommy, but himself. Just for a millisecond. Steve stared, now seeing Tommy. The child looked back, innocently. It was the eyes. Tommy had the same steel blues eyes he did. But in that instant he saw himself and not Tommy. Again, electricity streamed between them. It flowed in the room. Steve felt a definite sizzle in the air, like static electricity that allows fine wispy hair to float seemingly independent of gravity.

The man was uncomfortable. Something was happening inside him, something bubbling up, all the way to the surface. Tommy wasn't sure what was going on, but he could see that Steve was almost dazed; certainly something was going on inside his head. He tentatively asked, "Steve, are you okay?"

Steve shook his head to clear it, hardly hearing the question. He couldn't take his eyes off Tommy— he was seeing Tommy— but the images in his head were now filled with himself. A kaleidoscope of a thousand memories of moments— painful moments. He didn't answer. He was being bombarded with a gusher of emotions and sensations, flailing in a mental whirlwind.

Tommy reached over and touched his arm. A spark jumped between them which served to bring Steve back a bit, enough to regain some equilibrium. He took some deep breaths, a technique Samuel had taught him. *Okay, O'Shaughnessy. All kinds of things coming up here. Don't let them drown you. Let them come. Put them on a shelf in your mind, deal with them later, more slowly, one thing at a time. Thinking this way helps a great deal. And Samuel would remind me to never stuff anything, or bury emotions. Deal with them. Doesn't have to be all at once or immediately.*

Tommy wondered what was going on. He suspected something had happened to Steve, maybe when he was a kid, and somehow he was bringing back memories.

Steve looked again at Tommy, seeing a quizzical, worried expression on the small face; and the tall man smiled weakly. He put his hand on the boy's shoulder and squeezed, "I'm okay. I just remembered some things. I'll work them out. Don't worry about it." Tommy looked at him skeptically, but accepted what

Steve said. Tommy sensed and experienced the energy in the room, but was unsure what to make of it. Steve shuddered. He thought that someday, sometime, someplace, he would share at least some of what transpired with him and his own father with Tommy. Might be helpful to him….to both of them.

Steve thought about something he had long forgotten. He went to his room and opened the top drawer of the highboy. Back in the corner was a small box. He retrieved it and opened it, removing the chain of beads. Doc Burns' rosary. The last time Steve had touched it was just before he left for Korea. He debated bringing it along, but chose not to for fear of losing it. He wasn't sure what it was— maybe a smell or the feel of the black pearl beads, but somehow he felt comforted. And he knew that while he may have some serious work to do in dealing with his past, he would make it. Smiling to himself, he knew Doc would expect no less.

He studied the rosary. It didn't look quite the same as he remembered it. The beads had a kind of shine to them, a gold tint or hue — almost a shimmer. He remembered them being plain black beads. Pretty, and nice, but no shine or shimmer. Doc told him he had gotten the rosary when he was in the war and was stationed in Europe. He had made a side trip to Fatima one weekend, and some "very holy" priest had given him the rosary. Doc always had it with him.

Instead of putting the rosary back in the box and drawer, he pocketed it.

Steve had no idea that what was really happening here was the Holy Ghost was hard at work, using Tommy, a battered child, as a vehicle for healing for Steve. The same Holy Ghost that Doc had prayed to watch over Steve was hard at work. He finished making lunch just as Samuel and Marco arrived. The man and boy both got up to greet them. Steve introduced Tommy and Samuel.

The very first time Samuel had met Steve, it was a tense situation. To defuse some of the stress, Samuel purposely called Steve, "Stevie". A nickname anyone could clearly see was not a good fit for the stern, reserved O'Shaughnessy. But it worked in that moment and broke the tension. And Samuel — only Samuel — had ever used that name for Steve.

Looking intently at Steve and Tommy, and never one to beat around the bush, play games or mince words, Samuel commented, "Well, something powerful has been going on around here!" If you could see energy, the room would have been ablaze. Marco and Samuel both experienced the sparkle, the vivacity. The two friends noted that Steve looked washed out, totally washed out, but extremely peaceful.

Steve and Tommy looked at each other, grinned, and Steve said, "Yeah … you could say that…"

Nothing more was forthcoming. Making himself at home, Samuel plopped on the couch. "So, you want to expound on that, Stevie?"

Steve laughed. "Typical Samuel."

He went to the kitchen to serve lunch. He had made enough for all of them, figuring that Marco and Samuel would be eating with them. "In a bit. I don't know about you, Samuel, but I'm hungry. Let's eat."

As they lunched, Steve began. Looking at Tommy, he shook his head in awe and wonder. "Samuel, I still don't know who this kid is, why he came into my life, or a thousand other things. You know I'm not a religious person, 1 but I think God is at work here, using Tommy as a catalyst. And you and I may need to do a bit of work on me. Later." He proceeded to relate to his two best friends what had transpired minutes earlier, things becoming a bit clearer as he did. Tommy just sat and listened.

It is God who is bringing us together, bringing down walls and barriers. Thank you, Lord. I'll think about this more later, it's a soul— searching healing that doesn't belong to Tommy. He's an oblivious stimulus

— *an instrument of The Holy Ghost*— *but not called to be my therapist. He may act like an adult sometimes, but he's still a young child.*

After the recital, Samuel turned to Tommy. "Young man, sounds like you're been pretty helpful for Steve."

Tommy shook his shoulders, "I dunno, sir… I didn't do anything….."

"Call me Samuel, Tommy."

Continuing, he said, "You know, I'm tired. With the flight, the time change, all that sitting, I could use a nap. And, Stevie, you look good, but bushed as well. Tommy, a nap wouldn't hurt you either. Let's take a break for a few hours, recover."

His suggestion was met with approval. Tommy went back to the guest bedroom to nap, Samuel chose the hammock on the lanai (he loved sleeping in hammocks, he had one for his bed at home), and Steve went to his room. Marco left, promising to come by later that afternoon. All drifted off quickly and peacefully. It was about four hours later when Marco came back, Chinese take-out food in two large bags, to find them just rousing from their slumbers. "You guys must have been really wiped out to have slept so long!"

It was too early to eat the meal; he figured they could heat the food up later, and set out an assortment of appetizers for a snack.

Doc stopped in shortly after Marco's arrival. His face lit up in a smile when he saw Samuel whom he had met some years earlier when the man visited Steve. Doc checked Tommy, pronounced him well, doing fine. It had not escaped Doc's notice that Tommy favored his left arm, and limped with his right leg, but the physician chose not to mention it.

Samuel asked, "So, Stevie, you going to fill Doc in?" Doc Epstein knew some of Steve's past. Not all of it, as Samuel and Marco did. But when you have a back full of scars, keeping it a secret from your physician is impossible. He knew the bare bones, the basic details. He had never probed into the feelings, or the emotions with Steve. As per the psychiatrist's request, he complied, giving Doc a brief recap. He knew Samuel was okay with him sharing as much or as little as he wanted with Doc.

A break was needed after the story. Steve stood and stretched. "I'm going outside for a while." He went and sat near a large boulder not far from his house. Tommy watched. Then told the others he was going outside for a while, as well.

He approached Steve timidly. "Want some company?"

"Sure!"

Tommy sat cross legged on the sand opposite Steve. For a while he just picked up handfuls of sand and let it sift through his fingers, making a small mountain in front of him. Neither spoke. Then Tommy looked up sharply.

Steve met the stare. "Something's on your mind."

"Yeah. What's going on here?" Tommy had acquired a kind of "tough man" attitude.

Okay, so this kid is not just really intelligent, he's got street smarts, too. Not surprising.

"What do you mean?"

Tommy fired off questions rapidly. "Okay, here's what I mean. It seems you want me to stay here with you. Right? How long? Why? What's in it for you? What do you want from me? What are the ground rules? What is the deal with this Samuel guy?"

"Good questions, Tommy. Let me take them one at a time. Yes, I'd like you to stay here with me. How long? I don't really know. As long as necessary, maybe? As long as you need to? As long as it works for both of us? I don't know, but I'm thinking — and hoping — maybe a long time."

Steve mimicked Tommy and began sifting sand and making his own little mountain, but frequently looking up to gauge the boy's reaction and attitude to his answers.

"Why? What's in for me? I don't know that, either. But I'm thinking it has something to do with Fate. I think you and I were thrown together, unexpectedly, by a God who has something great in store for us. I do know this: in my heart, having you with me, living here, feels like what I'm supposed to be doing. I have learned that God sends little nudges to us now and then, and it's prudent to pay attention and follow them. I've been feeling nudged since the first moment I laid eyes upon you that day in my office. It's not just seeing that you're well taken care of. If that was all, I could pay someone to care for you, get you situated somewhere to live and go to school. That's not what I want, it's not what I feel called to do. I feel responsible."

Interrupting, Tommy countered vehemently, "You're not responsible for me!"

"Yes, you're right. That was a poor choice of words. I'm not responsible for you. But I do feel responsible for providing what I can, what you will accept. And personally, directly, not through some third party. I can't say why, Tommy, but that's the way it feels to me— like I'm supposed to be doing this personally. Does that make more sense?"

"I guess."

"Ground rules?"

"Yes, ground rules. For me staying with you. What am I supposed to do?"

Smiling Steve replied, "Tommy, usually I have answers. Again I'm going to hit you with, 'I don't know'. Ground rules? I never really thought about them. I've got a sister in California with two boys. She said something once that struck me. 'There's only two rules in my house: Respect people and respect property.' I guess if you want 'rules' I'd say that's pretty much it. Respect property is pretty straight forward, I think you'd do that naturally. Respect people— I guess for me to respect you would mean what I said after you'd gotten shot. I won't force you to do anything you don't want to do. That includes staying with me, or talking to

Samuel. I sense that you need and want to be in control of things relating to you. That's fine and understandable. I won't take that away from you. Nor will Samuel nor Doc nor Marco nor anyone, if I can help it."

"The flip side of that is you respecting me. That would mean things like not taking off and running away without talking to me about it first. Maybe also honesty. I'm not saying you have to share everything— or even anything— with me, or anyone else. But respect means being honest about what you do say. Maybe courtesy. Running away without talking would be rude. Just ordinary courtesy."

"We on the same page so far?"

Tommy shrugged. "I guess so."

"What do I want from you? That's a tough one. Again, I don't know. I haven't thought about it. The honesty. My off the top of my head thought would be that I want you to be the very best person you can be, who you want to be. And anything I can do to help , I will do. I think God has a plan for each one of us. And it unfolds over our whole life. We can cooperate with that plan or not. I guess I'd like it if you let me witness and be a part of the unfolding of your plan, your life. Is that a lot to ask? Could be. But staying with me doesn't mean you're locked into anything. What's it going to hurt to give it a try?"

Careful, O'Shaughnessy, don't push too hard.

Tommy shrugged again. He had gone back building to his sand mountain.

Steve chuckled. "This 'Samuel guy'? It was probably presumptuous of me to call him in without consulting you. Another one of those nudges from God, I think. I called him for help. Help for you, if you want it, if you allow it, help for me. A little or a lot, however it works out. I suspect that you have plenty of issues to work through and that is not even ON your priority list. But maybe it can be, maybe it could be."

"One good thing to know about me, Tommy is that there is a word I don't use much: should. Just now, I might have said, 'You should let Samuel help your with your issues.' I said, 'You could." Could implies choice, should implies obligation. Much of what we do is a choice. Anyway, I digress. Samuel is a good friend, he's helped me out with my 'issues'. I want you to have the same opportunity if you want it."

Tommy didn't reply.

"Bottom line, what's in for me? Knowing that I did what I thought was best. That's the key. That alone gives me a sense of peace, calm, and satisfaction. Beyond that? Tommy, I suspect that you are one tremendously interesting character and I think getting to know you would be a joy."

A bird landed on the boulder above Steve.

"It's your choice, Tommy. Ball's in your court. Hang on to it, serve it back, whatever." *Another little push, there, O'Shaughnessy. That's okay. I hope.* He regarded Tommy.

Tommy stared back at him. "Ball's in my court?"

Steve nodded.

"Tell you what. I'll hang on to the ball. That's all I will commit to now. Just hanging on. I won't run away. But no promises to talk to your friend or anything else. I'll just hang on to the ball. I don't have any place else I have to be just now." The boy grinned.

"Good enough for me. Nice sand mountain you've got there."

The two got up and headed back into the house.

Chapter 8
Tommy's Turn

Everyone had the feeling it was "Tommy's turn". Including Tommy. The boy felt uncomfortable— he was squirming, quieter than usual, not making any eye contact. Yet at the same time, he did seem to feel comfortable and safe. He had never experienced these kinds of feelings, and had no idea how to act.

The last thing I want is any pain for Tommy. Sam will help Tommy in the best way. Will Tommy open up? Is the time right? I want to tell Samuel to take it easy.

Marco and Doc looked at Steve and Samuel. They all expected big things to be happening here, and both wanted to be there for him, and Tommy. But they were sharp enough to realize they were two more people and that alone might be intimidating for Tommy, make him less likely to open up. Marco asked, "Steve, do you want Doc and me to stay? Or is it better if we left and came back later?"

Steve wasn't sure what was best. He looked at Samuel who simply said, "Your call, Stevie." Steve was more tuned in to the situation than the psychiatrist and could more likely make the best call. He said nothing, but studied the people in the room. He wanted Doc and Marco there; he wasn't sure if that was best for Tommy and the child's sense of security was most important to him.

No one spoke for a bit while Steve decided on an answer. Then, instead of replying, he did something odd. Looking directly at Tommy, his eyes conveyed kindness, empathy, compassion, sympathy, many things. This was a precious moment between the two of them and Steve had chosen to allow his few very good friends to witness it. They all knew Steve's history; Tommy was the only one who didn't.

Slowly he moved near him. He pulled up an ottoman and sat at eye level, almost knee to knee with the boy, all the while keeping eye contact with him. Unhurriedly he removed his necktie. He unbuttoned his white dress shirt and removed it with deliberate movements. He sat a moment in his T-shirt. His eyes never strayed from Tommy's. He didn't blink, nor did the boy.

The room had been silent since Marco's question, minutes earlier. Without words, Steve exuded calmness and tranquility. He kept his eyes locked on Tommy's. He reached over and gently squeezed the boy's shoulder. Then he slipped his T-shirt off and turned a little, exposing his back. Tommy's eyes couldn't help but be drawn to the scars criss-crossing the man's torso.

No one spoke. Tommy's lip quivered. The minute hand on the clock made two rotations. No one talked or moved. Steve slipped his T-shirt over his head, and put his dress shirt back on. Tommy's gaze had moved back to Steve's riveting eyes.

Without looking away, Steve quietly said to Doc and Marco one simple word, "Later."

The two left without comment. What Steve had accomplished— intentionally —was to let Tommy know it was okay for others to know about personal pain. The tall man accurately assessed the incredulity on Tommy's face. It wasn't hard to imagine his thoughts: that Steve let others— a few special others— know who he really was, what his history was.

Steve smiled softly; remaining right in front of Tommy. "It's going to be okay." Tears trickled down Tommy's cheeks. Steve wiped them away with his thumb.

"Breathe, Tommy," inhaling and exhaling deeply himself, as an example and for Tommy to synchronize his own breaths with. Tommy did as asked.

Steve smiled, "Good."

He got up and moved to the couch; patting the spot next to him, inviting Tommy over. Tommy complied, and Steve protectively draped his arm over him. Samuel remained quiet the entire time, sitting a few feet away, watching.

From experience, Steve knew Samuel employed rather unorthodox methods. His techniques were intense, and he made you do most of the work. His job was guiding and directing rather than providing answers. Often results were borne with months or years of therapy. People would always be plagued by new or old problems. If they could handle it themselves, he had equipped them with an invaluable toolbox. Then they wouldn't need him or any other therapist. Steve had gotten pretty good at this; having a sharp analytical mind like his helped.

The psychiatrist's years in a war situation taught him how to deal with emotional and mental crises quickly. A soldier in distress over seeing his whole platoon wiped out didn't have a year to sort it all out.

Steve looked at Tommy and said, "So, Tommy, tell us about yourself."

Tommy looked at Steve and Samuel. He slid closer to Steve (almost an impossibility, he was already up tight against him). Steve tightened his grip on the boy's shoulder, and whispered, "It's okay, Tommy."

Tommy pulled his legs up onto the couch, embracing them with his arm, trying to become physically as small as possible. They waited patiently.

Steve tried to make him feel more at ease. "Tommy you don't have to tell us anything. But if you want, you can tell us anything." Tommy nodded mutely. He curled up even closer to Steve.

Again, Steve could almost read the boy's mind. *He doesn't like this, he feels unnerved. The emotions are foreign to him. He's soaking up the physical closeness, but remains reluctant to talk. He wants to run away and not run away. He wants to trust me, but doesn't know how.*

It didn't take a genius for Samuel to realize the battle the boy was facing.

They waited.

Tommy looked again, long and hard at Steve, then at Samuel. Finally said in a quiet voice, "Okay."

Steve squeezed his shoulder. "Good."

Samuel got a large glass of water and offered it to Tommy, who accepted and drank.

To give him a possible opening, a starting point, Steve said, "You know, Tommy, you don't seem to like hospitals. Why?"

The boy thought before he spoke. "It's not really hospitals Steve, it's ….. well, I guess it's people who work in them…. sort of….."

Tommy stopped and chose a different route. The boy tilted his head and seemed to be somewhat more comfortable. "Let me tell you a story. Imagine a boy. Young. The only child of a man and a woman who are drug addicts, whose habits seem to go up and down. The father is able to often get off the drugs, not so for the mother. She dies of an overdose when he's five. So now it's just the kid and his dad. The kid is pretty smart, even at his young age he knows what a drug addict is, he knows there are times it is a good idea to become scarce and unseen. Life continues haphazardly for them. He's not enrolled in school. The father works some; peddles drugs a fair amount. They move around frequently to avoid the law."

"There are times the father, usually when he's strung out needing a fix, gets violent. And the boy is a handy target where he can express his anger. The boy learns what it is to be beaten, what that feels like. They don't live in a nice warm place like Hawaii; they live in a cold snowy climate. Like I said, he's smart. He figures out that when he's got a throbbing bleeding back, if he goes outside, takes off his shirt, and lays down in a snow bank, the cold mimics an anesthetic and numbs the pain."

Tommy stopped and swallowed a few times, squirmed uncomfortably, but continued. "Over the next few years, sometimes he gets to spend some time in school, but not usually. The schools he does go to have kind people, caring teachers, but they are overworked, and in an area where families are often transient, where students have hard lives, authorities can't really follow up on each one. This boy loved school, he loved learning, he loved his teachers. He also knew regular school attendance wasn't going to happen.

"The father was home at odd hours, often in the daytime; and the boy learned the smarter choice was to be gone. He discovered hanging out in stores often caused him to be profiled, understandably, by security guards as a potential threat, shoplifter, even though he didn't steal.. Well, there were times he did steal, that was always only food, and only because he was really hungry. He knew it was wrong, but sometimes when he had such bad stomach cramps from hunger, to snatch a candy bar off a shelf didn't seem so terrible."

"The boy figured out one of the best places to be was the public library. It was warm and dry inside, no one minded if you just sat around for a long time, and there were books galore waiting to be opened. He'd read anything, but especially liked fiction, because it transported him away from reality into some pleasant fantasy setting. The boy had discovered he could only frequent the same library about twice a week. If he went every day, as he wanted, the staff started to ask too many questions. And he could only go after school hours, even though he wasn't in school. So he'd find different ones and rotate his visits."

"The kid never got to be treated a doctor when he was hurt. His father never took him in to any clinic or anywhere. A few people nearby may have noticed the kid was around, but no one questioned a drug pusher. There were a lot of girlfriends who'd come by their place. The boy liked that— it distracted his father from him, and he felt a little safer, knowing he was unlikely to get a beating with a girl around."

Tommy stopped. There was more to the story, much more. They all knew it. But if Tommy needed to stop there, that was fine. He really had made a great start. There was nothing he said that really came as a surprise to Steve or Samuel.

Around mid-afternoon Steve made lunch for the three of them. They relaxed at the kitchen peninsula as he worked, and chatted about all kinds of things. Mostly Steve and Samuel talked, while Tommy listened. After they had eaten and cleaned up, Samuel suggested they go for a walk on the beach. They did; Steve lived in a secluded spot, free of other people. They stopped at a huge boulder a short way down the beach.

Looking at Tommy, Samuel said, "Tell us more."

Tommy shrugged and turned his head away. Non-committally, he replied, "Not much else to tell."

Samuel shook his head, not letting him get away with that. "Oh, yes there is. There is a ton more to tell, Tommy. And you know it and I know it and Steve knows it. What I have found working with people is that if you can get it out in the open, where it's real to you and to those you share it with, you can begin to deal with it, work with the issues. No one here is going to push you, and I can stay as long as I'm needed. But the sooner and more completely you can open up, the faster you'll heal. Don't be like Steve, here. What, twenty years and he's just discovering now that he still hasn't dealt with everything? You can do better, Tommy."

The psychiatrist smirked. "But then again, Steve didn't have me to help him back when he was a kid."

Steve started at Samuel's comment about hanging on to stuff for twenty years and huffed. *Well, okay. If Sam's going to use me as an example to help Tommy, I can handle a little sting. And he's right, as usual....*

Steve moved close to Tommy again, and touched his shoulder, but said nothing, just smiled. Tommy watched the waves; he also said nothing. After a few minutes, Samuel asked a question, "Tommy, do you think it would be easier for you to talk about things with or without Steve here? Either way is fine. I think you like having him here, but maybe it also makes it harder. Or maybe for some things you want him here, but not others. That's okay, too." Looking carefully at Tommy he informed him, "You do realize, don't you, that anything you say to me, or Steve, we will hold in strict confidence unless you say it's okay to tell someone else? This is all privileged." Tommy nodded.

And they sat longer.

Then quietly, without warning, Tommy continued, "As this boy got older, the father began to view him as a possible asset. He made him go out and steal things, high ticket items like electronic radios, things that could be hawked or resold for money. The boy hated doing this, but he felt like he had no choice. He learned more about the fine art of becoming scarce, making himself disappear...."

"Then there was that one time. Not yet ten years old, it was after he had gotten a pretty nasty beating. He had been going to school for about two months. His teacher knew where he lived. The boy never had told them, but his father must have filled in information on some form. When he didn't show up in school for a few days, she came looking for him. This was a wonderful teacher; he really liked her. He heard her at the door when his father answered; she asked to visit with him. His father refused, saying he wasn't available. The teacher, undeterred, suspected he had been beaten up and wasn't going to let it go. She came back later with Child Protection Services— CPS. They came into the apartment and found the boy, nearly unconscious, and called an ambulance. He remembered overhearing heated conversations with the social workers and his father. He was scared, more scared than he had ever been before. The attendants got him onto a gurney. As they wheeled him out, the look on his father's face was terrifying to the boy."

"He was medically treated in the hospital kindly and thoroughly by doctors and nurses. He was visited by social workers, CPS people, who all tried to get him to open up and talk about what had happened, to tell them his story. The boy kept completely mum. Unbeknownst to him, they were also having meetings with the father. Everyone believed the father had done the beating, but no one could prove anything."

"What they did was work out a temporary respite. The boy would go into foster care; the man would receive counseling and therapy to learn how to be a better parent."

Tommy looked now, for the first time since he started, at Steve and Samuel. "Foster homes aren't always very nice places." Then he was silent.

A few minutes later they walked back to Steve's. Steve had been pondering in his mind what to "do" with Tommy. Certainly it sounded like he was wary of any kind of "placement". That wouldn't work. Plus, that option just didn't "feel" right to Steve. At all. What he wanted was for Tommy to stay with him. He figured that was probably against some law, right now he didn't care about legalities. What he cared about was helping Tommy, doing what was in his best interests.

When they got back, Steve decided to head off to the office— he had some things that needed taking care of. He asked

Samuel and Tommy if they would be okay staying there. They were; Steve left. Tommy felt a little uncomfortable being around Samuel alone. Samuel was aware of his apprehension. He didn't do any therapy with Tommy, but he did begin to introduce some techniques that would be good for Tommy to know. He explained some relaxation methods to him, some deep breathing; things that helped calm a person. Tommy listened and paid attention. He did the things Samuel asked, but he was wary and on edge. Probably he thought about running away. But he didn't. Something was holding him there. Something good, even if he didn't understand it.

Steve raced to his office, took care of pressing business he had going. *I want to free up my time over the next few days. I want— need— to be with Tommy. For my sake and his. This word— almost a mantra— keeps popping up in my head: opportunity/gift. That's Doc Burn's voice, and Doc's face.* It made Steve smile. *What exactly is the opportunity/gift here? Certainly it has brought some old memories to the surface that I need to deal with. I didn't even know they were buried. So it's a gift to see that now I can handle it, then be done with it. Not an "easy" gift by any means, but a good one.*

But there's Doc again, shaking his head. He's saying something like, "There's more to it than that, Steve…" What the heck does that mean? Well, it will all work itself out, I'll figure it out. But sure as heck I'm not going to let this opportunity/gift pass by. I'll take care of office business then be able to devote my time and energy to "it"— the gift, and Tommy.

At the office he had a long talk with Marco, filling him in on what had happened earlier. He had asked Tommy if it was okay to share with Doc and Marco, Tommy said he could if he wanted. Marco was a good sounding board, helping him to see things more clearly sometimes. Samuel was not the only one who was good at asking questions that got you thinking.

Steve went back home hours later, calling ahead to let them know he was coming with take-out supper and Marco. The four had a leisurely dinner and evening, the three adults doing most of the talking. That was fine, they knew each other. By listening, Tommy was learning more about who they were, how they thought, and so on. Besides, he liked being around them, being part of their group.

Once again, Steve cleaned Tommy's injury. The pair talked as he did that. Steve said, "Today, there was that moment when I looked at you and saw myself as a boy. That threw me for a loop, Tommy. Let's just say that some unpleasant memories were brought back up for me. Something I'd really like to run away from instead of deal with. But I know dealing with it is best, what needs doing. So I will. I already did that some today, processing thoughts, and feelings. One thing I learned this morning was all those memories I had just buried long ago have been affecting me in ways I hadn't realized. I don't want you to make that same mistake."

Tommy said, "I was kind of scared to talk about what happened to me. Honestly, I didn't want to. But I thought you deserved an explanation, especially after you showed me your scars. Steve, that surprised me. You seem so together, so with it, so…. successful. I would never have imagined anything like that ever had happened to you. How did you … get over it…?"

Steve stood, "The answer to that, my friend, is long. And I'll show you, and tell you, over time — the answer's not a few sentences. Samuel played a big part. He's good, Tommy. Not easy, but good. I know I'm repeating myself, but it's true. Let him help you. Trust him. I do. Think about that tonight, about letting Samuel really help you. The more you can give him, the better it will be."

He then asked Tommy a specific question, instead of another general one, "Tommy, you favor your right arm. What happened?"

Tommy shrugged, "It got banged up a while back. No big deal." Steve knew there was much more to that story. He pushed just a little, "What about your leg? You've got a limp."

Again, no real information was forthcoming. Steve looked at him as he re-bandaged the arm, "You know, Doc could take a look at them very easily."

Tommy's rebuttal was instant, "NO! I'm fine."

Steve backed off, holding his hands in a position of surrender, "Okay, Tommy, you're the boss here. You don't have to."

Chapter 9
The Rest of the Story

    The next day Steve planned a relaxing fun day. He and Marco both took off work, and they, along with Tommy and Samuel, went sailing in Steve's boat. They left at seven a.m., stopping first to pick up supplies. The sun shone brightly, a pleasant breeze swayed palm leaves; no one could have asked for a more beautiful day.
    Steve's compact boat measured twenty feet and had a spacious open deck and enclosed lower cabin. Raised sheets filled with wind and they tacked along nicely in the easy sailing weather. Marco stripped off his shirt, so did Steve. Tommy noticed this, and Steve noticed Tommy look at them, him in particular. He laughed, "Tommy, I didn't take off my shirt in any kind of subtle message. I often do when I'm out sailing. I don't when people who don't know me—or my history—are around, but here on the boat I almost always do."
    Steve looked at Samuel, "But you know, maybe that's going to change. I've always hidden my scars and past from people. The only ones familiar with my history besides you all, and my sister, is Doc Epstein. I'm not going to broadcast my past

to everyone, but I think I'll stop hiding it. Do things like go ahead and take my shirt off at a pool. Probably a healthy step for me to take, right, Sam?"

"Yep." He honestly hadn't taken off his shirt for any ulterior motive. But as he thought about it, maybe it was good in a sneaky way— Tommy would be reminded that Steve had his own personal similar experiences — he would understand in ways others might not.

Samuel had talked earlier, privately, a bit with Steve about the day. The outing had been Steve's idea, but Samuel liked the plan. Privacy, no interruptions. He thought he'd let the day play out, possibly do some "therapy kinds of things" with Steve, or with Steve and Tommy together. Kind of ease the boy into talking and opening up. Steve's example could be helpful, and the older man was fine with that.

Samuel took this as an opening, "Stevie, why did you hide your scars? Why didn't you take your shirt off at pools? Why didn't or don't you want people to see the damage, to witness what you've been through?"

Steve thought for a while before responding. "I guess for lots of reasons, Samuel. I was embarrassed. I didn't want people to feel pity for me, to feel sorry for me. That's a big one. I didn't want to have to answer questions, to have to explain. Maybe I've been afraid people will be repulsed at seeing me, disgusted with me …"

Samuel asked, "So how will you explain it when people ask?"

Steve replied at once, "I'll simply tell them the truth: 'My old man had some mental problems and used me as a punching bag.' It's nobody's business but mine and asking would be rather rude. Some people will anyway. I doubt they'd persist, but if they did, I'd tell them it's not their business and redirect the conversation."

Tommy was silent, but listening intently.

They sailed along a while; the sound of waves hitting the boat and the soaring of sea birds overhead was soothing.

Samuel asked another question, "Stevie, tell me about yourself, what happened to you. You never really did, not all of it. I got bits and pieces, even a lot of it here and there. But give me the whole story."

Steve looked at Samuel. He understood the psychiatrist's purpose in these questions was twofold— to help Steve, and also to help Tommy. But this was the kind of thing Steve didn't like. He knew it was good, getting the feelings out, talking about the experiences, and that it would help Tommy, so he went along with the request.

Moving forward to the front of the deck, he leaned back and got comfortable. "Marco, take the helm." Then basically he repeated what he'd talked about with his friend earlier, sharing the details with Samuel and Tommy.

Steve told them about Doc, and how Doc would take care of him. Steve had reached into his pocket and fingered the rosary beads he had put there a few days earlier. Since taking them out of the box, he'd kept them in his pocket. He didn't pray with them right then, but for some unknown reason, he liked having the rosary on his person. And feeling the smooth beads reminded him of something he had long forgotten. He told his small audience about how Doc would pray for him when he'd come in to the man's office, battered and beaten, and hearing the prayers made him feel better. Looking pointedly at Tommy, but not saying anything, he decided then and there that he would start praying for Tommy, aloud at times but mostly silently in his heart.

Steve related how Doc tried to help him out of the mess he had surrounding his life, and that nothing happened until his father died. He wasn't going to, but suddenly felt compelled to explain in quite a bit of detail that last beating his father gave him, and the seriousness of the injuries inflicted upon him. He talked about how Doc took him in, and what a blessing that had been, his gratefulness.

The older man revealed how Doc taught him that he helped Steve not out of pity, but just because he could. Because he was there, and Steve was there, and there was no reason not to help him, take him in, treat him like a son. He told how he and his sister became very close.

Samuel asked how Steve felt when he was living all this.

Steve reminisced, again relaying the same emotions he had talked to Marco about.

Samuel questioned, "And you had lots of these memories and feelings come out yesterday. What are you going to do about it?"

Steve switched positions a bit, leaned forward, elbows on his knees, chin resting on his fists. "Well, Samuel, I realized everything that happened to me has played a part in making me who I am. Some of the bad experiences probably gave me a greater determination, stronger spirit, I don't know. I'm going to accept whatever helped me to be better, and then dismiss it. Toss it over board, just like this." He took the half glass of water next to him and dumped it out into the sea.

He explained, "I don't need that anymore. The picture of my past will always be there, but the experience doesn't have to be. And I can choose to put the picture away in an album and not look at it unless I want to. I can't erase anything, but I can choose to not let those years dictate or influence my life. That's what Doc told me long ago. I kind of understood the lesson then, but I understand it much better now."

Steve studied Tommy. "And Tommy's helping. Seeing him, knowing just a bit about him, makes me understand my own self—and past experiences—more completely. When I saw myself as him for that split second, I think it was the first time I really believed that what had happened to me wasn't little Stevie O'Shaughnessy's fault. I had been told that, repeatedly; by Doc

Burns, and by you, Samuel. And I knew—intellectually—that none of it was my fault. But inside, in my heart, I never accepted it, really. Until yesterday. Samuel, this is a huge thing. A good thing. I've been carrying guilt and didn't even know it. That is washed away now. And I feel better. Cleaner, lighter."

Samuel looked at Tommy, "So what do you think about what Stevie's been saying?"

Tommy shrugged, "Makes sense."

He had hoped for a longer answer. Well, he thought he'd give one more little shove. If it took, fine; if not, he'd let things go for now. Samuel said, "Tell me about the foster homes. Not good?"

Tommy hadn't planned on talking, but couldn't help but let a sneer escape. "Not good? No. Not good."

He was quiet, they were all quiet. Steve went and sat next to him, bare-chested. Tommy couldn't help but see the scars again. He finally looked up at Steve. Steve gave the tiniest nod of assurance, encouragement to go ahead. Tommy looked back down, then up. His gaze moved to Marco and Samuel. Steve could tell that inside part of him didn't want to say anything. But part of him wanted to tell these new friends just what it was really like in those foster homes.

He finally asked Steve, "You never lived in a foster home?"

Steve shook his head. "Well, not unless you call Doc's a foster home. I suppose you might consider it one, but not like what you had, I don't think. Doc's was good, very good."

A heavy sigh escaped Tommy's lips, as he struggled to decide if he should talk or not. He fidgeted. His subconscious rationalized to himself that telling what it was *like* didn't mean he had to share what he was *feeling* in regards to it. Telling what it was like was "safe."

He started, "When I was able to be released from the hospital after a few days, I was sent to a foster home. I'd never been in one; I didn't know much about them. The mother was nice enough. I had food to eat, a warm bed (even if the room was drafty). But the father was not okay. Two days passed before I wondered about some of the things he said and did when the two of us were alone. I was the only child in that home at that time. When I discovered what things he was thinking of, horrid things I had never imagined, and that he wanted me as part of that, I rabbitted, I ran, took off, terrified."

The adults had no trouble understanding what Tommy meant.

"Later, in the middle of the night, police officers picked me up. Nice men, well-meaning, not unkind, but I resisted. I didn't want to go back to whatever they had for me. Again I was not given any choice and was forced. I ended up in a group home, a residential facility. The plan was for me to remain there a month or so. Due to a shortage of beds, I ended up in a cottage with eight other boys, ages fourteen to seventeen, instead of one with kids closer to my age. The oldest boy was obviously king of the hill of the kids, everyone did what he wanted. He took one look at me, nine years old, licked his lips and smiled. 'This one's mine.' I was petrified at what he might mean. He took me aside and talked with me. 'Boy, you don't worry about a thing. I'm your friend; I'll take care of you. Nobody's gonna do anything to you. You're mine. And I'm saving you for a special time.' My blood turned to ice in my veins. For a week, things were fine. I was suspicious, on edge and didn't sleep much. I couldn't believe that what he meant by 'my time' really was what I thought it might be. Probably he meant he was going to make me steal something, or be mean to another kid, something like that. When you're on the streets, you learn about gut instinct and to heed its warnings. My gut instinct told me that wasn't what he meant, he meant something much worse. And so I ran away again. I couldn't let myself be …. hurt … that way. Ducking out became second nature to me."

In spite of warm sunshine, Tommy shivered. Steve put his arm around the boy's shoulders.

"I was alone, on the streets for a few days before the authorities caught up with me again. A social worker from CPS sat down to try to have a long talk with me. She was sure I had problems, all this was my doing, exaggerations, and outright lies. The woman had her mind made up about me; after a few minutes, I didn't even try to get her to recognize the truth. I realized she thought this way, 'I'm an adult, I know what is right and wrong, I know what is going on —nothing— and this kid is full of beans, making up stories to get people in trouble.' It was pretty frustrating, and sad."

"I was assigned another foster home. This place didn't have anyone in it that made me feel squeamish inside; but there was no love, no kindness. The couple had a small business, and housed foster kids as sources of free slave labor (I was the only one there at the time). Being summer, school was not in session. I had to get up early; and was fed a meager breakfast. They made money off the kids; the state provided for food and all, but the couple gave small portions of cheap food, pocketing most of the money. I had to work all day in their shop, doing all kinds of work, with only one small quick break for lunch. Back home twelve to fourteen hours later, some supper, then to bed. Repeat again the next day. Now, this existence was not pleasant by any means. But neither was it dangerous. I decided to stay, not run away, everything else had been so much worse."

"Almost six weeks total had passed. Eventually, I had had some sessions with a counselor, some alone, some with my dad. I never said anything of substance. I was too afraid. I think someone talked with my father. They told us both it was a 'cooling off' period."

Honestly, I was highly skeptical of all of it. I could see no changes in my father. On the surface he acted different. I'm sure he said all the right things at the right times. Played the game— he excelled at game-playing.

Tommy stopped here. Steve still had his arm around the small shoulders and squeezed gently, in a show of silent support. Steve, Samuel and Marco all figured there was still some heavy stuff Tommy was still leaving unsaid… that was okay. When the time was right, the revelations and telling would come. They all noticed Tommy had gone from previous disclosures using a third-person story-type telling to a first-person view. This was important. Samuel recognized the need for a break, "Hey, Stevie, what's the plan for grub?"

Steve brought sandwich fixings up onto the deck— more room there to make your lunch and eat. As they dined, Samuel asked, "Are we headed someplace in particular, or just out sailing?"

"We're going to a small deserted island I know." He had thought about taking Tommy snorkeling, but remembered his injured arm — being in the water would not be a good idea. A beautiful waterfall on the island, not too far from the shore, maybe ¼ mile, was a perfect spot to relax. He had been thinking about a hike there. Unsure how much of a handicap Tommy's "bad" leg would be, he thought when they got there, maybe he'd just ask him if he wanted to go.

Marco stayed at the helm after lunch; Steve broke out his chess board and he and Samuel played.

Steve asked, "You play chess, Tommy?"

"Yeah, but I'll watch you two."

Not much later they anchored at the island, and paddled ashore in a small inflatable dinghy. Besides the waterfall, the island had many things to be explored— finds on the shore, neat rocks and shells. Marco opted to take a nap on the beach; Samuel, Steve and Tommy did go to the waterfall.

They spent a leisurely afternoon on the island. Steve purposely hung pretty close to Tommy. At one point he asked him, "You doing okay?" Tommy nodded.

Sitting on the beach in a smooth cove, Steve was teaching him how to skip stones. Samuel came over and sat with them. Marco was close by, within earshot.

Samuel watched a bit, without saying anything. *My gut feeling is telling me things are getting stirred up in Tommy and if they don't come out, they'll eat away at him.* "Tommy, it's best to get things out, talk to us. Talk to me."

The boy said nothing, didn't make eye contact, and kept working on skipping stones. *Samuel's right. I do have things bottled up inside me, and it bugs me. Why haven't I been able to keep it stuffed the last two days? I've always kept it repressed just fine. I feel pretty good about Steve, I like him. Marco's nice, too. Talking with these guys is hard in one way, but it does feel good, helps. Steve seems to understand. And has been through torment himself, hard to believe; he seems so strong. When I first saw his chest and back I thought, 'Wow!' How can he be so successful and accomplished, after all that? I don't get it. I'll never be like that. It feels good when he puts his arm around me. Safe. Steve really likes this Samuel guy, seems to think he's proficient at helping, capable. Not just capable, but gifted almost. I know what they want. They want me to spill it all. Talk about my experiences and mental status. Maybe that is a good idea. Yeah, but I don't want to talk about it all. Too hard. Too ugly.*

When Samuel had come over and joined them, the hairs on Steve's neck tingled. Then when he heard with the beginning of questions where Samuel was going, wanted to go, he knew Tommy would be in turmoil. He reached into his pocket absent-mindedly, and touched the rosary beads. They felt warm. Warmer than they would be from just body heat. Not hot, just a little warmer than they "should" be, a few degrees at most. Steve dismissed his observation; he figured the hot sun had probably been shining on his pocket. *But maybe there is something going on here beyond human comprehension. Maybe it's time to pray.* In his subconscious, *he suspected something supernatural at work which spurred him to pray. Doc had said that to pray, you can just talk to God.*

As he skipped stones, and sat silently with Tommy and Samuel, he prayed in his heart: *God, you know I'm not very good at this. But I need your help. This kid needs your help. He's scared, he's hurting, he's confused. Heck, you know better than me where he's at and what he needs. Be with him, Lord. Help him to open up, let out all his pain. Help Samuel to say the right things. Help me to be there for him, Lord. I don't come to you very often, sorry about that. Somehow I get the feeling that may change and you and I are going to get to know each other a little better. Or maybe it's more accurate to say I'll get to know you better. You already know all about me.*

He threw a few more rocks. *Doc, if you're up there, lend a hand here. Help me out, help Tommy out. You saved me, now help me to save Tommy. God, Lord, make it better.*

A couple more rocks skimmed the water. *Oh, and Mary, you too, if you do this kind of thing. We need all the help we can get here.* Steve remembered Doc had told him sometimes God answer prayers clearly, in ways you expected and hoped, and ways you think are best. But sometimes he answers them differently than you want, and you don't understand how or why or even if he answered your prayer.

He looked over at Tommy. At that very moment Tommy drew in a deep breath and started talking.

"The goal of CPS is to reunite broken families into one friendly happy cohesive functional unit. To get the parents the help they need so families can be together. Well, la-de-dah. Lofty ideals. Maybe it works for some, maybe it works for most. But not for me and I knew it. Anything I had to say would not be considered, so I opted to say nothing. I sat and listened one morning, in the office of one of these 'helpful' social workers, as she explained how my father had changed, that he learned better methods of parenting, how things would be different. And how she was happy to be able to send me back home. How follow up sessions would be scheduled and so on. I was terrified. This wasn't okay. Not at all."

"On the drive home, my dad and I were quiet. And that night. And the next few days. A social worker did come on the second day to check on things. I said nothing. She cheerily found everything fine. Maybe I should have spoken up of my fears. Past history with CPS told me they wouldn't be considered, rather dismissed as invalid, unwarranted. They'd say that I had a problem, it was all inside my head."

"Now CPS has well-meaning people. They truly do want to help. And like I said, maybe lots of times they do. But they are also overworked. They can't keep track of all their 'finished' cases. Especially of those people who move out of the county, or even out of the state. They don't have time or resources to track them down, and follow up. And in this case, my dad and I did move. Exactly for that reason. My father harbored some intense rage and anger. At CPS, at me, at having to go to follow up sessions and therapy, at all of it. He wanted out from under their scrutiny. Moving presented no difficulty. And so we moved. To another state. I lived in fear. My father was a smoldering cauldron. I feared 'a day' would come. And it did."

"My father had lost his regular job due to the trouble with child services. He was a drug pusher, but also had a menial job to bring in some regular money. When his peers discovered he was being required to attend therapy and all, the ridicule aggravated his fury. He detested that. He loathed the therapy sessions, having to 'make nice' and say all this garbage. He knew he had to play the game. He did want me back, only because he began to realize how he could use me as an asset, to steal, to run drugs for him, and more. He just saw me as a pawn to be used. So he had to play their silly games and talk sweet to the nice ladies. It all just made him madder inside.

At this point Tommy had to stop. He sat trembling next to Steve for a long time, breathing ragged, attempting to compose himself before continuing.

"And 'the day' came. Like I said, imagine all the rage and anger roiling and building beneath the surface. Who was responsible for it? The father? No way."

"Me."

"I was the reason he lost his job. I was the reason he was ridiculed at work and by those who knew him. I was the reason he had to go to all those stupid sessions. I was the reason that 'stupid broad' came out to visit when we were still in the other town. I lost him money with less business; less stealing because I was off having fun in some foster home somewhere. I was the cause of all his problems. Everything was my fault. Or so he thought with his skewed assessment."

Tommy shook more. Steve held him tight. No one spoke. Then Tommy slowly and quietly continued, "So when that fury reached the boiling point and exploded like a volcano blowing its top, who do you think the target was?"

"And how do you think it might have been expressed? Maybe break a leg? Maybe dislocate a shoulder? Break an arm?"

Tommy faltered, but continued, "Maybe all three?? And let's throw in some good kicks to the chest — see if we can crack a rib or two!"

Tommy's lip quivered. He waited some minutes until he recovered a bit. He had been looking down, but now he looked at each person directly, his eyes full of tears. "Imagine the scene. Imagine me lying on the floor, fading in and out of consciousness from pain. Alone, no help coming. It wasn't just the pain of the injuries. How was I supposed to get a drink of water? Food? What about using the bathroom, the toilet? That was twenty feet away, I could barely move. How long do you think it takes, how many days, before I could even get to the bathroom? I drank out of the toilet because it was too hard to stand up and get water from the sink. How long do you think it took until I was able to get out of my filthy clothes, full of my own body waste? A week? Two? What do you think it smelled like?"

Even nature silenced itself out of respect and reverence for Tommy's "confession". No birds chirped, the soft waves reaching the shore rolled themselves out noiselessly.

"I considered if I even wanted to live.... why bother? Just slip away. It's too hard, it hurts too much. But something, I don't know what, kept me alive, wouldn't let me slip away. Time passed. Slowly, very slowly, very painfully. After a few weeks, I was able to get up, sometimes, more or less. I could use the bathroom, clean myself. Open a box of crackers to eat, get a drink of water. Moving still caused considerable pain; I spent most of my time lying on the chilly bathroom floor. I still remember how soothing the cool ceramic tiles felt on my cheek or back."

Tommy surveyed the teary somber faces of Steve, Samuel and Marco. "Eventually, over months, I healed. Sort of. Bones don't knit very well if they're never set. They can easily break again, maybe several times over the next few years. Just one day, snap. Then you get to spend more time crippled."

There was another pause here. Steve sensed the worst had been told, now Tommy was re-centering himself before continuing.

"I learned many things from that whole experience. First off, a kid that age should not even have any idea of what ... some of those things mean.... what they are...... much less have been very close to being a victim himself. I learned how to stay out of trouble, how not to trust adults. I learned how CPS is deadly. That was a big one."

The boy's voice changed a degree from somber to businesslike, more impersonal.

"Steve, you asked why I don't like hospitals. Well, it's not hospitals, it's CPS. It's them jumping in and trying to fix things, make family situations better. When a kid who is a minor is seen in a doctor's office or hospital, if there is no parent of legal guardian, CPS takes over. Complicate matters by medical professionals being required to report abuse. So, in a case like this, if I go to a hospital, I'll be under the 'protection' of CPS in a flash. And I just told you that is a bad thing. Something I'd avoid at all costs— pain, suffering, another beating, even death maybe. Unless I'm really dumb, there is no way I'm going to go anywhere near any situation where they might be. And I'm not dumb."

"So, say, for example, years later, someone comes along who wants to help. I'm a bit older now, wiser. We have moved again. To a pleasant place like Hawaii. In so many ways, Hawaii is wonderful. It's not cold, so if you're … out on the streets… you won't freeze to death… lots of fresh fruit can be found in dumpsters and places. Maybe some is spoiled, but a lot isn't, or part of it is okay. You've got water to clean with, a whole ocean full. Salt water isn't the best for washing, but it works. Maybe my father is still around, but I spend little time at 'home'. It's okay being out because the streets aren't bad here. Being home means having to steal for my dad, probably getting a beating now and then. Being on the streets means scrounging, staying out of trouble, not getting caught. It's easier than being at 'home'. I find it not bad at all."

"But then this man comes along… another whole story. And he wants to help. And he thinks he knows how to best help. Somehow we manage to connect to each other. I can tell the man is honest and sincere, that he is trustworthy, and that he will listen to me. And I have to ask myself, why? Why is he trying so hard to help…me?"

And Tommy finished. No one spoke for a long time. Slowly the adults began to come out of what was an almost trance-like state. Tommy had completely captivated them with his story. One sighed, Marco cleared his throat. The birds seemed to twitter again. Steve remained silent and motionless, gazing on

Tommy's face. The boy's look didn't waver from Steve's steel blue eyes.

Chapter 10
Steve's Response and an Answer

Steve had been sitting, leaning forward, forearms resting on his knees during Tommy's recitation. Everyone took a few moments to digest the account. Finally Steve said quietly, "You know, Tommy, if I was that man, and I met a kid like the one in your story, here's what I'd do. First, and most important, I'd do anything I needed to to make sure he was safe. I believe strongly in the laws of this country, but laws are made for people, to protect them. If I thought something needed to be done differently to protect this boy, I wouldn't hesitate a second to do it. Second, I'd figure out some way around the dilemma, so he could get any medical care he needed. Without CPS. In a way the boy felt comfortable with. I would figure out a way."

Drawing a deep breath, Steve continued. "And I'd tell him a story. But the story I'd tell him isn't about 'a' boy. It is about a boy, but a certain boy, a little boy named Steve O'Shaughnessy. It's a true story. You know the story because I just told it. How a Good Samaritan gave him what he needed, turned his life around, allowed him to grow and become a good person, the person he is today. How a doctor taught him many

many things about life, about why we're here on this earth, to help one another."

"If I were the man, I'd tell the boy that I'd want to help him. Really help him, not for a while in passing, but to make a lasting changing difference in his life. A permanent change. To share a life together, like that doctor did with me. I'd do it not out of obligation for some debt, nor out of pity, but just because I could do it. Because it needed doing. Because Divine Providence brought us together. I am here, he needs me, and I can help. Because I'm 'the' one who this came to. I would want the boy to know that if he allowed me to help him; he would be helping me to help myself, to heal myself even more. I'd want the boy to say, 'Yes' because I don't think I could bear it if he didn't."

"I'd tell the boy that I have a small handful of wonderful friends who I trust who would help us navigate through things. They would be there with their love and support, he's not alone, I'm not alone. We have a team, a family. I have a team, a family, and I want him to be a part of it. And each one of those people will welcome him with unconditional love and open arms. He doesn't need to be alone anymore. Or afraid anymore."

"That's what I'd tell the boy."

And Steve and Tommy looked at each other for a long time, while Samuel and Marco were silent.

All the while Steve was saying this, he thought about Doc Burns' wisdom. *Doc said not to let opportunities pass you by. Well, this one's here and it's great and I'm hanging on to it. This is right, I know this is right and good. Maybe I need to slow down, but that doesn't feel right. This is unfolding faster than I can imagine, but that's the way it's happening. This gift is here today, it may not be tomorrow. I'm scared, but that's okay. I guess I'm scared because I don't understand it all, don't know where this is going, where I/we will end up. I have no idea what I'm getting myself into here. But that won't stop me, I need to jump in and stay in. Good Lord, more than once in my past if I had known where some choice would lead me I'd have turned tail and run like a scared chicken in the opposite direction, full speed. But each of those times, they were gifts/ opportunities from God and led me to good and great things, good and great discoveries, good and great people. Okay God, prayer time: You know, God, I have no idea what's going on here. But I'm going to follow my heart, I believe that is your will, and you'll take care of it all somehow.*

Doc's prayer, said decades before, for the Holy Ghost to watch over and guide Steve was bearing fruit.

Samuel' accurate knack of reading people and situations showed him that Tommy was doing well with talking, but he also avoiding much— in particular his feelings. That's okay; Samuel wouldn't expect him to open up that part of him just yet. He surmised Tommy was unaware of these influences at work within him. All in good time. Time for a change of atmosphere. "Steve, I'm going to go for a quick swim. You going to make us some supper? And why don't you guys drink some of that lemonade you made earlier?" Samuel was a real stickler for people staying well hydrated. He believed it made them feel better and therapy go better.

Steve had made earlier some packets of what he called hobo stew, which were basically chunks of meat, veggies and seasonings folded into foil squares to be set in a fire to cook. He had started a fire some time back and put the packets in now to begin cooking. Tommy sat nearby watching, he asked if Steve needed any help. He didn't, and they went back to skipping rocks, after he had served each of them a tall glass of the lemonade.

They talked about sand crabs, the birds they saw, and made small talk. Marco joined Samuel in the water. After they ate the delicious meal, they packed up and headed back. It had been a good day, long, exhausting mentally— for all. They dropped Marco off and then went to Steve's.

Even though it was not that late, Samuel announced, "You know, it probably would be best if you two went to bed. You're tired. It's been a roller coaster day. I don't know why I'm here anyway. You seem to be doing an amazing job of handling this yourselves."

Steve grinned, "Samuel, you're here for mop-up and to catch the parts we miss!"

Samuel grinned back, replied in mock indignation, "Oh, thanks Stevie, nice to know I'm appreciated. But now, sleep." Looking at Steve and Tommy, he amended his suggestion, "Okay, Tommy, you sleep. Steve, you need to sleep, but you won't. Your mind is going to mull over this problem about CPS until you've got an answer or drop from exhaustion. So, think, my friend." They all laughed.

Again Steve washed Tommy's arm, running through a similar ritual of talking about things they had covered that day, asking if he was okay, all that. It had been a good day, all things considered.

Tommy went to bed shortly after and Steve joined Samuel on the lanai. Samuel was relaxing comfortably in his hammock, enjoying the Hawaiian sunset. Neither man spoke, nothing needed to be said. Steve was deep in thought, Samuel let him be, knew that's the way he worked best.

Steve spent the next several hours walking slowly along the beach, gazing at the stars, listening to the waves, ending back at his house when suddenly the light bulb went on for Steve. "Samuel, I've got it! Listen, will you stay with Tommy? I need to go someplace."

Knowing his friend well, he didn't press for details, "Sure, Stevie."

Steve went inside and made a phone call. Because of his job and company, he knew many people and had friends in high places, good connections. "Hi Brian, it's Steve. I know it's late, I hope I didn't wake you. Listen, I need to see you."

The voice on the other end of the line said, "No, Steve, I'm still up. But it's past 10:30. You want to see me tonight?"

"Yes. Please, Brian."

"Okay, come on over."

Steve drove to his friend's house. While he didn't encounter the man often, they were well acquainted and respected each other, as individuals as well as skilled professionals. Brian was waiting for him and opened the door as Steve hurried up the walk.

He extended his hand and shook his friend's. "Thanks for seeing me so late."

"Come on in. You want some juice?"

"No, thanks. Look, I need some information and some help. I think you can do it for me."

Brian was a Family Court judge, a competent and fair man. Steve briefly explained the situation with Tommy, leaving out most details, but giving his friend enough information to know the score.

"The problem is that Tommy is a minor. Amongst other things, he won't accept any medical help because of well-founded, I think, fears of CPS. Because of the abuse, and lack of a legal guardian, they'll be called in. He simply won't cooperate with anything if CPS is anywhere near."

Looking his friend solemnly in the eye, Steve continued, "Brian, he has every reason to hate and fear CPS. What I want is to know if you can make me his legal guardian, so I can make medical decisions without CPS being involved. I want to be named as his legal guardian. And I want it to go beyond that, to adoption, but for starters, for now, legal guardianship. And soon— this can't drag out. Can you do something?"

Brian let out a long sigh. "Wow, Steve. Normally for legal guardianship a home study is conducted, along with detailed investigations, psychological evaluations and more. The data is presented to me, usually by CPS; then I review the reports and make a decision based on that information. You're asking me to sidestep that process and just grant you custody, correct?"

"Yes. I can tell you this much: This is the right thing for Tommy and for me. You can talk with Marco, Doc Epstein and Samuel Goldberg, a psychiatrist. They all know the situation. While they don't know my solution, yet, I'm sure they'd all agree it is a good one, the best, the best for both of us. This needs to happen, Brian, and now. Can you do it?"

"Steve, if I want to, if I think it's best for the child, I can decree you as Tommy's legal guardian without following any of the steps I mentioned. Effective immediately."

Steve was wasting no time in his questions and answers and fired back, "Will you do it, Brian?"

Brian studied his friend a few minutes while Steve remained silent. "What does Tommy want? Have you asked him?"

"No," Steve replied. "He was sleeping when I left. I haven't asked him but I know what his reaction will be. First, he'll be flabbergasted. Then awed. Brian, I'm sure he'll be overjoyed and relieved if such a thing were to become a reality for him. He will never have imagined things working out like this."

"Okay, Steve, I'll do it. IF... three things. First, legally, I can only grant temporary guardianship. For six months. After that, I can do a review and make the placement permanent. Along with adoption—but we can wait with that— slow down, doesn't have to happen right away. Second, legally, we're required to make a 'thorough investigation' to find any living biological relatives. I can't dismiss that."

Eyes twinkling, the judge hinted, "But if the child doesn't provide us with any information, it's kind of hard to investigate. I mean we don't have anything, really, other than a first name, which may or may not even be real. Now, Tommy could choose to open up and give us all kinds of detail. Or he could choose not to divulge any information of that sort. To follow the law, I will need to at least ask him about his family situation. Third, I want to talk with Tommy alone. I want to make sure he knows what this is, what a placement means and so on."

"Fine on all counts, Brian. Only one thing — I have no problem with you talking alone with Tommy. But he may be insecure with that. Is there some place where we can meet, where you can talk with him privately, but I can be within sight? Like a park, maybe? He'd feel a lot safer if I was there and in his sight, even if you two were having a private conversation. And it means a lot to me to have him feel safe."

"Okay, Steve, how about if I come by your place early in the morning before work? Tommy and I can talk on the beach, or on your lanai. You'd be inside, in sight. I can do the paperwork when I get to the office, then file it, and it's a done deal."

Steve gratefully shook his hand! "Brian, you're a lifesaver. And I mean that literally. Thank you!"

Steve left feeling on top of the world. *An investigation. I'm sure there won't be one. All Tommy has to do is say nothing. He'd do that even without prompting, but I think I'll give him a heads up on it. Maybe I should conduct an investigation. No, I can't do that without Tommy's okay. Not even consider it. But probably if I wanted I could find out who his father was. There is a lot I know already: they're from out of state, the mother is deceased, there are hospital records, and CPS records, somewhere. Tommy is an only child, he's ten or eleven, I'd guess. The fact that the father was a drug user and dealer narrows the field considerably. Especially when you add in that he would only have been in the islands a year or two. If I investigated and found the guy, I think I'd kill the bastard! Whoa! Where'd that come from? Reminds me of when my dear Andrea, my fiancé, was murdered, a few months before our wedding. If Marco hadn't caught up to us and pulled me off the murderer, I'm not sure I wouldn't have beaten him to death. And what has been done to Tommy is worse in some ways than outright murder. O'Shaughnessy, stow those thoughts, deal with them later. No way am I going to investigate.*

Back at the house, Steve entered quietly. Samuel asked sleepily from the lanai, "Well, how'd it go?"

Joy gilded Steve's voice as he replied, "Great, Samuel, I'll tell you about it in the morning."

He headed to bed, but first stopped off in Tommy's room. *Funny. I'm calling my guest bedroom, "Tommy's room."* He looked at the sleeping boy, went over, planted a light kiss on his forehead, and murmured quietly, "It's all going to be fine, Tommy. Just fine." And said a quiet prayer aloud — one of thanksgiving for Tommy that he was able to open up, and of protection over him, and for strength, support, whatever they or he needed. The words he spoke came easily and comfortably to Steve, and that surprised him.

Chapter 11
The Legalities

Steve got about five hours of solid, restful sleep, which was about all he generally needed. He woke early, and woke Tommy, as well. "Get up, buddy, you've got a busy morning ahead of you."

Tommy looked at him questioningly. All Steve said was, "Get cleaned up and dressed, we're having company. I'll tell you about it at breakfast."

Tommy obliged. They sat down to eat the breakfast Steve prepared. Samuel also was up and dressed. Steve grinned broadly. Samuel said, "So……..? Spill it, Stevie."

Steve answered, "Okay, it's like this. The problem, well, the immediate problem is that if Tommy gets medical treatment, officially, in a hospital, CPS will come in because he's a minor without a parent or legal guardian. The answer is so simple, right in front of us. Why didn't we see the solution right away?"

Samuel asked, "And the answer is….?"

"He simply needs a parent or legal guardian. That will keep CPS away."

Tommy scoffed cynically, an unusual attitude for him, "Oh, yeah… sounds good…. what do we do? Hustle down to the five and dime and pick one out?" Looking down, he poked his eggs with his fork.

Steve had stopped talking, stopped moving. He waited. He waited for Tommy to figure it out. Tommy gazed at Steve's face, trying to read the message the man was sending. Nothing made sense for a second, and then it clicked!

Eyes wide, mouth agape, the boy stammered, "STEVE? YOU? You want to be my legal guardian??"

Steve smiled. "Yes, Tommy. More than that, later we'll talk about adoption, but for starters, legal guardian."

"A friend of mine is stopping by this morning. I went to see him last night. Brian Tracer. He's a Family Court Judge. He wants to talk with you, Tommy, and if you want this arrangement, he'll file paperwork this morning and it's a done deal. Due to the laws, I can only get custody on a temporary basis for six months, pending a review to make it permanent. But he will if we want it, Tommy. I told him some general information, he knows what is going on but I left out the details."

Steve warned him, "One thing he's going to ask you, he's required to ask you, is for details on any biological family. Tommy, you can tell him as much or as little as you like. It's entirely up to you. You certainly can say nothing. He'll have to look into any details you give him."

The boy's brow furrowed. "Tommy, it's okay, it will be okay. You don't have to say anything."

Tommy felt marginally better, but still far from comfortable with all of it.

A few minutes later, Brian rang the front doorbell. Introductions were made; the judge gently suggested they—he and Tommy—go out on the lanai to talk a bit. Tommy's eyes were wide and fearful; Steve nodded his encouragement. "Tommy, go with him. I'll be right in here. You can call me if you need me."

Brian started out by trying to put Tommy at ease. "Tommy, Steve told me that he wants to be your legal guardian, and eventually adopt you. What are your thoughts about that?"

Tommy honestly replied, "I am overwhelmed. I can't imagine what life with Steve would be like, but it would be the very best thing that could ever happen to me."

"So, you like the idea? No hesitation?"

"The only thing I can't figure out, and Steve said not to worry about it, is how he can fit me in. Steve says he has time for whatever he wants in his life, we all make time for what we want. And he wants me in his life and will make everything fit. Not that I need anything, but he is busy with a job, I don't want to get in his way or anything. I don't want to be a burden to him. Steve says that would never happen. I believe him, but I can't figure out how...."

Brian chuckled, "Steve can handle that just fine."

Then he said to Tommy, "I've got another question. I need to ask this. I want you to listen carefully to exactly how I ask this, exactly what I'm asking. Understand?"

Tommy nodded.

"I need to ask you if there is anything you will share with me regarding any biological relatives you have?" Brian was careful not to ask if there was any information, or if he wanted to share info, but if he would share.

Tommy was scared here. "Sir, does your decision depend on my answer?"

Brian thought, "No, not really. But in one way, yes. I'm required to conduct an investigation in a case like this to find any biological relatives and possibly place the child with them. If I have no information on any biological relatives, I can't conduct an investigation, can I? If there is information, then I'm obligated to investigate."

Slowly, he asked, "Do you understand what I'm saying?"

Tommy got the message loud and clear. Without any hesitation or batting an eye, he said squarely, "There is no information available on any biological relatives."

Steve was right, Brian thought, this kid is smart.

Brian grinned. "Okay, that's it then. Any questions for me?"

"Yes, sir, one. With all this legal stuff, what about a name? Do I get some sort of legal name? "

"Yes."

"What is it?"

Brian answered, "It can be anything you want. Is there a name you have in mind?"

"Yes, sir. I'd like to ask your opinion about it, though, and Samuel's…"

Sliding open the sliding glass patio door, Brian requested, "Samuel, could you please come out here?"

Steve was about to follow when Brian stopped him. "Just Samuel, Steve."

Studying the people on the other side of the door, Steve pondered. *No one looks upset. Why don't they want me out there? What the dickens are they talking about?*

He observed through the glass as Tommy appeared to be stammering, unsure about something.

Meanwhile, outside Tommy talked with the two of them, "You both know Steve well. Judge Tracer said I can have any legal name I want. There's one I'm thinking of, but I am not sure if Steve would like it or not. I want to ask you what you think."

Tommy took a deep breath, held it, and said, "Thomas…… Thomas Steven O'Shaughnessy." Letting the air out, he scanned their faces anxiously.

Samuel and Brian had huge smiles on their faces. Samuel said, "Tommy, Steve would be very touched, honored and proud if you choose that name." And Brian agreed.

And now the smile spread to Tommy face.

Still watching, Steve saw the broad smiles, and slid the door open for them as they moved to enter.

Brian said, "Steve, I'm heading off to my office now, my secretary can start right away on the paperwork. She'll need to call you to get some facts, Social Security number, similar data from you. It should take her an hour or so to process it. Why don't you stop by around ten, we'll get everything signed and notarized, then file the papers?"

Brian was pleased to be able to finish with, "Then it's a done deal." He made two people very happy that morning!

He left, and Tommy and Samuel grinned looked at each other, thinking about the secret they shared.

Steve noticed the exchanges. "What's up?"

Tommy slowly drawled, "Well, Steve, Judge Tracer said that with all the paperwork, I get a legal name. It can be anything I want. And I have one in mind, if it's okay with you."

"Okay…. what is it?"

And Tommy just smiled and looked at Samuel.

Steve looked back and forth at the two of them, "Come on, give…."

Samuel laughed, "I think you should tell him, Tommy."

"Okay….. Thomas…… Steven …… O'Shaughnessy."

Steve was speechless, overcome with emotion and love. Tommy misinterpreted Steve's face and was immediately afraid that Steve didn't like it!

Hurriedly he said, "I don't have to use that, Steve. I can use anything. If you don't like it…"

Steve grabbed him in a bear hug and with moist eyes, reassured him, "Tommy, it's perfect! Absolutely perfect!" And he truly did think it was perfect. He loved it!

Steve and Tommy left some time later to go to the courthouse and deal with the legalities. Samuel headed off to visit some local friends.

Documents were completed, signed, notarized, and filed. Brian was pleased to be the first to congratulate them. Steve had his arm around Tommy's shoulders as they walked out of the building. He stopped and sat on the top step of the courthouse, needing to sit a minute and absorb the significance of the moment.

The two sat there, just be-ing. Inside he felt really wonderful. Tommy shared his joy. It felt good for both of them.

Tommy said, "Steve, I know a big reason you did this was so Doc could 'check me out' and work on some things. And that's fine, but can it wait a day? It won't make any difference to me, and I really would rather not have my first day as Thomas Steven O'Shaughnessy spent at the hospital having tests and being poked and prodded."

Steve totally understood and agreed. "Tommy, that's fine. But I want you to know that while I am relieved that you will now be able to get the medical care you need, that is a very small part of why I'm happy about this. I'm just glad that you are part of my life. It's absolutely wonderful!"

And they sat longer in the sunshine. The rosary in Steve's pocket was warm.

Chapter 12
Introductions and More

Finally Steve got up from the stone steps. "C'mon."

He wouldn't tell where they were going, but drove to the office. The workload was down, his being gone a few days wasn't a problem, his staff was perfectly capable of picking up the slack. He knew Marco would be at work and wanted to share this with his kaikiana first! He went into his office with Tommy, both of them smiling broadly. Lisa noticed, as did all the rest in the outer office. Lisa Barker, Steve's competent and excellent secretary, had gotten married a few months back to a wonderful accountant named Simon. Steve expected any day for her to announce a pregnancy and retirement. Rapping on Marco's open office as they passed; he indicated with a hand motion to join Tommy and him in his private office.

Marco sensed the electricity, jumped up and went into Steve's office. Steve closed the door. "Steve, what's up? You two look like you just swallowed the canary!" Steve and Tommy grinned but didn't answer.

"Come on Steve, GIVE!"

Unable to contain himself, Steve stood behind Tommy, put his hands on the boy's shoulders, and announced, "Marco, there's someone I'd like you to meet."

Marco's brow furrowed, ocean blue eyes questioned. Steve and Tommy's smiles widened.

"Marco, meet Thomas Steven O'Shaughnessy! I am now his legal guardian."

Astonished and speechless for a few seconds, Marco digested the introduction.

Pure joy spread over his features as he rushed over to hug them. "Steve, Tommy— WONDERDFUL! I'm so happy for both of you! What… how… when?"

Steve explained. Marco was truly overjoyed for his friend, and Tommy. This was so good!

Steve had noticed before, and again just now, that Tommy would slightly flinch when hugged. *Hugging him hurts, his back hurts, or something's not quite right. I'll find out more about that later; for now I'll watch it carefully.*

"Marco, for now, we're going to keep this quiet. Tommy and I are taking the day to enjoy life; I don't want word out to everyone yet."

Having revealed the information first to his best friend, Steve now invited Bobby and Keo into the office. Bobby, the fourth man on Steve's team, was young, energetic, and detail oriented. Steve had known both these men almost since the start of his business, and they were like family. He proudly shared his news with them, positioning himself directly behind Tommy, close, which prevented anyone from giving him a full bear hug. Tommy looked at Steve quizzically, and realized that his body posture had been intentional. His new guardian was pretty observant and smart.

Bobby and Keo had known something was up, but had no idea of the depth of this radical direction their boss's life had been taking. Marco at least had had a clue.

Next was Lisa. Steve again maintained the same stance. To the casual observer, it was just where he was standing, nothing out of the ordinary. Tommy was grateful. It wasn't just his back that hurt when he was hugged hard; it was also his arm and shoulder. And that arm had a nasty way of popping out of the socket easily if any pressure was applied the wrong way. Lisa was happy for him. Accepting all the best wishes sincerely, Steve and Tommy smiled.

The man and boy departed, leaving an order for the staff to, "Mind the shop," and headed over to the governor's office. Steve considered the governor a personal friend and wanted to share the news with him. The unexpected visit surprised Bill Hendrickson. Steve did the same intro, and they both enjoyed the look of shock on the governor's face which was, of course, followed by sincere congratulations! Like the rest, he was truly happy for his friend, and Tommy.

That was it for the day for meeting people and spreading the news.

"We'll see Doc tomorrow and tell him."

Running his hand through the boy's locks, Steve questioned, "Would you like to get a haircut?"

Tommy shrugged. "Sure."

The barber cut Tommy's hair to a respectable length, and gave Steve his regular trim.

"Next stop, clothes for you, kiddo. You need more than what Marco picked out for you, plus what you want, what fits your tastes."

Tommy shook his head. "I'm okay, I can get by. I don't need anything."

The boy, unused to having things bought for him, was overwhelmed. But with Steve's help and guidance, they purchased a complete wardrobe. As they shopped and browsed, they talked about plans for things to do together and short trips, many other things. The day was getting long and it had been busy. They went back home, a word with new meaning for Steve. Samuel was back from his day out and about. They visited while all shared in the supper preparations then ate.

Steve touched base with Doc and asked if he could bring Tommy in in the morning. Doc was surprised, but pleased. He didn't ask how or why, he just wanted to see this patient and fix whatever needed fixing! 9:00 was set up, in Doc's hospital office.

After Tommy went to bed, Samuel and Steve sat up very late talking.

Samuel made it a point to cover all kinds of things, go over again feelings, memories, everything with Steve. He realized many major things had occurred in a relatively short time. He thought all was well and good, but wanted to touch base with each issue. And so they talked. All was well with Steve, as Samuel had expected. He had worked through many things himself in the last few days. *I taught him well....*

Tommy's going to need more help... certainly with the medical procedures ahead of him, memories would be brought back. Steve will be good at helping, but it'll take more than his efforts. "Steve, I thought about heading back to Singapore, but I'm going stay longer. I'm not sure how frequently you're going to need me, but I enjoy Hawaii."

"Thank you, Sam. We do need you. I hope Tommy will get out what needs addressing."

The psychiatrist was really beginning to feel Tommy out. He had been watching him keenly since they had met, and was beginning to get a good handle on the boy. An amazing kid, from what he saw. Yet Samuel was doing most of the talking; what Tommy had been saying was still of little substance. At this point, anyway, he remained guarded and resistant to any kind of real help. The opposition was expected; had it not been there, he would have been concerned.

He realized that Tommy, naturally, not intentionally, was very subtle in his resistance. And he almost made it appear as if he was cooperating fully. He shared all the details of his past.

That was hard, no doubt; but it was also mostly story telling. He did allow himself to be more a part of it toward the end of his telling. Samuel figured that was a slip-up on his part, he hadn't — meant to do it— to go into the first person, "this is about me" mode.

It was much harder to get into feelings, expressing them, and then handling that. And that's where they needed to go. He expected to apply a combination of using the boy's intellect and logic to begin to name some feelings.

Chapter 13
The Medical— Doc

Next morning, on the way to the appointment, Tommy's nervousness showed. Both Steve and Samuel had picked up on that at breakfast. They discovered that mostly what was bothering him was the ugliness of all of it. And that it would be hard for Steve. Steve was worried about the day being hard for Tommy. Samuel, not unkindly, dismissed them, "Listen, just go. Do what needs doing. We'll talk this afternoon, decipher things then. No sense worrying over it now, when you don't even know what's going to happen or how…."

The good advice made sense, but did little to relieve tension.

They went into the outer office and found Doc waiting. Steve had his arm around Tommy's shoulder and a smile on his face. A twitch of a grin managed to peek through Tommy's apprehension, as well. Doc asked, "So, are you going to tell me what this is all about?"

Steve glanced at Tommy. "Hey Doc, when you get a new patient, officially, isn't there all kinds of paperwork you need to fill out?"

Doc looked at Steve like he had grown horns. Steve never cared about medical paperwork.

Noticing, and expecting that reaction, he continued, "So, what's the first thing on your form? Name???"

Doc had opened the clipboard folder, now he shut it, leaned back in his chair and waited. Two could play this game. He'd let Steve say whatever he had to say, he wasn't going to be baited.

"Right, Doc? The form asks for name, right, Doc?????"

Changing his mind, deciding to play along, he said, "Okay, Steve. Yes, it asks for NAME. What do you want me to fill in?"

Steve and Tommy are bursting. "Here, Doc, let me fill it out!" Steve grabbed the clipboard from him, wrote in big bold letters in the name slot: Thomas Steven O'Shaughnessy, and handed the papers back to Doc, beaming triumphantly.

Doc took it, read the name, began to ask, "What?" then realized the significance of this. "Steve, do you mean…. what…"

Steve interrupted him, "Doc, I'd like you to meet Thomas Steven O'Shaughnessy!"

Doc choked up, came around the desk and gave them both a hug. "My God, Steve… this is… wonderful! I'm so happy for you, for both of you." He shook his hands, pounded Steve on the back several times. Gently he shook Tommy's head.

He sat back down and took a minute to absorb this news. "My God…."

Finally he said, "Okay, so this means, what— you're his legal guardian?"

"Yes, so I have complete authority to make any and all medical decisions. You can call CPS if you need to, but you will also tell them that any abuse you encounter occurred before I became his legal guardian, so they have no need or jurisdiction in this case."

"Steve, that's perfect."

Then Doc, looking at Tommy with a heavy heart, knowing things would be hard, probably painful (physically and otherwise), sighed, "Okay, son, come on," indicating moving to the exam room.

Tommy was scared for those very reasons. He gravely met Doc's eye and got up.

As did Steve. Tommy turned and said, "No, just me."

This didn't sit well with Steve at all. He surmised Tommy didn't want him with him because he wanted to spare Steve the pain of seeing his injuries. And anything that Doc might need to do that hurt. As he began to speak, Tommy cut him off. "Steve, NO. It's ugly, really ugly. I don't want you to see." His eyes pooled with tears.

Steve shook his head and clenched his fists as he thought about his words before he spoke. "Tommy, I'm sure it is ugly. And I'll hate it. And I'll hate the man who did this to you and that it was done. And yes, son, it's going to hurt for me to see it. I'm afraid it's going to hurt a lot. But I want to be with you. I don't want you to be alone. Tommy, you're NOT ALONE ANYMORE, no matter what. Yes, Doc'll be there, but that's not the same. ***I*** want to be there. ***I*** want to be the one holding your hand."

Steve's eyes had misted over, but he continued, "Tommy, when you hurt, I hurt. I promised I'd never make you do anything you don't want to. And if you really won't let me come in with you, I'll stay here. But I want to be there with you. I don't want you to be alone. We're family now. And family shares the good and the bad together. Please let me stay with you." The tears trickled down Steve's cheeks.

And down Tommy's, as well. He did want Steve with him. He knew he would be a great comfort. But he also didn't want to hurt Steve.

Doc huskily added at this point, "Tommy, I think it'll be worse for Steve if he doesn't see. Horrible as things might be, he may imagine worse." Tommy couldn't conceive how anyone could imagine things worse than they were. He bit his quivering bottom lip so hard a trickle of blood came down. Steve gently took his chin in his hand and wiped it away with a sad smile on his face. Tommy shut his eyes and nodded a yes.

Steve took him in his arms, hugged him gently for a few seconds, then took his small hand in his large one and they walked in to the exam room.

Doc witnessed the interchange. *God, this IS what I wanted, but it's going to be hard…. Lord, help me, help all of us.*

Tommy donned a hospital gown and climbed onto the table. Steve locked onto his eyes; Doc kept his full attention on the chart. He was going to try his hardest to be all business but knew he'd be unlikely to maintain that façade.

"Okay, young man, let's start at the top." *Innocent enough place to begin.* He checked eyes and ears, throat; all seemed okay. *Things are going to get tougher now.* "Tell me about your arm, Tommy. When was it first hurt, can you tell me what happened, how it feels now, can you use it at all?" he asked as he slid the gown over the shoulder to expose it and the arm. Steve was still right there, in front and a bit to the side. Neither he nor Doc had looked at his back yet, now exposed with the gown down to his waist on one side.

Tommy gulped. "What happened first was it was pulled out of the socket. Then it got twisted and the bone snapped. There is some pain, some of the time. Doc, it— the shoulder— gets dislocated real easy. It doesn't take much at all, sometimes just getting bumped. Doc, please be careful," he pleaded.

Doc fully intended to do exactly that, be careful. He took the upper arm and gently felt the bone. As he lifted it just slightly away from the body, he felt the shoulder snap out. Tommy turned white as a ghost, gasped, and began to sweat. Tommy took a deep breath, firmly grabbed his left upper arm with his right hand, and pulled it forward and in, unable to stifle a scream as he did so, turning even whiter.

Horrified at what he had just done, Doc gently eased the boy to a lying position on the table. The boy trembled, Doc was shaking as well. "Tommy, I'm sorry…..I didn't mean to…"

The boy drew in a deep breath and regained some composure. "I know, Doc, you didn't know… it's okay." But Doc knew it wasn't okay. Tommy's tears continued to flow silently, he continued to breathe deeply. And Steve could do nothing but stand there silently, squeezing the child's good hand in what little support he could give.

Doc gave them all a few moments to recover. *Geez, I was being gentle. I was! This boy is very delicate, at least in some ways….. No wonder that arm was useless, I did no more than move it an inch, less than an inch, and the shoulder dislocates….* Doc listened to his chest next. As he moved his hands (so very gently) along the rib cage it was apparent there had been multiple fractures, bumps from bones that were never aligned but managed to heal to some degree anyway. There must have been a half dozen of these fractures in the front alone.

Hoping Tommy was doing a bit better, he asked, "Can you sit up for me, son?" Tommy nodded and Doc helped him up. He moved around to his back, and taking his first look at the battered torso let out a very audible gasp. He tried to recover from the shock of the sight of Tommy's back and had a hard time doing so. It took him much longer than he expected. Steve and Tommy were eye to eye. Steve knew this was important. And he was terrified. Doc's reaction alarmed him. "Tommy, I'm going to look." Tears flowed down Tommy's face. Steve slowly moved to the side so he could see, yet still kept his eyes on Tommy's. Doc placed his hand on Steve's arm and squeezed, in support and warning. No one spoke. And slowly Steve let his gaze go to Tommy's back. He inhaled sharply. He took some long seconds to really look, so Tommy knew that he saw, saw it all. Then he returned his own pain-filled eyes to Tommy's. His voice cracked but had confidence and conviction, "It'll be okay." It would be okay. He'd make it okay! He moved forward a half step and pulled Tommy's head (probably the only part of him without serious injury) to his chest and they both cried. And Doc had his own tears falling behind them.

Tommy's back looked like raw hamburger. Lacerations, deep, everywhere. Some healed, many unhealed, raw, red. Not a square inch of uninjured skin.

Steve decided they needed to rally and keep going. He pulled back and lifted Tommy's chin to meet his eyes, "Come on, let's get on with this," indicating to Doc to continue.

Doc, again ever so lightly examined the back, and the back rib cage (surprised that Tommy's back didn't seem more tender when he touched it). More apparent fractures, poorly healed. Some at skewed angles. Doc had no doubt that there had to be certain positions that caused a jagged rib end to press a sore spot when Tommy twisted or bent certain ways. Or was hugged.

Continuing his exam, he asked next about the leg. "It was broken the same time as the arm fracture and shoulder dislocation," Tommy said. "I can't walk normally on it. And sometimes, for no reason, it just snaps and breaks again. That has happened twice now, the last time maybe six months ago."

Doc gently, very gently, examined the boy's leg. It didn't seem to be overly painful. He could feel where the break had been, he could feel the bone ends knitted together, but not held by much. No wonder it would snap on him. Feeling Tommy's bones was so easy because he was so thin.

Mostly finished now, he asked, "Tommy, I'd like to check you for sexual abuse." Tommy warily asked, "How do you do that?"

Doc concisely explained about a simple digital rectal exam. Tommy said he hadn't been abused that way. Doc acknowledged that but added, "Sometimes when terrible things happen to us, we block out memories… I just want to check to be sure…"

Tommy looked at Steve for guidance, who encouraged, "Humor him, Tommy," hoping against hope that what Doc wondered about hadn't happened.

Tommy rolled his eyes. "Geez! Okay," and turned on his side, curling his knees up.

Doc did an exam quickly without much discomfort, and announced, much to Steve's relief, "No problems there. Everything's fine."

Doc drew blood for all kinds of tests, and got a urine and stool sample. He expected to find the patient anemic, he probably had parasites, maybe infections, who knew what else.

"Okay, here's what's next. I want X-rays of that shoulder, chest and back, abdomen and leg. Then I'll have Mark Dante go over that. You remember him, Steve— he's the one that did your hand. And then we'll consult and listen to what he recommends. Also by this afternoon I should have some of your test results back. So, for now you go to X-ray, then take a break, get some lunch, relax, and come back here about two. Any questions?"

"Sounds busy, Doc, but I think we can manage."

Steve was grateful Doc was pulling Mark Dante, a feisty Italian doctor, in on the case. Steve had had his hand shot at point blank range by a crazy woman a few years back when he was held hostage. And it had been weeks before he was rescued and able to be treated. Mark Dante was the expert orthopedic man who worked on the injury. He realigned bones, muscles, tissue, and over time assisted Steve in full healing. His hand was good as new. Steve had to laugh as he remembered how puzzled Doc was with certain things. Steve obeyed Dr. Dante's orders to the letter, wearing the hand guard, the sling, the brace, all faithfully for as long as Mark recommended. Steve never decided that enough was enough, as he always did with Doc's orders.

It was simple. First off, Mark Dante was very straightforward with him. He told him his hand had been seriously injured but he thought he could repair the damage and with therapy and adherence to his orders, full mobility and 100% use of the hand — his right hand— his dominant hand— could be recovered. He treated Steve as an adult, explained the reasoning behind all the caution (the guard for almost six months, the brace, and other things). He told him what consequences were likely to be if he didn't follow orders, which would be limited flexibility and function. Steve wanted full use of his hand, so obeyed the orders, as cumbersome and tedious as they were. He spent many hours in therapy and working with Mark, having each little element assessed and reassessed. And was rewarded with the desired outcome. Mark was a stickler for detail, and highly regarded in his profession. To have him work on Tommy would be a relief.

So Tommy had his tests, they had lunch, and went back at two.

Chapter 14
The Medical— Mark Dante

"Mark, good to see you! How are you?" Steve offered his hand to the man as he entered the exam room. Mark went far beyond the social handshake, to Steve's amusement, and took his hand, twisted and manipulated it, prodded and pushed spots, doing a quick cursory exam.

"Good, Steve, how's the hand? Looks great!"

Steve smiled, held up his hand, flexed the fingers and muscles, "It's perfect, Mark," And sincerely added, "Thanks again."

Mark turned to Tommy, "So, who do we have here? Steve, I didn't know you had a son."

"It's a long but great story, Mark. I didn't have a 'ward' until yesterday! Mark, my 'ward', Tommy. Tommy, Dr. Mark Dante."

"So, buddy, looks like some parts of you are messed up. That's my specialty, fixing messes. Just ask Steve. When I met him, his hand was a mess, a royal mess!"

"He's right, Tommy, my hand appeared hopeless. Mark's a genius at his profession. He'll do well with you."

"Yes, we'll get everything all oiled and working properly."

Becoming businesslike, yet compassionate, "Tommy, why don't you call me Dr. Mark? We're going to be seeing a lot of each other, I want to be friends. Okay?"

Tommy nodded yes.

"Okay, I reviewed all your pretty pictures. Can I examine you?"

Tommy was impressed that he would ask him for permission instead of just doing it. It set him at ease a bit. He didn't mind the examination, but he remembered what had happened with Doc that morning and his shoulder and was scared. Doc had clued Mark in on that fiasco. Mark sensed the fear. "Tommy, Epstein told me what happened this morning. I'll be very, very careful with that shoulder. Believe me, the last thing I want is for the joint to pop out again!"

Tommy was still scared, but consented. He again disrobed and climbed onto the exam table. True to his word, Mark was very gentle. Barely touching the shoulder, he didn't try to move it. He tested all kinds of things, muscle strength, range of motion, flexibility, and more. He was much more thorough with the leg. He had him walk, stand, watched how he bore weight on it (or didn't). Tommy liked the careful, considerate physician. He always precisely explained to Tommy what he was going to do next, which relieved some of the tension. When Mark first glimpsed Tommy's back, he did a sharp intake of breathe, but composed himself and went on, making no comment.

Mark also carefully but completely palpated each individual rib, all the way around, back to front, and examined all the rest of Tommy. He came across what he suspected had been a fracture of his right forearm. Tommy recalled nothing of that, but Mark was pretty sure there had been a fracture. "Feels like it was just the one bone, you may have just thought you had a sore arm or something...."

Finished, he told Tommy he could get dressed. While waiting in the office, he made many notes. Tommy and Steve came back in. Mark looked at them and said, "Tommy, I want to give you a nickname. I want to call you Humpty Dumpty. Because 'you had a great fall'. But… but, but, but, my boy, I am tons better than all the king's horses and all the king's men because I can put Humpty Dumpty back together again!"

This brought laughter from Tommy and Steve and Doc, doing much to relieve the thick tension! "Fine with me, Dr. Mark!"

"Here's what I suggest: First off, you need your strength built up. You're weak and anemic, which needs to be addressed. Doc also may find other things indicated by your lab work requiring attention as well. But, I don't want you to sustain any additional injuries while we fatten you up." Tommy liked the way this doctor talked.

"I want to get you set up with a leg brace, an ankle to hip plastic brace you can strap on and will wear 24/7 except when you shower and bathe. And when you're in the shower or tub you will be very careful not to hurt yourself. I'm going to give you one allowing knee movement; but the brace will almost guarantee that your bone won't break again. It will provide the stability and support needed. So one thing I want you to do is to begin to try to build up some muscles in that leg. To try to walk normally on it. The bone needs repairing; we'll do that in surgery by adding a plate later when you're stronger. But for now, you can begin to work the muscles. They are atrophied from lack of use. I'll set you up with Physical Therapy to help you get started."

Steve interrupted here, "Raleigh?" Mark nodded yes.

Raleigh was a physical therapist Steve (and all his team) knew well, and had worked with personally, often more than once. He was a huge hulk of a man, 6' 4", easily 280 lbs. Raleigh would take a new case, study the medical record, X-rays and so on, and consider the doctor's recommendation. Then he'd examine the patient's hand, arm, leg, whatever, schedule a consultation with the doctor and plan and implement the best course of action. He was skilled at knowing exactly what needed working on, and how to best work to achieve optimal results. An unmerciful task master, but he helped patients achieve excellent results. Raleigh would push longer and harder and farther than anyone thought they could go. And if for some terrible reason the unfortunate subject hadn't done his "therapy homework" (exercises), of course he'd realize, and they'd pay the price the next session as he cranked up the intensity, sweetly reminding that had they done their exercises, this wouldn't be so hard. No excuses were allowed. Steve learned quickly not to let the groundwork slide. One wonderful thing about Raleigh, though, was that after each "torture session", he finished the session with the most soothing, wonderful, healing, relaxing massage. That reward really did make the pain worth it. It did cross Steve's mind that he couldn't do a backrub with Tommy, but Raleigh would figure something out. And Raleigh loved working with Mark Dante's patients because he was so good at "putting things back together perfectly", making his job of rehabilitation so much easier and more effective. Raleigh's patients loved and hated him at the same time.

  Mark continued, "I also want your shoulder and arm immobilized. I'm going to apply a plaster cast. Each time that pops out it causes more damage and scar tissue, not to mention pain. We'll do surgery later to repair both the upper arm, and the shoulder socket. I'm going to leave your wrist and hand free. This will allow you to begin using them, building those muscles. You won't be able to hurt yourself, to reinjure the shoulder, because of the cast, so you're free to begin to use your hand some." He proceeded to explain some of his thoughts for the surgeries, their options, timing and so on, all of which would be dealt with in more detail later.

  Steve and Tommy spent the remainder of the afternoon with Dr. Mark getting a leg brace fitted and adjusted, cast applied to shoulder and arm, which ended up covering more than half his chest as well, then meeting with Raleigh and learning some exercises. Mark stayed, watching to see how Raleigh got Tommy set up with the walking, the leg and hand exercises, and how Tommy handled it. It had been a long and stressful day and they were tired as they headed home. Things were awkward for Tommy with his brace and cast, but he began to learn to manage.

Chapter 15
What Else?

Okay, so medical was covered, not finished by any means, but the process begun. Mental was being covered, some progress being made. Legal was completed, for now. A big thing left was education.

Tommy was smart, really sharp, Steve had come to realize. It certainly wouldn't do to plunk him into a classroom with kids his own age. Between the lack of formal education, and Tommy's experiences, regular school would be an awful choice.

Steve had been thinking about a friend of his — a man he had met some years back on a case. Bob Carson was an elderly, kind old retired professor who had worked his whole career in education. Steve had taken an instant liking to the gentleman with the twinkling eyes and no-nonsense yet jovial manner when they first met. Perhaps he could assist with Tommy, at least for starters. One thing they needed was to know what his abilities were, what knowledge he had acquired, and his grade level. Often, the vocabulary Tommy used, and the way he used language, startled Steve. Professor Carson could spend some time with Tommy, evaluate him, and suggest some options, sharing the pros and cons of each. He'd make a point to talk with him today.

Despite poor sleep, Steve was buoyant. He had spent some time considering how Tommy would fit into his life along with work. The man harbored no doubts that Tommy came first, the priority over work. But, the boy was pretty independent; it wouldn't do to have Steve hovering over him. He'd want him to have his own life, his own work. There would be things and times they'd share, but not everything, and not 24/7. Steve decided to just let that area flow allowing the situation to work itself out, with Tommy becoming busy with school or education, while he was occupied by work.

Steve realized he, in essence, was a single parent now, of an eleven year old boy. *I don't even really know how old he is!* But Steve was far from an ordinary single parent and Tommy was far from your average eleven year old boy. *Nope, might as well not even try to compare.*

Steve was content to let these thoughts incubate in his mind to develop into more concrete ideas as time passed.

Steve was reluctant to leave and go jogging. It would be a tough day for Tommy, if he really opened up with Samuel. *God, help Tommy to cooperate. Help him to heal. Guide Samuel in his work. Help me to do what I can to assist either of them.*

Steve set out in his sweats and running shoes. He was covering the same route he often took. On his way back, still early, he heard the church bells from St. Bartholomew's ring out the Angelus. Slowing, he began to walk in that direction. The bells pealed out every morning at the same time, but today they called to him. He recalled from the sign in front of the old Gothic church that morning Mass was at six a.m. Arriving at the church, just a block off the beach, the bells wound down their clanging. He walked into the nave and automatically blessed himself with holy water, genuflecting before he went into one of the last pews. Steve was surrounded with memories that flooded back, engaging nearly all of his senses — sight, sound, smell, touch, even (it seemed) taste. Early morning sunlight streamed through stained glass windows, casting colored shadows on the dark wood pews and gray marble floor. Flickering candles burned at a side altar, and the red sanctuary flame glowed in front by the tabernacle. The lingering odor of incense from some ceremony wafted over him, filling even his throat. A few older women sat here and there, heads covered by veils. Darkness infused the nave, but it was a comforting darkness, not an oppressive or sinister one. Typical for a weekday morning, attendance was sparse, with maybe a few dozen participants scattered toward the front or off to the side.

Steve had been to Mass now and then, mostly for funerals and weddings, and once in a while he went for Christmas or Easter. Growing up those few years with Doc Burns, Steve had practiced the Catholic faith and attended Mass weekly. He had been baptized as an infant, but until he moved in with Doc, he never went to church or had any kind of faith formation. The man taught him the basics of the faith, the reasons behind all the rituals and sacraments. But much more than that, Doc showed him, by his life and example, what faith was all about.

So here he was, suddenly finding himself in a church, with Mass about to begin, totally unplanned. Despite being sweaty, and not properly attired at all for Mass, he stayed. Steve and the priest knew each other, they had worked together on a case some years back and had become friends. He was a good man whom Steve liked; more than once he had consulted him with some question. Steve followed the Mass, sitting, kneeling, standing as normal, easily remembering the Latin responses to the prayers. He remained in the pew during Communion.

After the short Mass, he remained kneeling in the pew, unsure quite why he stayed. The others knelt and prayed a minute or so, then left. It had been about five minutes when Fr. Phillips walked out of the sacristy and back to him. They smiled at each other in recognition, and Fr. Phillips motioned Steve out. He left the pew, genuflecting out of habit. Once in the vestibule, Father warmly shook hands with him. "Steve, how nice to see you!" Father genuinely was happy.

Admittedly surprised to spot him at Mass, the priest knew it was obviously a spur-of-the-moment thing, given the way Steve was dressed. Suddenly Steve was self-conscious and apologized for his attire. Father good-naturedly laughed it off. "So what brings you here?"

Then, he quickly amended his comment, "I'm glad you're here, Steve. Very glad. You're welcome anytime. But I can't say I recall seeing you here for daily Mass before…"

Steve laughed, "Father, I'm not sure why I'm here. I think your bells drew me in. Like a Pied Piper thing."

He considered the priest carefully, who returned his gaze. Father said, "So, what's up?"

Steve didn't say anything. Father took him by the elbow and escorted him back into the garden behind the rectory. It was a beautiful spot, quiet and peaceful, ablaze with tropical and traditional flowers and greenery, with gravel walkways spreading away from a three-tiered fountain at the center shedding bubbling water down to a glittering pool at the bottom. As they walked along the pathways in the small space, the priest waited for Steve to talk. Steve didn't feel uncomfortable but, rather, surprised and startled with himself.

What the dickens am I doing here? What am I supposed to say? What do I want to say? Good God. Soon, Fr. Phillips knew the whole story, including Steve's past. Steve had related a condensed and sanitized version, but the gist of it was there. "Father, I'm not sure why I'm here. Why I'm talking to you. I don't expect answers from you. I'm not sure there are answers." But it did feel good talking to the man, who did nothing but listen carefully.

Fr. Phillips smiled. Even though the two men were close in age, the priest laid his hand on Steve's should in a paternal gesture. "You'll figure it out, Steve. I think God has a plan here. The Holy Ghost is at work. Touch base with God."

Steve didn't discuss it more, but wondered. *And exactly how do I touch base with God?* He smiled as he stood from a bench near the fountain to leave, "We'll see, Father. Sounds good."

They walked back around front, the priest shaking his hand before Steve left, and chiding playfully, "Don't be such a stranger. Come anytime. For Mass. Or to talk. I'm here for you, Steve."

Somehow that invitation made Steve feel warm inside—a soothing warmth. His hand went to the pocket of his sweats which held the rosary beads. *Am I imagining this, or are they warm again? O'Shaughnessy, are you going bonkers? Nah, but this is weird with the rosary. Maybe I'll ask Father about it. Forget it for now.* Slowly he jogged back the last quarter mile home, then headed to the office, leaving Samuel and Tommy to work.

After checking messages, Steve placed a call to Professor Carson. While waiting for an answer, he reflected on the man's solitude and loneliness. University and state budget cuts had meant early retirement; his wife had died six or seven years prior. Steve was aware he did some volunteer work, but also surmised that his vast talents, knowledge and experiences were underused, being wasted. "Bob, Steve O'Shaughnessy. How are you?"

"Steven! How nice of you to call! I'm fine, just fine. What about you?"

With a hint of excitement, thinking maybe Steve needed his help on a case or something, "What are you calling about? Can I help you with something?"

Steve picked up his eagerness, again suspecting his hunch was right, and the old man had a desolate existence. He and Tommy may be a quite suitable match. "As a matter of fact, Bob,

I think you might be able to help me. I'd like to come out and visit you, if I may?"

"Fine, Steven, fine! When? Today? Why don't you join me for lunch?"

That hadn't exactly been in Steve's plan, but figured it would be a good idea. Take his mind off thinking what Tommy might be going through with therapy, make an old man happy by visiting with him, and discuss Tommy. "Sounds perfect, Bob! Thank you. 1:00?"

"That would be wonderful, Steven, I'm looking forward to it."

The morning passed for Steve. He did get a few things done, organized, but his mind wandered from his work. He got a call from Doc regarding the results of Tommy's lab work. Results were what they had anticipated, no surprises. The physician was aware Tommy and Samuel were working together and asked Steve how that was going.

"Well enough, I guess Doc. They're really just getting started." And decided he didn't want to get into the matter.

But before he let him go, Doc wisely asked, "And how are YOU doing, Steve?" well aware he had his own issues.

"Yeah, Doc, well...." He didn't want to say more, but did anyway, "Samuel's going to a have a go at me as well in a day or so."

Doc knew what that meant, but he was still glad to hear it. "Good, Steve." And then, very sincerely, "Let me know if I can help in any way."

"Thanks, Doc. I will." Steve hung up, being grateful for wonderful friends. He was a very lucky and blessed man.

Bob Carson lived in a quaint little cottage, clean and bright — but cluttered everywhere with books. Steve chuckled. Tommy would love this place. The two greeted each other warmly. "Come, Steven, sit. I've made some mango smoothies for us."

Steve moved with him outside to the lanai. "Delicious, Bob. Thank you."

In a while the professor served a wonderful lunch of typical Hawaiian fare, marvelously prepared. As they dined, Steve shared the story, telling enough for the professor to fully understand, but omitting details.

"My goodness, Steven, this lad sounds most intriguing. I'd love to meet him, talk with him, work with him. Do you think he'd like to?"

"Professor, I think if he stepped one foot in your house and saw all these books, he'd be thrilled! Not to mention I think you and he would hit it off well."

"Well, then, by all means, bring him by when he's better, when he's up to it! I'm excited, Steven, this will be wonderful!"

"Very well, Professor, I'll call you. I'm not sure when, maybe tomorrow."

"Anytime, Steven, anytime. You have a terrific afternoon, now, young man!"

Steve walked back to his car, smiling and pleased with the idea.

Meanwhile, Tommy and Samuel had another somewhat fruitful day, about what Samuel had expected. There was progress, but still lots of work left. They'd been at it steady and hadn't eaten since breakfast (albeit a late breakfast). Breaking for the day, together they prepared supper. Samuel encouraged Tommy to help as best he could, even limited by only having one good hand. They chatted as they worked.

Steve came home, they all ate together and had a peaceful quiet evening.

Chapter 16
A Visit with the Professor

At breakfast the next day, they discussed the plans for the day. Samuel had a few errands to run, and then he and Steve would meet up, after he took Tommy to the Professor's for the day.

On the drive out they chatted comfortably. Tommy had a million questions, most of which Steve didn't have answers to, about what they'd be doing and is he a teacher, and this and that. Steve just laughed, "You'll see, he'll answer you."

They arrived and were warmly greeted by the professor who had excitedly stepped out his door as he heard the car drive up. "Come in, come in!"

And as Steve had expected, Tommy's jaw dropped at the sight of the man's libraries and books all over. "Wow!"

Amusedly, Professor Carson said, "So, Tommy, Steve says you like to read."

"Oh, yes, sir! I love books!"

Glancing at Steve, the professor said, "Tommy, we're going to get along just fine!"

Before turning to leave, Steve carefully made sure that they both knew he could be called anytime, for any reason if they needed him. A part of him was unsure about leaving.

The professor laughed, "Go, Steve. We're going to have fun today."

Steve smiled and headed back to his place; the few worries he had about Tommy for that day dissipated in the breeze on his drive home. He found Samuel enjoying the sunshine on the lanai with a cup of coffee. The psychiatrist looked directly at him. "So, Stevie, how goes it?"

Having worked extensively with Samuel before, he thought a moment, then didn't beat around the bush at all, "Honest to God, Samuel, I really don't know."

And Samuel, typically, didn't say anything, just waited for Steve to move forward. Steve laughed as he realized his friend's tactics. "God, Samuel, you're the same as always!"

Steve began, "Let me work through this. First, I am very glad Tommy came into my life. Yes, it's been hard in ways that I never imagined. Samuel, I never expected anything like this in my life. But it's good, very good. I can see lots of wonderful times for us together. Sharing a lot of our lives. I'm excited about it, Samuel."

Samuel asked, "What about your memories, Stevie, your scars? And the new ones Tommy opened up the other day?"

Steve pursued his lips tightly closed. He hated hurting, hated being in pain. What he often did was bury it, hard and deep. Which he knew wasn't best, and which he also knew Samuel wouldn't let him get away with. "Aww, Samuel. Yes, they resurfaced. Shall I say moved from the side of the road into the middle? And a bunch of new fallen trees jam smack front and center. But you know, they don't seem to have much strength, much staying power. I went for a long jog yesterday and worked a bunch of things out."

Samuel pressed on, "Enlighten me, Stevie. What was that all about?"

Steve thought about it. "Samuel, what it was, was that I believed my father loved me. That he did what he did because he loved me, wanted me to be better, and wanted to teach me what I needed to know, what was important. Never mind that his methods were wrong. If he MEANT to be helping, that was what counted. And in a split second, I'm still not sure why and why's not important, I realized that was all baloney. My father DIDN'T love me. And that meant I was unlovable. This belief was firmly lodged in my subconscious all along. I mean, if your own father doesn't love you, how can anyone? And in the next second, I realized that too was baloney. My father was incapable of loving. He didn't love me because he couldn't. He had no idea how or why. Again, I don't know why he was that was way; I never really knew anything about his upbringing. But he didn't love me not because he choose not to love me, but because he couldn't, he didn't know how. And that, Samuel, was what was buried. Believing myself unlovable. Believing that in my deepest core. That's why the walls are there. If there aren't any walls, and someone doesn't love me, then it would just validate my mistaken belief. The walls don't allow the possibility of love in, so there is no chance of not being loved. No opportunity to be unloved. But, I know now how wrong that is. Somehow, I saw Tommy and realized easily that what he deserved was unconditional love. And then I saw myself and realized that I had deserved the very same thing. Every kid does. And that was healing— deeply healing. The realization that I didn't get what was supposed to be there, not because of something wrong with me, or something I did wrong, but because someone— my father— was incapable of giving it. This has been tremendously curative and soothing. Like I said, I didn't even know that wound was there."

He paused, then stopped to look at Samuel instead of out at the waves. "Samuel, I truly think that's all of it. There's nothing else hiding, lurking, beneath the surface. We both know those days many years ago when we fought through this, we didn't get it all. I don't know why it was hidden so deep; maybe the pain was too great. Maybe I knew that, as good as you are, you couldn't give me what I needed. Maybe I just knew Tommy could, and would, and that's why it erupted. It's done, Samuel. I'm sure of it." Steve was confident, his voice was strong.

Samuel believed him and agreed that he was right. "Quite the lad, isn't he, Stevie?"

"Understatement of the year, my friend!"

Then, just to be sure, to confirm his feelings, Samuel asked, "So, the scars are back at the roadside? Stevie O'Shaughnessy is whole and sound?"

Steve grinned, "Yes, Doctor."

"And can you deal with Tommy's pain?"

"That's a tough one. It hurts me when I know he's hurting, that he has hurt and been hurt. And seeing his physical scars was no picnic. Nor the pain I know he still faces. But, yeah, Samuel, I think I can deal with it."

Samuel affirmed that. "I think you can too, Steve."

Steve thought more. "I've got a lot of anger, Samuel. Anger at what has happened to Tommy and at the man who did it, impotence at not being able to 'fix' it, frustration with not being able to take away Tommy's pain or burden. A lot of anger, Samuel. But I recognize it. I'm not quite ready to let go of it yet, but I can see that I will be."

"Well, that's honest. And good that you can see it honestly."

As Steve was thinking about Tommy, he wondered how he was doing with the Professor and chuckled.

"What's so funny?"

"Oh, you don't know the fellow I took Tommy to today, but he's a kind crusty old academia type. Loves books. I knew he and Tommy would hit it off. The look on his face when he walked into the professor's home, thousands of books everywhere, was priceless. He looked like a kid in a candy store. I have a real good feeling about those two."

They sat in comfortable silence.

"And you know, Samuel, I'm also real pleased that I've got Doc and Mark Dante to look after him as well. Did he tell you Mark gave him a nickname, Humpty Dumpty? That said he saw that Tommy had 'had a great fall', but that he was lots better than all the king's horses and all the king's men and would put Tommy back together again. He will, Samuel. When that crazy woman shot my hand it was obliterated. Bones, muscles, blood vessels, nerves, all of it. A huge hole right in the palm. And it was three weeks before I was rescued and got any treatment for it. And Mark took that mess and made it whole again."

"Sounds like a competent man."

"Yes, and so is the therapist. He makes a world of difference as well."

Samuel had been thinking, then explained to Steve, "You know, Stevie, it's like there are two Tommys. Not a split personality or anything, but I see two sides to him. It's a good thing, I think. On the one side, you have a little boy. A smart kid, real smart, but still a little boy, with all the needs and immaturity of an eleven year old little boy. And one who has been missing a lot of very key things that are critical to being happy and well adjusted. I think you will be able to make those things up to him, to a large degree, and his intelligence also helps, but it's something to pay attention to. On the other hand, you've got this hard, armored tough, savvy kid. The one who survived the abuse, the one who handles whatever is thrown at him. What the goal is here is to let the little boy come out, he's pretty hidden. Keep the good, positive and strong traits of the warrior, but allow him to more fade into the background. He's not needed anymore; you're here to do the protecting. It's going to take some work on Tommy's part to let that happen, to meld the parts of himself into a good cohesive whole. It can be done, and he'll do it I think; I'm just telling you how I see it. I can also see that I'm not going to be doing any highly intensive therapy with Tommy right now. He's still too guarded for that. Natural self-defense mechanisms and all. But that will come; I'd guess maybe in a few months. That's where the real work needs doing, though, Steve. He has talked about things, and that's good, but he's not gotten very personal. All in good time."

That made sense to Steve, "Well, Samuel, he'll have your help. That's a tremendous asset."

Samuel nodded. Then asked, "Stevie, you feel strongly about adopting Tommy, don't you?"

Steve replied affirmatively. "Yes, I do, Sam. It just feels so right that we belong together, as a family. I know it will take some time to figure out how to do that, me as a single parent, Tommy as an 'ordinary' kid. As ordinary as he can be, given his history. And brains. But we'll get it.

Samuel agreed, "Yeah, you will."

Steve's stomach rumbled and he suggested, "Samuel, remember the last time you were here, we went to that tiny oceanside café off King Street? I'd like to take you there."

Samuel was pleased with that, and they left. After enjoying a nice meal, Steve dropped his friend downtown, and went to the office to tackle more work. He was finally able to focus on work for a while and time flew as he efficiently finished tasks. They had been fortunate in that no big cases were pending; nothing came up that was critical.

Realizing it was six p.m., past time to call it quits for today, he gave a quick call to Professor Carson, asking how things went and telling him he's be by in a bit to pick up Tommy. "Steven, we've had a marvelous day, both of us. I'll fill you in when you stop by."

Smiling, Steve was not surprised, and appreciative of yet one more thing. Curious as to the professor's findings, he made his way there quickly.

"Steve! Hi. I've had a great day. Professor Carson is the most extraordinary guy. And his books! He has tons of books! Some really rare ones. Ones they don't have in libraries. Some are antiques."

Steve was amused as Tommy gushed on in excitement. "And we talked about the most amazing things. He told me he'd teach me all kinds of stuff. He knows more than anyone else I've ever met!"

The professor instructed Tommy, "Son, go get that book from earlier, plop yourself down with it, while Steve and I talk." He led his friend out onto the lanai.

"Well, Steven, I have not had this good a day in many years. Tommy is amazing. You're absolutely right; he does have photographic visual memory and hearing. And he is smart, as you suspected. I didn't do any kind of formal testing, I will in time, but I'd expect the genius level."

Steve was stunned. He knew Tommy was smart, but genius? Wow. And to be that smart, retain that intelligence in spite of the horrible things that happened to him was astonishing.

The professor continued, "He's well read, Steve, in some areas. We discussed some of the classics, he's sharp with deductions, inferences, logic, all of that. He said he never really had much regular school, just spent time reading in libraries. Is that right?"

"That's right, Bob…"

"Remarkable. Absolutely remarkable." His mind was elsewhere — thinking about Tommy.

"Steven, I think there are considerable gaps in his knowledge, which is not surprising without having been taught. Mathematics, physics, some science things. He says he doesn't really like history, except for biographies of historical figures.

These are just some initial impressions I have. As I work with him more, talk more, I'll get a much better idea. When are you going to bring him back? Tomorrow?"

Steve laughed and was pleased with the man's eagerness. "I don't think tomorrow, maybe the next day. Let me call you." He was thinking that perhaps tomorrow would be a day for he and Tommy to talk together with Samuel.

"Anytime, Steven, soon, though!"

They walked back through the house to the front door, collecting Tommy as they went. "Professor, may I please take this book home with me? I promise to be careful with it and bring it back when I come again!"

Then, looking at Steve, asked, "Steve, when do I get to come again? I do get to come back, don't I, Steve?"

"Yes. Yes, Tommy, you'll be back. Maybe not tomorrow, but soon. Don't worry."

Before getting into the car, Steve shook the professor's hand, "Thank you, Bob."

"Believe me, it was my pleasure!"

And then added as an afterthought, "Steven, have you ever played chess with him?"

Perplexed, Steve replied that he hadn't.

Grinning, the professor said, "Why don't you try it? And Steven — let me advise you. Don't give him any leeway. Don't hold back at all!!"

Now Steve was curious.

As he made a nice supper of meat loaf, mashed potatoes, and tomato soup, Tommy regaled him with a non-stop flow of talk about Professor Carson and his day. Seeing Tommy smile and be so animated warmed Steve's heart to no end.

Before Steve went to clean up the dishes, he reminded Tommy about the physical therapy exercises Raleigh had given him. Tommy typically rolled his eyes. "I know they're not dumb, Steve, but …."

"A pain?" Steve supplied. "I know, Tommy. But I'd suggest you do them anyway. Raleigh's going to know if you did or not. And from my experience, if he knows you didn't do them, he'll turn up the heat on your next session to make you sorry for your slip-up! Now, maybe because you're a 'kid', or maybe because you're new with him, he might grant you a bit of mercy, but I wouldn't count on it."

In the kitchen, Tommy ran through the routine Raleigh had assigned as he talked with Steve. It wasn't hard, or painful, just tedious.

After he finished, Steve got the chessboard out of a cabinet. "So, where'd you learn to play chess?"

Smirking, Tommy asked, "You really want to know?"

"Yeah."

"A bunch of old geezers in the park. They'd play in the afternoons and I'd watch. Finally they started letting me play. We'd have a lot of fun. They'd end up betting when I'd play. Silly things, like a stick of gum, or donut. "

Steve asked, "Did the guys who bet for you win or lose?"

Tommy slyly refused to answer, as they set the pieces up.

Steve liked chess. He liked the intrigue of the game, the infinite possibilities, plays, styles, techniques. He was a fairly accomplished player, and seldom lost. *I think I'll follow Bob's advice and be very careful.* Steve played very aggressively, his typical game, attacking strong and hard from the beginning. All the while he was watching Tommy. Steve learned that you can tell a lot about a chess player from his body language. You can often figure out your opponent's style, where he might be going with his game plan from watching him.

Tommy seemed unfazed by the direct attacks. He'd apply clever defenses, and more than once surprised Steve with a move. About ten minutes into the game, Steve realized he was in deep trouble. Very cunningly, Tommy had been positioning key pieces for an assault. Already much was in place for Tommy; it was going to require some clever strategy for Steve to get adequate damage control and defenses properly situated. He looked at Tommy, hoping maybe it was all just 'dumb luck' or something. Tommy met his eyes and Steve knew it wasn't 'dumb luck'. They played the game out, Steve lost.

He challenged the boy to another game and was much more careful this time paying close attention to each of his opponent's moves, trying to discern his plan of action. Tommy knew what he was doing and was amused. He could tell Steve wasn't used to losing at chess. Every now and then, just for fun, he'd hesitate or fumble. The third time he did this, Steve looked at him and said, gruffly but friendly, "Knock off the act! You know exactly what you're doing, kiddo!" That game ended in a draw, barely.

"One more?" He knew his chess playing skills were rusty; he also admitted to himself that was a minor factor in his lack of wining. It wasn't late yet, and they both seemed to be having fun. Steve was relishing the mental workout. Samuel came in before they started the third game and sauntered over to watch; Steve quickly brought him up to date.

In this game, Tommy decided to change his strategy a bit. The last two games he had designed attacks to be stealthy, sneaky, and at the same time set up defenses that usually protected several key areas simultaneously. This time he did that, but also focused on some direct frontal confrontations, more a la O'Shaughnessy style. This confused Steve a bit, as Tommy had intended. Steve asked him about it, "What're you doing this time, Tommy?"

Tommy replied innocently, "Oh, I dunno, I thought maybe I'd try it your way this time."

A few minutes later, Steve just about got suckered into a jam before he realized it. "Tommy, you little sneak!"

Tommy laughed. Steve was able to rally, but not enough to come back and win. Tommy took that game.

"The professor was right, you are good. And no mercy for you from now on when we play!"

Tommy drawled in a sing song voice, intentionally using poor grammar, and mocked, "Hey, Stevie, you want maybe I should give you a handicap?"

To which Steve replied, in the same sing-song voice, but with a twinge of annoyance (at himself, not Tommy), "Nooo, Tommy, I don't want maybe you should give me a handicap!!"

They all laughed. "Apparently I need to hone my skills a bit!" Steve expected to enjoy being pitted against a challenger who was better than he was and would bring him up to a higher level of competence. A competitive man, he would expand his abilities so he would sometimes come out on top. He also knew it wouldn't be easy.

Steve and Samuel talked more that evening after Tommy was bedded down for the night about how to proceed with things. Tommy still had lots of work to do. He was beginning to open up and trust Samuel a bit, but it was only a beginning. Sometimes the boy slipped very easily into the role of being a brilliant eleven year old boy, like when they'd play chess, or when he'd complain about doing his physical therapy exercises. Sometimes he was still the armored warrior.

What they decided was that Samuel would go back to Singapore. He would touch base a few times a week with Tommy by phone. Return visits for long weekends would be scheduled every four to six weeks or as needed. Besides his business doing well financially, Steve had made some very profitable stock market investments so financing Samuel's trips wasn't a concern.

Steve and Tommy would get much needed time to begin to really establish a relationship. It was obvious they had already bonded, but they needed to work on just figuring out how their lives would mesh, how to relate, that kind of thing.

Phone conversations weren't as ideal as talking in person, but would do. Samuel headed back home to Singapore the next day. Tommy and Steve took him to the airport and gave their friend a warm sendoff.

Chapter 17
A Bit More Medical

The boy's health was coming along; the anemia was better, They had an appointment to see Mark again in a few days to discuss surgery. Twice weekly visits with Raleigh were also part of their newly established routine. When Steve watched Tommy and Raleigh together, it seemed to him that the therapist was awfully easy on him compared to the almost brutal treatment he seemed to get when he was in therapy and mending!

Steve took Tommy in to see Doc about his arm, have his stitches checked. Doc wanted to do more blood tests. As Tommy sat on his exam table he seemed nervous. Fidgeting, and looking back and forth at Steve, Doc, and his lap, he finally said tentatively, "Doc, there's something I really want to tell you."

Doc stopped getting ready to draw blood and looked at him, patiently waiting to hear what it was. Steve went on alert. The boy took some deep breaths and said shyly, "Doc…..I really don't like needles."

It was only Doc's decades of experience that gave him the reserve not to burst out laughing. *This kid had been hurt so many ways, and he's afraid of needles?*

"Oh, Tommy, that's okay. Lots of people don't like needles. You know Keo, the big Hawaiian who works with Steve? More than once he has passed out cold on me when he sees a needle coming his way. Really! If I ever need to give him a shot or draw blood, I make him lie down first. He's not a tiny fellow and when he goes down, it's hard!"

Then, glancing at Steve, "And he's not the only one. Steve and Marco aren't so bad, they don't faint on me, but they flinch pretty easily, too."

Steve grimaced a bit at this betrayal, but understood it helped Tommy to hear it.

"Here's a trick, Tommy. Don't look at the needle, focus someplace else. Say Steve's face." Ready to draw the blood, Doc said firmly, "Okay, I'm going to do this quick. Look at Steve now." He didn't ask if Tommy was ready, just went ahead and did it. And it went okay. Doc hit a vein on the first try (he usually did) and Tommy cringed but held steady.

Studying Tommy carefully for paleness or dizziness, he said, "All done. You okay?"

Tommy shook his head yes and let out a deep breath. Doc removed the stitches, while Steve kept a hand on the boy's shoulder in silent support. Doc gave Tommy a quick once over, said he thought he was doing fine.

Next stop was physical therapy with Raleigh. Steve watched carefully as they ran through the paces. This was Tommy's third visit with him. He sadly wasn't the lucky recipient of backrubs the first two times, with his cast and all. This time around, though, Raleigh had it figured out. When the session was over, he smiled at Steve, then Tommy. He ushered them into his massage room, a tiny space that had nice low lighting, quiet soothing music, and a warmer temperature. He helped Tommy up onto his massage table, face up. Arranged a comfy pillow under his head, another under the neck, and a third under his knees. Asked him if the lighting, music and temperature were all okay, if he was comfortable.

"Okay, Tommy, I can't quite give you the backrub I normally do with my patients, but I have figured out something that I think you'll like. I'm going to give you a massage. You'll become very relaxed and comfortable. When I'm finished, I'll just leave. Steve, when I'm finished with Tommy, if you could come out with me, there's something I'd like to cover with you. Tommy, you may well fall asleep during the massage, that's fine. Regardless, you can lie here as long as you like, sleeping, resting, whatever. When you want and feel ready, you can just get up and leave. Understand?"

Tommy nodded, curious as to what Raleigh was going to do. So was Steve.

Raleigh instructed Tommy to just relax, close his eyes if he wanted. Then he started massaging his left leg, the "good" one, beginning at the thigh, working his way down. Very strongly, kneading the muscles, but also gently. He was careful to go slowly, hitting each spot with his large strong fingers, including working the back of the leg as well as the top. He did the whole leg, ending with a complete foot massage. Then moved to his right foot, just the foot on that side. But a nice foot massage. This was very relaxing. Then he moved and did the right shoulder and arm, completely, including the hand. He did the left hand as well. Then he moved to the top of Tommy's head and began some very gentle head and scalp massage, covering every inch, just as he did elsewhere. And lastly he moved to his face. There he just used fingertips, massaging in circular motions, then with strokes. Tommy was completely relaxed. Steve found it amazing.

Raleigh noticed Steve's look as he finished, just smiled, and headed out, very quietly. Steve followed. Raleigh led him to another small therapy room with a massage bench in it. Raleigh instructed, "Steve, take off your shoes, strip to the waist and lie down, face down." Steve looked at him, puzzled.

"Look, you're not my patient, and you haven't 'done' anything therapy wise to earn a massage, but you sure look like you could use one. You've had a tremendous amount of stress over the last few days, your neck and shoulders are probably one big knot."

Steve grinned, Raleigh was absolutely correct. And he'd never turn down a good back rub from this guy. He did as instructed and got settled. (Raleigh was the one other person who had seen the scars on Steve's back, he never asked about them, Steve never volunteered any information.) This room wasn't one Raleigh had ever used with Steve before, and it didn't have the nice low lighting, but he had plugged in a cassette player and had some nice music going. And Steve didn't really need all the trappings. Raleigh started in and was met with low moans of soreness from Steve as he worked the taut muscles. He wasn't getting quite the results he wanted as quickly as he had expected (he had underestimated Steve's level of tenseness.) He quietly and calmly led Steve through some relaxing deep breathing exercises, still working on his muscles, but more gently, slowly. And little by little he could feel the relaxation begin and grow in each area. Steve's moans gradually turned to sighs and then sounds of comfort, of one being soothed. He thought to himself, "O'Shaughnessy really needed this!" He spent a long while working on Steve. He had alerted his staff where he was and to ask Tommy just to wait if he came out before he and Steve were done.

Eventually he finished, satisfied that the muscles were relaxed, and left. Steve lay in peace a few more minutes, then got up, dressed and came out. Raleigh and Tommy were sitting and talking as Steve came up. He placed a hand on Raleigh's shoulder, "Thank you, Raleigh, that was absolutely wonderful, and I needed it. I really appreciate it." And he did.

Raleigh smiled, said he was glad to be of service, and said goodbye to the two of them.

Chapter 18
Surgery

Steve found himself drawn to prayer much more often these days than he had in many years. He also thought about returning to regular Sunday Mass attendance. Perhaps it was some sort of inner realization that he needed God's guide through this turn the maze of his life had taken. He wanted to do what was best for Tommy, and thought he had a pretty good idea of what that might be, the part he could play in the boy's life, but also felt a need for reassurance from God, something he was finding through prayer.

Another morning after his jog, he went to Mass. His heart was being drawn to the holy service like iron to a magnet. And again, afterwards he knelt in a pew midway towards the front in the empty dimly lit church. Several rays of colored light played over the large crucifix which hung prominently at the front center. He wasn't sure just why he was here, or how he actually got to this point, kneeling at church, with a desire to pray. That much he did know— he wanted to pray. Why, how, about what, that's the part he was confused about.

Steve thought back to Doc Burns. He remembered asking him how to pray. Doc chuckled and told Steve to just talk to God like a friend. Just pretend he's sitting right there next to you, Someone with all the answers, Someone willing to, and wanting to, listen to all your problems and concerns. Just start talking. Steve had tried it a few times, it seemed weird to him as a teenager.

It still seemed odd to him, but maybe a bit less so, and he figured he'd give it a try. *What's going on here, God? I don't get it. I don't get why Tommy came into my life. What am I supposed to do, what am I supposed to learn? Where do I go, where do Tommy and I go from here?*

Steve also recalled that Doc said a big part of praying was also "listening". Not in terms of hearing voices, but more like getting a feeling about something, a sorting out of a direction or answer in your head. So Steve stopped "talking" to "listen".

He wasn't surprised to not really "hear" anything, get any answers. He prayed more over the next ten minutes; his gaze was drawn to the crucifix. He studied the statue upon it — that of a man who had been beaten and suffered, one who died. *Lord, that's another thing I don't get.* Doc tried to explain it. Steve remembered so clearly so many things Doc said, which surprised him. Things he hadn't thought about in decades, yet it was just like hearing Doc's voice and seeing his smiling face.

Doc used to say, "Offer it up." When Steve asked what that meant, he said that you would "unite" your pain and suffering to Christ's, which made it more valuable. To "use" your suffering to help others. *Well, I remember what he said, and maybe I get it a bit more, but not really.*

Steve studied the corpus on the cross. *How many times have I heard the story of the Passion? How much Christ suffered. Why did He do that? You're God, why did you allow them to do that to you?* Doc would have said Christ did it for him. *Well, whatever. I don't get that part. But Christ — the man — knew what it was to suffer. He could identify with me, and Tommy. Or maybe vice-versa? I can identify with him?*

Steve wasn't angry with God; he never blamed Him for what had happened, either to him or Tommy. And He knew he could find some peace from, or through, God. He figured that was what he was really looking for here. He prayed longer, trying with some success to use Doc's technique of just talking to God as a friend.

What ended up pouring out was anguish. Over his own pain as a child. Over the pain he knew Tommy felt. Physical pain, but also the emotional pain. That was worse. It had been worse for him. And he knew it was for Tommy, also. He looked upon the cross. *God, whyyy??? Why this suffering? Why did it happen with me? Why did it happen with Tommy? WHY, Lord? WHY???* Tears escaped his eyes.

After a few minutes, he realized he was listening, like Doc had advised. And "hearing", so to speak. The message coming to him was that his suffering, in part, had made him who he was. Maybe that had led some of his 'poor' qualities, like his guardedness, and walls, but also much of his good— his strength, his perseverance, and more, He could see how without having that, he would have been a very different person, certainly less in some areas.

As he knelt there, more of Doc's wisdom came back to him: "Steve, if a person allows it, suffering can bring you closer to Christ. And, in my opinion, anything that brings you closer to Christ is good."

Steve remembered thinking at the time that seemed quite ridiculous (he didn't say that to Doc, not wanting to offend him, but he suspected the old man knew what he was thinking). But now, here he was, kneeling in a church, praying. That put him closer to Christ than he had been for a long, long time. *Maybe Doc was right…*

More thoughts came to him. *Are these inspirations from the Holy Ghost? God LOVES me. He truly, completely and unconditionally loves me. I've known this a long time, but it was always an intellectual belief, in my mind, my head. Now I know it in my heart. And that's where it matters.* Steve felt a deep penetrating warmth spread through his chest and body. For a second he wondered if he were having a heart attack. It was strong and fiery, but not at all painful. God's love burned deeper and deeper and more intensely into him, infusing him with what could only be called true heavenly joy. He had never expected anything like this when he stopped into the church. Suddenly he smelled the fragrance of roses, though there were no fresh flowers anywhere in the church that he could see, and his rosary was warm. Steve had never felt as overwhelmed as he did this minute. Even when he and Doc shared some very significant moments, they were no comparison to this.

Taken aback by the awesome power he was feeling, it was all he could do to sit and allow himself to be bathed in it. He didn't need to think, to pray, to act, he just needed to "be". And how wonderful that was. Time passed, slowly the intensity faded. But Steve knew he would never, never forget this time.

He was home in plenty of time to get cleaned up, eat, and still make the appointment Tommy had with Mark Dante. As usual, the doctor began by meticulously examined Tommy, asking how therapy was going and how he was feeling, what he was doing, etc. He ordered additional tests, and said he believed Tommy was ready for surgery. Mark's plan was to operate first on the arm, resetting the bones and stabilizing them with a small plate. Then he would move to the shoulder in the same surgery and work on restoring it. He was fairly certain he could work with what was there, repair it, and Tommy would have 100% use of it (after therapy, of course).

Mark wasn't sure about the leg; he said it was unlikely they would do that the same day. That would extend the surgery by several hours and may well be too much of a burden at one time on the body. That surgery involved a procedure similar to what Mark would be using on the arm. However, Mark said if he got in there with the arm and shoulder and all was going well, he may just decide to do the leg, as well. He'd just have to wait and see. If not that day, he said he'd expect to follow the arm surgery with leg surgery about two weeks after. He did warn both of them that Tommy's leg would be immobilized in a heavy cast for a month, and that he would not be able to use crutches with only one good arm. He'd be wheelchair bound. At Tommy's crestfallen look, he tried to lighten the mood with the comment that it would be temporary, only a few months. Steve just figured they'd deal with it. Doc Epstein also gave the green light and the operation was scheduled for two days later.

Tommy was admitted the next afternoon. To Tommy's embarrassment, yet relief, Steve had shared with Mark his dislike of needles. News which Mark took without any ridicule or judgment. Matter-of-factly, he replied, "Okay, we can deal with that. You'll have some needles with surgery, but we'll handle it."

Steve's keen eye picked up on little things Tommy did that told him he was a bit scared— quirky laughs at odd times, jerky motions. The boy was trying to act very matter-of-fact, but major surgery is never matter-of-fact. And he was also uncomfortable with all the attention directed towards him— he had always preferred not to be noticed much. Yet in one way, he was touched by being treated so warmly by so many.

Father Phillips stopped in for a quick visit. Tommy was given pre-op meds after supper which made him groggy and he slept.

Next morning, when Tommy was getting ready to be transported to surgery, Steve was emotional. He knew and expected all to go well, but it was hard to see him wheeled off. Doc Epstein was there in his scrubs, ready to assist as needed in surgery, and laid a hand on Steve's shoulder in silent support. And Marco also showed up before Tommy left.

The waiting began. They remained in Tommy's room, instead of some impersonal waiting room with other people. Steve paced. He and Marco talked some. Doc Epstein came down about three hours later to talk with Steve. "Steve, Mark's going to go ahead with his leg. Things went very well so far with the arm and shoulder, Tommy's doing fine, his vitals are good. He feels it will be best to do the leg now, as long as things are going so well. I'm heading back up; I just wanted to let you know. It'll be at least another two hours before we're done."

Steve was glad Tommy was doing well, but it felt like agony to have to wait longer still. He distracted himself by thinking about how they'd manage with a wheelchair, working out some challenges and planning to keep things simple, and about how Tommy would manage being so dependent on him.

There was a knock on the door and Fr. Phillips came in to check on things. "Hi, Steve. How's it going?" After Steve's concise report, Father stayed a while longer. As he left, he promised Steve he'd say Mass that evening for Tommy, a gesture Steve found touching and which brought tears to his eyes.

A couple of hours later, Mark and Doc sailed into Tommy's room. Steve immediately noticed the upbeat looks on their faces. Mark reported that Tommy did really well through it all, which was why he decided to go for the leg surgery as well. All plates, pins, wires were in place. Mark's prognosis was that it was very likely he'd have full and complete recovery of the use of his arm, shoulder, and leg, in time, and with faithful therapy. He said Tommy was in the recovery room now and they'd be bringing him back to his room in about fifteen minutes, but that he'd still be groggy from the meds and would sleep.

Steve's eyes watered. He turned away from the men for a moment and stared out the window. After exhaling deeply, swallowing, and running his hand through his hair, he turned back. He shook hands with each, but it was his eyes that really portrayed his deep gratitude and expressed his appreciation.

Tommy came down, and was asleep. The nurse asked Steve to leave while they got him moved in and settled. Steve said he'd stay out of the way and took up a position leaning against the wall. The nurse scrutinized him carefully, then determined the battle of getting him to leave was not worth it. Steve assessed her as she went about the task of transferring Tommy and checking him. She was thorough, methodical, and efficient. Of medium height, maybe in her late forties, he could tell she was highly competent; no medical detail would be missed with her in charge. She was kind and gentle, but he wouldn't use the word "warm" to describe her. When finished, she gave him a concise report of Tommy's status. She had introduced herself earlier as Miss Watkins, Steve mentally dubbed her Nurse Cratchet. She came across in a not unfriendly manner, but very business-like. Before she left she told him if he had any questions to feel free to ask anytime

Before Marco left, he reminded Steve to call him if there was anything he needed, and that he'd be back later. And to tell Tommy hi.

As Steve sat and waited for Tommy to come to, he prayed, thanking God for a successful surgery then thought back and thanked God for all that had happened so far with Tommy and himself.

Tommy woke up a bit later, sleepily looked at Steve, and smiled. "Hey, Tommy, how'd you feel?"

"Floating…. Fine…"

Steve knew he probably wouldn't remember, but informed him anyway, "Tommy, Dr. Mark took care of everything. He did your arm and shoulder and leg. He said everything went smoothly, that you did really well, that you should be fine with time and therapy."

"Hmmmmm…"

A minute later he opened his eyes more, focused on Steve, spoke a bit more clearly, and asked, "Steve, can you come here, close?"

Steve moved right next to the bed, put the railing down, and leaned close. Tommy murmured fuzzily, "Closer…."

Steve studied the situation a bit, kicked off his shoes (his suit coat was already on the back of the chair), and ever so gently climbed in the bed next to Tommy and put his arm around him. *Good grief, Nurse by-the-book Cratchet is going to come in here in a minute and have a hissy fit! Well, too bad.*

He knew Tommy liked to have him be physically close — hug— that kind of thing. But the young man also was afraid to get close, and certainly not ask for it. But under the guise of drugs, it was okay to say something like that.

The man studied the lad. Tommy angled his head a little closer to him, turning his gaze up to Steve meeting his guardian's look with clear, lucid, aware eyes. The message Tommy's eyes contained was, "I trust you." He sighed deeply and easily fell back to sleep. Steve pulled him a little closer and also relished the growing familiarity they were developing. *He's so different now than the first time I saw him. His hair is cut and short, I never noticed before how delicate his eyelashes are. All those lines of fear and worry I saw that first day in his face are erased. His face is soft and delicate, not harsh and troubled. My God, my life has taken such a dramatic and unexpected turn. Tommy's mine! Not mine in the sense of ownership, but mine in the sense of family. I have become responsible for him— that's scary. But yet it's not, because I know it's right. It feels so right, and in my prayers it's the only— and strong— answer that comes to me.*

He's so much like me. He's got those walls built up, just like I do. Can't let anyone in, you might get hurt. But sometimes, in little ways, like just now, the gates open. Yes, part of it is the drugs, but not all of it— he intentionally and with awareness invited me to be close to him. He can sense the family bond as well as I can. This was good. Life was good.

By the time Tommy was released from the hospital a few days later, the bond he and Steve were building was growing by leaps. They naturally evolved into more physical contact, as there were so many things that Tommy couldn't do; he helped him get ready for bed, move around, do pretty much everything. It annoyed Tommy, but in one secret way he liked the comfort and security of being taken care of so completely.

Steve took some time off work during Tommy's initial few days back home. He hired a private nurse when he did return to his work schedule. He could have stayed himself and continue caring for Tommy, but figured that might be a bit too stifling or confining for Tommy. It also occurred to him that Tommy might well think he was a burden if he was around 24/7; and Tommy needed to have some independence and control over his recovery. A private nurse was a good arrangement. After a few weeks recovering, the boy started back with the Professor for a couple hours each day. The teacher came to Steve's home to make it easier for everyone. He gave Tommy plenty of work to do to keep him occupied during the long days of mostly sitting.

Chapter 19
Getting to Know Each Other

One morning after daily Mass, Steve as usual stayed a few minutes to pray. He spied Father still in the sacristy and went and asked him if he had time to talk. The suggestion delighted the priest and soon they were sitting with coffee in the garden.

Steve started, "Father, Doc Burns used to say Communion gave him strength. I don't get that. Never did. But it made sense to Doc."

The priest thought before he replied, "Well, Steve, the Holy Eucharist is a mystery. And we can only understand mysteries so much. But simply put, when you receive Communion, you actually become united with Christ, 'one' with Him. And that imparts His strength to you."

Steve raised one eyebrow with skepticism. Father's explanation didn't satisfy him. "Ah, Steve. How else can I put it? Sometimes the Eucharist is referred to as 'food for the soul'."

The man remained unconvinced. The priest said, "I think it is something you need to experience to understand." No one spoke for a few minutes. Then Steve asked, "Father, what do I have to do to receive Communion? I used to all the time when I was with Doc and went to Mass every Sunday, but that was fifteen years ago."

The priest was elated with the way things were going with Steve. He had been praying for him, and Father interpreted these questions as a good sign. Instead of answering he came back with his own question, "Steve, do you believe that during Mass, during the Consecration, the bread and wine literally BECOME the Body and Blood of Christ?"

After thinking for a minute he gave an honest answer. "I don't know. I know that's what Doc had believed. I can't say if I ever really believed that or not."

Another period of comfortable silence, birds chirping, water tinkling as it cascaded down the fountain. The priest asked, "Steve, when was the last time you were to Confession?"

Steve looked up quickly, startled. He chuckled and vaguely replied, "A while. A long while." The priest recognized this concluded today's conversation, but a mirthful smile appeared on his face. "I could hear your Confession now if you wanted. We can go right over to the church..." He understood Steve wasn't ready for such a step, but figured he'd plant a seed for nurturing later.

Steve stood and stretched, in preparation for leaving. His hand went to the pocket with the rosary. Warm again. He almost asked the priest about this, then thought the man would think him daft. Knowing Fr. Phillips didn't expect him to say yes to his Confession question, he smiled back and was going to say, "Another time, Father." And instead, to his utter surprise, the words that came out were, "Okay, Father."

Both men stood there shocked, wondering where in the world that came from. (And it didn't come from "the world"—it came from a place beyond "the world", a divine place.) Steve blinked, his mouth dropped open. He was stunned.

The priest looked at him with questioning eyes. He didn't want to ask outright, "Are you sure?", but he did want to affirm that Steve did want to do it. In response, Steve nodded, still dazed.

The two made their way to the church and entered. Fr. Phillips suggested that Steve pray a bit before confessing. He told him not to worry if he didn't remember the formula, that wasn't important. He told Steve just to come into the confessional when he was ready; he went into the center section.

Steve knelt down. He was shaking. *Good Lord, what have I gotten myself into? Lord, I have no idea why I'm doing this. Where are you leading me? This has got to be Your doing. Doc, you've got to be behind this somehow, too! Are you up there in heaven laughing, smiling at my predicament? CONFESSION??? It's been probably fifteen years!*

Slowly Steve regained some equilibrium. He remembered a formula Doc had taught him about Confession. Five fingers: on your thumb you "know your sins". On your index finger you "make up your mind not to sin again". On your middle finger you "confess your sins to the priest". On your ring finger you "are sorry for your sins". And on your pinky you "do the penance the priest gives you." He was surprised how the blueprint came right back to him. He even remembered the words you used in the confessional.

So, he spent some time thinking about his sins. Fifteen years is a long time. A few minutes later he stood, ready as he'd ever be. He was shaking again. Steve parted the heavy violet drape on the penitent's side, entered and knelt. He heard the divider screen slide sideways and the priest began, "In the name of the Father, and of the Son, and of the Holy Ghost."

"Bless me, Father for I have sinned. It's been at least fifteen years since my last Confession…"

They finished. Father came out of the confessional after Steve had left the cubicle, and knelt across the aisle. When Steve was finished with his prayers and penance and rose, Father also did. He asked Steve quietly, "Would you like to receive Holy Communion?"

This most unusual offer delighted the man; he nodded vigorously. Something exceptionally strong was moving him today. He really and truly did want to receive Holy Communion, more than he could ever remember. It never occurred to him that he might be offered this Gift at this moment.

They walked to the front of the church. Indicating to Steve to wait at the Communion rail Father went to get the Blessed Sacrament. Steve knelt and waited. He gazed upon the crucifix as Holy Communion was placed on his tongue for the first time in many many years. The priest returned the ciborium to the tabernacle and left via the sanctuary. Steve remained praying in the church, alone. Well, not really alone, but devoid of human companions. If one was able to see, they would have witnessed thousands of saints and angels rejoicing over the lost lamb who was finding his way home. Doc Burns and the Blessed Mother were leading the cheering.

A full hour passed before he left. Checking his watch, he was surprised how long he had been inside. As he walked down the steps, Fr. Phillips was leaving the rectory. Steve went over with yet more questions. "Father, what do you make your hosts out of?"

The priest was perplexed at the odd question, "We don't make them, we buy them. They're made from plain wheat flour and water. Same as everyone else, we all pretty much purchase them from the same place— a convent in Alabama. Why?"

Steve shook his head. "It's been a long time, Father. And I've received Holy Communion hundreds of times. But it never tasted like it did today. It's always been plain and bland."

Fr. Phillips got a tingly feeling. "So what did it taste like today?"

Steve's face beamed a broad smile, he was radiant. "Sweet. Wonderfully sweet, like the most delicate but richest honey. Absolutely wonderful."

The priest said nothing but paled a bit. He knew a small miracle had happened. Then Steve said, "Another thing was weird, Father. Suddenly I noticed the odor of roses. It was an aroma hard to describe. Best word I can think of is heavenly. I looked around— there were no roses anywhere, Father. The same thing happened the other day, too."

Fr. Phillips sat on the rectory step to catch his breath at these revelations. Steve glanced at him, wondering what was wrong with him. "Father, are you okay?"

He nodded and studied his friend. Indicating a spot next to him, he said, "Sit down."

Steve did so, watching the man. The priest finally said, "Steve, I think God has blessed you with a small miracle. As for the rose smell, I've known two other people who said they experienced that. Apparently sometimes, once in a very great while, someone might notice a fragrance of roses. It is said to be an indication of the Blessed Mother being present."

He stopped and swallowed, "But the sweetness of the Eucharist, actually tasting a sweetness, I've heard of that— very rarely, mind you— very rarely, but never known anyone who experienced it. Steve, tell me more about it."

Steve did, there really wasn't much to tell. Staring into space, smiling, he could still taste it, far and away the best thing he'd ever had. The priest scrutinized him once again. "Steve, I've been praying for you the last day. Earlier I said, 'I think it is something you need to experience to understand.' I think the good Lord saw fit to grace you with an 'experience' though I never dreamed it would be something like this! Steve, I'm in awe."

The two men sat side by side in silence a while longer. Then, referring to what had happened, Steve asked, "Father, is there something I'm supposed to do?"

The priest shook his head, "No, but understand you have been given a great gift."

They talked a few minutes longer, then each headed his own way. Steve headed to his office, but Fr. Phillips made a quick stop into the church first, to pray a prayer of thanksgiving.

Next morning Steve went to 6 a.m. Mass. He wanted to go. He wanted to receive Communion. Energized by the thought, he had trouble waiting. At the Consecration, he felt shivers in his spine. Due to the small congregation at the early weekday Mass, the Communion line went quickly. He knelt at the rail, waiting for Father to get to him for his turn in receiving. And when Father got to him, he slowed, and very carefully, clearly held up the Host a few seconds and the placed it on his tongue. Steve bowed his head, remained a few seconds, and then rose to return to his pew. Today the Host tasted sweet, like it had yesterday, but not as much so, not at all. Much much more "taste" than an "ordinary" Host, but nowhere near as wonderful as his first time after his absence from the Sacrament.

After Mass, Steve stayed to pray a bit. His thoughts turned to Doc. He didn't think the man ever experienced anything quite like he had the last two days. Maybe he did, but Steve thought he would have shared that at some point if he had. He had the eerie feeling that Doc was there with him, in spirit. It gave him the willies, but also felt comfortable. Steve was beginning to understand why Doc went to Mass more than when he just "had" to on Sundays. There was something to this whole Mass/ Church/ Sacraments bit. He planned to continue getting to Mass — and Confession— frequently.

Chapter 20
Moving Along

It had been about three weeks since his surgery, a month since Samuel had left. The psychiatrist had kept tabs on the boy with regular phone calls. Steve felt he and Tommy were getting along fine, beginning to know each other better— the quirks, personality traits, that kind of thing. His physical healing was coming along. Tommy was anxious to be rid of the cumbersome casts and wheelchair. Despite being weighed down by the plaster, he was scheduled for physical therapy with Raleigh a few times each week to work on those things he was able to exercise.

The man and boy often were together in the evenings. Sometimes they played cards, Steve bought a Monopoly game, sometimes they watched TV. Tommy loved learning, which pleased Steve immensely. Chess games were also often part of their evenings. Steve had been keeping track mentally (he was sure Tommy was, as well). He'd manage to pull a draw about one out of four games, a win only about half as often. Not very good, in his book! But he paid close attention as they played and was indeed slowly picking up some things and improving. Steve talked about things he'd like to do with Tommy, things to teach him— sailing, horseback riding, and more. Marco wanted to teach him surfing; it sounded exciting to Tommy.

Steve planned a surprise afternoon of boating one day. Tommy had been pretty cooped up in the house, time to get out. He loaded the boy and some supplies into the car, picked up Marco and headed off. Tommy couldn't use his wheelchair on the boat, but that was okay. They had been going a few minutes, were well out of the harbor, when Steve and Marco matter-of-factly stripped their shirts off, something they usually did. Tommy watched, thinking about that. Neither Steve nor Marco noticed him looking at them.

While he was handicapped by having only one good arm, he could do some things. And he managed to wiggle out of his own shirt, sitting there in the sun bare-chested and bare-backed. Steve and Marco had both been preoccupied with a jammed fitting, so didn't notice his actions. They got the part unstuck, then Steve went back to the helm, while Marco stayed back to check the other ones. Immediately Steve noticed Tommy, who was looking directly at him. Steve smiled broadly but said nothing. Tommy smiled back. It was a significant moment. Marco knew about his history, but had never seen his injuries. And in taking his shirt off, Tommy was physically as well as mentally, saying, "Hey, this is who I am and what I look like." He was opening himself up, to Marco at least. Marco had spent lots of time with them, Tommy knew he was a good friend, family in essence. Marco came around a second later, and did a double take when he saw Tommy with no shirt.

"Whoa!" He stopped, then moved over and sat right next to Tommy. He studied the battered body. The wordless message his actions conveyed was, "Okay, let me see who you are." After looking carefully, and accepting him as he was, without revulsion or disgust. he gave him a hearty but gentle shove and said, "No big deal." Tommy grinned, so did Steve. And nothing more needed to be said. A pleasant day was spent on the water.

Eventually Tommy's leg cast was removed and the brace put on in its place. Raleigh was an exceptional physical therapist. He had an intuition about him of how best to help each patient. Tommy needed to work a lot on things; many of the exercises and routines were dull and boring. And understandably Tommy wasn't real thrilled about doing them. Raleigh talked to the doctors and Steve about an idea he had and they all gave him enthusiastic approval. At the next therapy session, he had a large box wrapped up for Tommy. Smiling, he said, "Tommy, when you're done today, you can open this present I got for you."

"What is it? Let me open it now? Please!"

Raleigh was adamant that he had to wait until he was done for the day. Not surprisingly, Tommy worked well and fast running through the routine. He was making progress, but it was slow. He had been off the crutches a week but still was very weak in his injured leg, and walked with a pronounced limp. It would take effort to overcome that. Steve would normally drop him off and pick him back up an hour later. Today he made a point of getting back early, so he could watch Tommy as he opened his present, knowing what it was and that it would thrill him.

Finally finished, Raleigh presented him with the box. Tommy ripped the paper open and the lid off. Inside was a nice, bright shiny skateboard! Skateboarding was a relatively new sport, and he had seen some amazing maneuvers done on them. Raleigh told him he had a friend who would help him learn the basics.

Tommy excited asked, "When?" Steve and Raleigh smiled— this was going to work well. The key here was that to be able to skateboard well (and what kid didn't want to be able to skateboard well) you had to be strong, flexible and balanced. All things Tommy needed to work on with his injured leg. Steve produced his own present for Tommy— a set of knee and elbow pads. The last thing anyone wanted was for him to be injured again.

Steve's mind kept drifting back to this whole religious thing. The next day he got up extra early, 4:30 a.m. Steve found he could often get by on little sleep, a 4:30 rising didn't bother him. Donning his workout clothes, he jogged early. Back home by 5:30, he showered, dressed and walked to St. Bart's for Mass. Lingering as usual after Mass and praying for a while, he checked in the sacristy before he left the Church to see if Father was still there. He was; Steve looked carefully at the priest. "Fr. Philips, I have another question for you. About rosaries. I know they are just beads, not any magic charm or anything. That the power comes in the prayer, the devotion. But… I have a rosary." He took it out of his pocket to show the man, and continued, "It belonged to Doc Burns. Father, I swear that when he gave it to me just before he died it was plain black pearl beads. He told me he got it from a 'holy priest' in Fatima when he was there during the war. But it was plain black, Father. Look at it now, there is a gold shimmer to it. Maybe my memory is faulty, but I really don't think so."

The priest took the rosary and studied it. He smiled broadly at Steve as he handed it back. "Yes, definitely it has a gold shimmer to it." He looked up, trying to formulate a "good" answer. He said, "Steve, I think you're being favored by someone…again."

Steve was startled by that reply, it had never occurred to him that he, Steve Connor O'Shaughnessy personally, was actually being "favored" by anyone in that way. He never even really thought they— anyone in heaven— thought about him. This idea of someone really looking out for him, watching over him, was strange— foreign, a bit unsettling, yet highly comforting at the same time.

Well, so far Father has not thought me bonkers, might as well go all the way here…

He added almost shyly, "So, Father, if I said that sometimes the rosary feels just a bit … 'warm'… in my pocket, you'd probably say the same thing... that I'm being 'favored'? I mean the first time I'd been sitting in the sun and I thought that was it. That wasn't it, Father."

Father Phillips smiled and nodded. Someone up there was doing a great job with his friend. The clergyman said a quick private mental prayer of thanksgiving. Then he suggested to Steve, "What say we make a quick five-minute stop in church together before you go, to pray a prayer of thanksgiving?"

Steve nodded affirmatively; he certainly had plenty to be thankful for.

At breakfast the next morning, Steve talked to Tommy about Samuel coming for another visit to work with him more. "I think it's time to begin to tackle some things, Tommy." The regular phone calls were going fine, but they both knew, and Steve as well, that it was time for some serious work. Tommy had been doing adequately, emotionally, but hadn't jumped all the way into the pool of his emotions. He skirted along the edge, testing the waters a bit, but not jumping in. It was time to swim. Arrangements were made.

Steve and Tommy picked him up from the airport. There was friendliness and camaraderie, but also tenseness. Back at home they shared supper, sat and visited a while, made small talk. Tommy excitedly showed off his skateboard skills. He often sang as he skateboarded and did so today. That was another thing Steve had learned about the boy — he had an exceptional voice and liked to sing, sounding like a lark. Samuel was suitably impressed with both skills.

Tommy liked Samuel and enjoyed his corny humor and easygoing demeanor. He wanted to please Steve, and did think it was a good idea, but he was also scared. Steve knew that; he wanted to say a thousand things to Tommy, but kept his remark short. "It's okay to be scared Tommy." The boy sat looking dejected.

Samuel came out from the bedroom after freshening up and joined them. They both looked somber and no one spoke. Samuel had heard voices and realized that his arrival stopped them and had a pretty good idea why. "Hmmmm. Been talking about me?"

Looking back and forth between them, and then only at Tommy, he finally said, "So, Tommy, you going to let me get inside your head?"

Steve rolled his eyes. *GEEZ, you've got the bedside manner of a turkey!*

Tommy wrapped his arms around himself. "What're you gonna do there?"

"Oh, dig around, toss some rocks out, turn over a few layers of dirt, fertilize a bit, then maybe plant some nice flowers…"

Tommy didn't meet Samuel's eyes, and only glanced at Steve. Then he simply said in a resigned voice, "Okay."

Chapter 21
Tommy and Samuel Work

The next morning, Steve didn't want to leave. He wanted to grab Tommy and run away and hide, hide them both away from any pain or suffering. He went for his jog and returned. The trio talked over breakfast. "Tommy, Samuel and I think it would be best for you to talk with him alone, at least for now. I'm going in to work this morning and leave you two here. Either one of you can call me anytime if you need me. Okay?"

Tommy swallowed, and shook his head up and down.

Steve lingered. Samuel took him by the arm to usher him out the door, "I'll call and update you later, Stevie."

Despite the firm escort, Steve stopped, unmovable. He turned, went back to Tommy, and gave him a huge hug.

Once in his car, he made his way to Mass. Not the usual six a.m. Mass at his beloved St. Bart's, but a later Mass at a parish downtown near his office. He stayed a while to pray afterwards. On the rest of the drive to the office he said some more prayers for Tommy, and Samuel. Tommy couldn't be in better hands, it was just heartbreaking that Tommy even needed to be in anyone's hands like that.

Walking through the outer office, he greeted everyone curtly. Passing Marco's cubicle, he looked at him. He wasn't going to, but couldn't help himself. Marco read the anguish in Steve's face perfectly. Steve didn't say anything, didn't stop or slow down, just went into his office. Marco dropped what he was doing, followed Steve in, and closed the door behind him. Steve had sat behind his desk, Marco sat on "his" corner of the desk, close, facing Steve. "He's with Samuel?"

All Steve could do was screw his eyes shut, clench his jaw, ball his fists and nod. Marco actually moaned in sympathy. He got up, put his hand on Steve's shoulder, attempting to reassure him saying, "Steve, that's good. You know that. Samuel's the best; he'll take care of him."

Steve nodded in silence. They just sat there a while. "I know, Marco. But God, it's going to hurt! That poor kid has been hurt enough. I know it has to come out so he can heal, but God, Marco.... Why Whyyyyyy???"

And there was nothing they could do. There was nothing Marco could do to ease his friend's pain. There was nothing Steve could do to ease Tommy's pain. All they could do was be there when they were needed. Marco now for Steve. Steve (and Marco) later for Tommy.

The minutes, the seconds, dragged by for Steve all morning. He tried to do some work; he'd start filling out some forms, and completely lose this train of thought, which was always back to Tommy. He kept checking the clock, willing Samuel to call; and wanting to call home himself for a report, knowing that wasn't wise. Samuel would call when it was right.

Marco brought in take-out for lunch. Steve didn't even look at it. "Marco, it's 1:00, he still hasn't called!"

Needlessly replying, Marco said, "He will, Steve. You have to wait."

Steve had left his house at 7:30 that morning, it was just after three when Samuel finally called. "Steve, we're doing okay.

Tommy's taking a nap right now. Steve, we're doing okay," he repeated knowing Steve was overwrought. The man was so focused on Tommy, he didn't even notice that Samuel was calling him Steve, not Stevie.

And Samuel continued, "It's coming. Lots there, we both knew that, but it's coming. Tommy's doing well, Steve. This is hard, very hard, but good. He's okay. Exhausted, spent, but okay."

When Steve was honest with himself, that's about what he expected to hear. Samuel sounded plenty tired himself, Steve knew this was taxing for him, also.

Samuel continued, "Steve, I expect him to sleep a good three to four hours, but then I want to keep going with him."

Expecting opposition, but firm in his resolve, "The two of us alone, Steve. Not you, not yet. Go home with Marco tonight."

"SAMUEL! NO!"

Samuel wouldn't let him continue his protests, cut him off, and playing the broken record, "Steve, the two of us alone. Not you, not yet. Go home with Marco tonight!" Steve wanted to strangle him. He wanted to hang up on him, but knew that if he called back, Samuel wouldn't answer, he'd take the phone off the hook. Damn that man and his tactics!

Drawing a deep breath, Steve begged, "Samuel, I want to be there for Tommy. I want him to know that I am here for him. Samuel, a huge thing is not being alone."

"I know, Steve. You're right. But you and I both know Tommy doesn't feel abandoned by you. He's not alone. He's got me, and right now, I am what he needs most. You being here would make things much harder for him, Steve, much harder. You know that, I know that, Tommy knows that."

Back to the broken record, "Steve, the two of us alone. Not you, not yet. Go home with Marco tonight!"

"SAMUEL!"

Getting mad, tired himself, Samuel yelled, "Okay, Steve, look. If you want, I can come and soothe your poor psyche. Help you deal with your pain. That means I stop working with Tommy to tend to you. Now we both know Tommy needs me right now a whole lot more than you do. So, damn it, Steve, suck it up, work through it. I've taught you enough how to do that. You take care of you; let me deal with Tommy.... Steve, I won't kid you. It's rough. It's dirty and ugly. It's painful, excruciating, agonizing. You know that already. And you know that if we take a break from dealing with it, it's going to be harder to come back to, if we even can come back to it. You coming in now would take us off course, Steve. What Tommy needs, what we both need is for you to be waiting with open arms on the beach when we land. We need you, Steve, solid and strong, ready to scoop Tommy up and to exchange his agony and ache with your love. That's what we need, Steve, that's what Tommy will need. Steve, Tommy's doing well, really well. He's strong, courageous, a real trooper. This is gruesome work, hideous therapy, but he's coming up with what he needs. Steve, I've got to tell you, I'm impressed. It really is going much better than I had expected. Damn it, Steve, I'm tired. I don't want to have to deal with you being difficult!"

Resigned, trusting Samuel, who he really did trust, he quietly asked, "I'm sorry, Samuel. Can you please tell me when? Tomorrow?"

Relieved, Samuel assured him, "Yeah, I think we'll be ready, not done with everything, but ready for you by tomorrow, probably afternoon, maybe later. I will let you know, Steve."

Choking, Steve said, "Thank you, Samuel.... Tell him... tell him I love him.... that I want to be there with him and hold him... that I will be there when ... when it's over... when the time is right.."

"I will, Steve. And he knows. He'll know. I'll make sure. I'll tell him."

Samuel fell asleep in his hammock. Tommy awoke several hours later, and saw Samuel sleeping. It had been a hard day so far. And he knew it would continue, but wasn't looking forward to it at all. Tommy knew what they were doing was good, and necessary, but it was very torturous and grueling. He grinned. *No way am I going to wake him so we can go at it again!* He went in the fridge and fixed himself a sandwich and some juice. As he sat at the counter eating, he reflected on some of the things they'd covered. Samuel was very sharp, he knew what to ask, and he knew when to stay quiet. Dad was right, he was good. Tommy was glad Steve had called him in to help. Finished with his snack, he went (very quietly so as to not wake "The Monster") out to sit in the sunshine on the lanai. And just sat quietly, thinking, resting, getting ready, he supposed, for Round Two. He thought about calling Steve, but figured that probably wouldn't be a good idea without Samuel's okay.

Samuel quietly woke without Tommy realizing it. He watched Tommy just looking out at the ocean. Samuel was very tempted to jump right in and ask him what he was thinking about. But decided it would be better to wait a bit, ease in, maybe.

"Hey."

Tommy turned, rolled his eyes, "Oh, the Monster awakens!" Samuel laughed; this boy still had a sense of humor! Amazing. He sat up, stretched. "That nap felt good. You hungry?"

"No, I just had a sandwich."

"Okay, I am. Let me get something."

Tommy accompanied him into the kitchen; they made small talk while Samuel heated up some leftovers. "I talked to Steve while you were sleeping."

Tommy cheered at this, "What'd he say?"

Samuel chuckled. "Well… he's got a pretty good idea of what's happening here. And he's not happy about it. He knows it's good, but he's not happy that it's ugly and dirty and hurts like hell. And that there's nothing he can do to help, to make it better."

Then, carefully watching Tommy, "He got especially ticked when I told him not to come home tonight, to stay at Marco's."

Tommy looked crestfallen, said nothing. "Tommy, we're doing really well, I think. You're doing really well, fantastic. Honestly, I am really impressed with you, with your courage, your strength. Geez, you even still have a sense of humor. It's coming, you're working through it. But I think if Steve comes, it's going to sidetrack us. And getting back on track would be very hard."

He waited a bit, "I know you know this already, but Steve made me promise to tell you that he loves you, he'd like to be here with you, and will be waiting when it's over, and that you're not alone."

"That's pretty reassuring, Tommy. Steve's an amazing man."

Tommy just nodded, aching to run away, just hide away in a deserted cave somewhere with Steve, get a huge hug and never come out. Knowing that wasn't right, and wouldn't happen. He shared these thoughts with Samuel.

"Kid, I don't blame you one bit. I'd feel the same way."

Still waiting for the food to finish heating, Samuel thought about something. "Tommy, if you want, I think it would be okay for you to talk to Steve on the phone for a few minutes."

He did think if they connected a bit, just connected, not enough to get off track, it would strengthen them both.

Tommy brightened considerably!

"Let me call him and talk to him first."

The phone was answered on the first ring. "Stevie, Tommy and I just woke up and are having something to eat. I was thinking that maybe you'd like to talk to him on the phone a few minutes. I know he would. And I think a few minutes on the phone would be good for both of you. Everything I said earlier still applies, but connect with each other."

With that he handed the phone to Tommy, who eagerly took it, "Steve?"

Steve was overcome with emotion at this from Samuel he didn't know what to say, "Tommy! How are you, are you okay?

"Yeah, I'm doing okay. There's this Monster here who keeps clawing around in my brain, but I'm okay."

Steve laughed through tears to hear that bit of lightness. He knew he wouldn't have much time, "Tommy, I love you. No matter what, I love you. And I'm here for you. You need me, you need anything, you just holler and I'll be there. Tommy as soon as you and Samuel are finished, I'll be there. Samuel told me you're doing great, that I can be proud of you, that you're a strong and courageous person."

That choked Tommy up, and he didn't want to, but he couldn't help saying, "Steve, what I want to do is run away right this second with you, curl up in a ball in your lap with your strong arms around me and never leave."

Steve's heart broke. He knew he didn't have much time. "Tommy, soon… I will scoop you up in my strong arms and hug you tighter than you've ever been hugged before. And you and I will both love it. But you won't want to stay forever. You're going to stay long enough to get recharged and then you're going to go out confidently into the world and live. You're going to live a wonderful, exciting, beautiful life. You're going to have ups and downs, but the pain and memories of your past will have faded away. Not be erased, but hold no more power over you. And you'll always like my strong arms around you, and I'll always like putting them there. But you're not going to need them, Tommy. You're going to be fine soaring like an eagle on your own. I love you, Tommy. Now go kick butt with that Monster!"

And Tommy laughed, "I love you, Steve. Thanks!"

And in closing, "See you tomorrow, I think. Unless the Monster devours me. If you don't hear anything by suppertime, call out the troops!"

And with that he hung up.

Marco had been with Steve, listening, when this call came. He only heard Steve's side of it, but surmised the other half. "Steve, that was awesome! You did great."

And Steve's heart hurt like never before at the pain Tommy was going through, but he knew Marco was right. The right words had come out of his mouth.

Meanwhile, back at the ranch, Samuel had heard Tommy's side. When the boy's voice cracked, Samuel was instantly worried. What was Steve going to say? But whatever he said, it must have been good, it pulled Tommy back. "So, Tommy, you've got this gift of remembering things. Tell me what Steve said."

And Tommy relayed word for word everything Steve said. And Samuel smiled as he was inwardly relieved. Steve had been perfect. He came through with flying colors when put on the spot, even though he was hurting tremendously himself. *Way to go, my friend! Way to go, Stevie!* With that, Tommy and Samuel began Round Two.

Steve was trying to recover. He was grateful, very grateful for the call. Tommy did sound like he was making it— that it was tough, but making it. And Steve knew Samuel wouldn't let him drown. He knew Samuel was an expert and would be able to tell where the edge was, and not go over it, nor let Tommy fall over it.

"Marco, I'm going for a run, a long one, I think." Steve figured a long physical workout would help body and soul. He donned his sweats and running shoes and took off. And ran. Hard. For many miles. And alternated when running between crying and cursing. Finally he slowed, walked ten minutes or so to cool down a bit, then stopped and sat on a rocky outcrop, looking out at the ocean, smelling the salt air, hearing the surf crash —

thinking, planning, figuring. Steve really had no idea how far he'd run, nor what time it was.

When Steve jogged, his mind seemed to work well. Often this was the time when he had insights or was able to reason things out in his mind. Today his thoughts were obviously on Tommy, but also himself. He thought back to his own miserable childhood. All of this had brought up his own demons, his own pain and insecurities. He had to face them, square off, and eliminate them. Okay, first off, this whole bit about being unlovable. He recognized that he had indeed felt unlovable, believed himself to be unlovable, until his recent understanding that it was his father's problem, not his. Steve realized that he had lived his life without being aware of this, and that it had affected how he was, who he was. And realized, again, really absorbing and accepting that he WAS loveable, he could be, and WAS loved. He could give and receive love. He had a fiancé who he had loved and who had loved him as a woman loves. He had friends, like Marco who he loved and who loved him as friends. He had Doc Burns whom had he had loved as a father-figure and who loved him as a son. And now he had Tommy, who he could love as his son, and who he hoped could come to love him as a father. This was good.

All these pieces had always been there, Steve was just putting them together all the way. Kind of like puzzle pieces in a box, the whole picture was becoming clearer as the pieces fit in. Steve mused to himself that he thought he already knew what the whole picture looked like. Obviously there were shades and vistas that he was just beginning to see.

There was the pain of his own childhood. He knew that the big thing with that was the aloneness he had talked about. The physical beatings were no picnic, nor many other things. He was able to put all that in the past. Steve realized it had been there, under the surface, smoldering for a long time. Tommy was the catalyst that brought it all out. The wound was opened and had drained well. All he needed to do for complete healing was a little cleaning around the edges, and letting it remain open to fresh air. Not to hide it, or squelch it anymore. *Okay, I can do that. I am who I am, that is part of me, I can accept it as it is, allow it to be. It can heal over, it already has a great deal, and it will finish healing over. While I don't intend to highlight the scar, I don't need to hide it, either.* As Steve worked through this, he felt as if a burden was lifted, and it felt good.

The other big "problem" Steve was having was Tommy's pain. He was so angry and felt so impotent. He was angry at what had happened to Tommy. Angry at the man who did it, but he had already worked through that, pretty completely. Angry at the pain the boy suffered, and was still suffering. He felt impotent because there was so little he could do. He couldn't take away the past. He couldn't take away the current pain. He couldn't "do" therapy "for" Tommy— he couldn't work it out for him. And his impotence made him angry. Not with himself, but with the whole situation. *Okay so, I have this anger. It's a feeling. Feelings are neither good nor bad, they just are. That's fine. I can accept that. Now, what am I going to do with this feeling? I have choices here. I can let it consume me. I can let it rule my life. Or, more constructively, I can choose to let the feeling go. I can say that I don't need it anymore, it serves no useful or constructive purpose and I will it to leave, I choose to be finished with it.* Now Steve knew the last option was what he would do. He also knew that one of the best ways to "get over it" was some sort of intense physical activity— a marathon or something. He'd have to think more on that, he wasn't quite ready to take that step yet. More of Steve's burden was lifted as he ran and worked through his thoughts.

Finally he headed back at a steady jog— it felt good, cleansing somehow. Marco was grateful to see him return, concerned about his friend. He was pretty confident he'd work it all out, but knew it was a rough time.

The run tired Steve, yet he didn't sleep well. He tossed and turned, wondering if Tommy was sleeping or if Samuel was "working" on him. He couldn't wait for this to be over.

Samuel called the next morning around nine to report. "Stevie, we're okay. It's going good, Stevie. I'm thinking we'll still use most of today alone together, Round Three, but I'm pretty sure by tonight we'll have it wound up and you can come back."

Steve was elated at that last bit, dismayed at the first part. "Samuel, is he really okay?"

"Yes, Steve, it's been hard on him, we both expected that. He's drained, and will take some time to recuperate, but he will. Especially with you there."

Steve knew this was taxing on Samuel. When he worked with him in the past, it was almost as if the psychiatrist would actually take on and shoulder some of your burden himself, not just lead you through it. "Fine, Samuel, we'll work it out. You need to take care of yourself, too, buddy."

Later that day, Samuel said to Tommy, "You know, Tommy, I think we're just about done. Pretty much wrapped everything up. What do you think?"

Tommy had realized that day they were getting towards the end of this ordeal, and was grateful. To hear Samuel say this gratified him. "Yeah, I think so, too."

They had begun eating supper, and Samuel eyed Tommy carefully. He was very good at doing that, watching you, and you knew he was doing it, but at the same time didn't realize it. "So, everything okay with you?"

"Uh huh."

They finished the meal in silence and took a few minutes to clean up.

"So, whaddya say we call Steve and tell him to come home?"

"YES!"

Steve was still with Marco at the office, they both knew he'd probably go home tonight. Steve was afraid that maybe Samuel would call and postpone the reunion for some reason like more therapy needed! He was nervous, had been all day, pacing, antsy. Marco had ordered in Chinese and was trying to force Steve to eat. "Look, Steve, you really haven't eaten all day. You need to nourish yourself, get some calories in. Last thing you'd want is to see Tommy then pass out from low blood sugar or something!"

Steve saw the sense in that and stopped his striding to sit down and eat. And absent-mindedly ate about a half carton of Chinese noodles and hopped back up again. "Marco, it's almost six. Why hasn't Samuel called? I haven't talked to him since nine this morning!"

"Steve, relax! They're okay. If anything was wrong, Samuel would have called."

Steve knew Marco was right, but this waiting was torture for him.

"Marco, let's go to your place, it's closer to mine than here. That way, I can get there faster when Samuel calls."

Indulging his friend, sincerely trying to make it easier for him, "Sure, Steve." Marco grabbed the take out to bring home for later.

Shortly after that, the call came. Steve zipped out without a word. Marco wasn't offended; he knew his friend had to go.

After Samuel had called Steve, he encouraged Tommy, "Tommy, I've been amazed with you. You have worked through all this with courage, faith, conviction, dedication. You're going to be fine. And you've got Steve here with you. I really don't foresee any problems. But, I want you to know that anytime, anytime, if you need me, call. I'm here for you. Understand?"

Tommy began to be overwhelmed with all Samuel had done for him, all he could do was nod his head yes,

Samuel smiled and gave him a big hug.

At that moment Steve rushed in. Tommy had all these things in mind that he was going to say when he saw him. But nothing was said. Steve looked at him wildly, as if he expected Tommy to have turned orange, grown another head or something. He ran over in about two steps to the couch and snatched him up in a hug. And Tommy just melted into him. No one spoke. Samuel smiled, went out on the lanai and lay down in his hammock. Steve and Tommy sat together for hours, wordlessly, just connecting, just letting love flow. Tommy feel asleep with his head on Steve's shoulder, Steve was starting to nod off himself. He carried Tommy to bed, but couldn't bring himself to leave him. He sat next to him on the bed, still cradling him in his arms. And they both slept. Morning sun was streaming in through the window as they began to stir. Steve got up, Tommy woke up with the movement and he also got up. They walked into the kitchen, hand in hand, where Samuel was starting coffee. Hair mussed, it looked like he had slept well, also.

"Good morning, you two! Looks like you slept well!' Samuel had noticed that Steve had stayed with Tommy that night, he expected it and would have been surprised had he not. They just grinned. All three of them went to get cleaned up while the coffee brewed. Steve helped Tommy remove his brace so he could shower.

They met back in the living room, looked at one another. Now what? Steve suggested, "You know, I don't usually go out for breakfast, but let's do it." He called and invited Marco to join them at one of Steve's favorite places. For Steve, breakfast was usually a hurried necessity, not a time to be enjoyed, but today they ate leisurely and enjoyed good food and company. Steve was always right next to Tommy.

The meal finished, settled in their stomachs, and the question again, now what? He decided to make it an easy lazy day. He'd stop in at the office (with Tommy) to do a bit of paperwork he had to attend to. Then they would let the day lead them where it did.

And the day passed gently, quietly, smoothly, easily, happily about as Steve thought it might. Samuel had been on his own, his day had been fine as well. Steve and Samuel talked, alone, late into the evening. "I'm eternally grateful for my good friends, Marco, you, Doc. I'm so glad I called you when I did. I appreciate your coming, Samuel. You've been a lifesaver, truly."

Samuel humbly answered, "You're welcome, Steve. It's rewarding for me too, to see someone overcome a tragedy. To see you and Tommy happy is a great reward, all I need. Really, Steve."

Steve was quiet a minute, then questioned him, "How was it, Samuel? I suspect pretty bad."

If nothing else, Samuel was honest. Taking a long time before he answered, "Steve, it was horrid. Tommy's been beaten to a pulp and battered in so many ways, not just physically. I am truly surprised he hadn't given up years ago. Especially for so long with no help. I'll admit I was scared more than once in those days we worked together. The ocean was so deep, the currents so strong, I wasn't sure I'd be able to hold him, hang on tight enough without letting him slip away. Quitting, backing off, crossed my mind more than once. But I knew if I did that, he'd never be fully healed, he'd never be what he could be, what he was meant to be. Steve, I made a call, I gambled. I thought that I should consult with you before I did that, but I knew you'd want it all. You'd take the risk to get it all. And to have stopped at that point would have not been good. It really was hell, Steve. And Tommy trusted me. He trusted me because you did, because you do. You told him to. And I was scared, really scared, that this time I might not have what it took to pull him through."

Samuel silently relived some moments and minutes and hours from the last few days and shuddered. So did Steve as he digested Samuel's report.

"But you did, Samuel, you did pull him through. Right? I mean, Tommy looks great, he 'feels' great. I can sense his healing, a burden gone. Maybe not entirely gone, but a tiny molehill now, compared to the mountain it was a few days ago, a few months ago. Tommy is okay, isn't he, Samuel?"

"Yes, Steve, he is. There will always be scars, you know that. But they're just there, lying at the roadside, not blocking his path, not causing him pain or trouble. Steve, Tommy truly is amazing. His strength, his resilience, his will, his drive."

Chuckling, he continued, "You know, if I had to 'pick out' a son for you and a father for him, I don't think there'd be a better match." Looking at Steve directly, "You'll do great together, Steve, I'm happy for you both. Very happy."

They sat in silence a while longer.

"Samuel, it's mostly over for him, right? I mean, that's what those two appalling days with you were all about. I guess I'm really sorry and upset that he had to experience that. But I can help him see it's over. I'm sure he knows that."

"Yes, Stevie. But if you need to, call me. If it's not working itself out for you, I can help. I'll come. I told Tommy the same thing. You know I mean it."

With heartfelt emotion, Steve said, "Yes, I do, Samuel. Thanks. And Samuel— I doubt this would not have ended well if not for you."

"You're welcome."

Chapter 22
Steve's Turn

The next day was spent doing errands, wrapping up some odds and ends, and so on. Samuel stayed at Steve's soaking up sun and resting. That evening after supper the three of them were sitting around. Samuel was thinking. "Hmmm… Stevie, Tommy, maybe now's a good time for us to talk."

Steve looked at Tommy, then Samuel. "I don't know, what do you think, Tommy? As good as any, I suppose? Or are you too tired?"

Tommy shrugged his shoulders, "Fine with me."

Steve looked questioningly at Samuel, "So…. what?"

"Whatever you guys want. Is there anything you want to say to Steve, Tommy? Any thoughts or feelings you want to share?" Samuel asked, not really expecting much. With Tommy, he thought Steve was pretty clued in to everything.

Tommy couldn't really think of anything, "I guess not, I can't think of anything. I mean, Steve's seen my back, he knows my story. I guess I don't think he'll ever really know how grateful I am for what he has done for me, and will." Looking at Steve wisely, he amended, "But then again, maybe he does."

"I guess maybe I'm not sure how things are going to work out. Steve works, and that takes lots of his time and energy. Not that I need it or anything, I just don't want to take away from his work. But we've talked about that already and he said not to worry about it, so I won't."

No one spoke for a few minutes; Samuel waited.

He turned to Steve, "What about you, Stevie? What do you want to share with Tommy?" He strongly suspected there was something there, Steve had mentioned anger.

Steve sat tight-lipped for a while. Samuel wasn't willing to let something lie if he thought there was any substance to it.

Steve uncomfortably looked at Tommy, and then Samuel and then back and forth.

Samuel figured that there were things here that needed addressing, but not in front of Tommy. So he ordered, "C'mon, Steve, let's go outside." And headed out the door, where he walked a fair ways up the beach, in silence, with a reluctant Steve.

He needed a push. Samuel shoved, "Come on, Stevie, get it out."

Steve still hesitated, then plunged ahead. "Okay, Samuel. This isn't very nice, and I am not happy with the way I feel about it. When I first went to see Brian about the legalities of guardianship and all that, and he mentioned an investigation, I thought about conducting one. Really, I knew quite a bit and if I wanted, I could probably find Tommy's father. I had thought about it even before I saw Brian."

Steve knew this would have alarmed Tommy. "The main reason I did not do it was because it would have been a betrayal of his trust in me. And I won't do it, ever, unless he wanted me to."

Steve didn't continue. Samuel pushed more. "So, Stevie, why did you want to do that?"

The two men had stopped and were leaning against the large boulder.

Steve balled his fist, tightly pursed his lips, jumped up and paced. Samuel waited him out. Every now and then Steve would glance at Samuel.

Finally he shouted, "OKAY! The reason I wanted to find him was because I wanted to beat him to a pulp with my bare fists!"

He drew a breath and continued animatedly, "I hate that man for what he did to Tommy; I'd like to see him dead and rotting in hell!" He pounded the boulder, and looked nastily at Samuel, "Satisfied?"

Samuel accepted his outburst without comment, and remained silent. Steve just glared at him.

"Okay, Stevie, how does that make you feel? How do you feel about having those emotions?"

Not wanting to give more, Steve curtly replied, "I don't like it."

"Stevie, I think Tommy hates his father some, but figured out that really more than hate, he feels pity for him. That he is so screwed up. I know he never wants to see him again. That chapter of his life is over, he can and wants to move on with things. And Tommy knows that he can't do that if he has hate in his life. I think you need to figure out a way to deal with your feelings and anger."

He meant now, not tomorrow or next week or next month or next year. "Can you figure out how to do that?"

Steve hadn't expected this little session to go this way. And was not real happy with it. And also knew he couldn't get away with skirting or avoiding the issue.

Still wound tight, all Steve said was, "No."

Samuel looked at him for a while, then said. "Let's go back to the house."

They did. Tommy had been waiting for them and wondered what had happened. "Steve, fill him in a bit…:

Steve sighed, "Basically, Tommy, I've got a lot of anger and hate towards your father for what he did to you. But I'll work it out, get over it. Don't worry about it."

And with that, Samuel said, "Yep, that's right, Tommy. Don't worry about it. Stevie's going to deal with it— now. Are you okay staying here alone if we go out for a while?"

Steve eyed Samuel warily, a bit concerned about Tommy, but more fearful of some plan Samuel had concocted.

Tommy rolled his eyes, they all knew it was a silly question; Tommy had been alone on the streets for years, to stay here alone was nothing. "Yes."

Steve was more wary. Samuel simply asked, "You belong to a gym, right?"

"Yes."

"Do you keep gym clothes there, or bring them from home?"

"I bring them."

"Okay, get your gear. Tommy, we'll be back late, don't wait up."

Steve wanted to remain rooted in his spot, but knew that was futile. He got up and got his things.

He and Samuel left. Samuel instructed him to drive to the gym.

They got there; Steve changed and went back to Samuel. He knew this wasn't going to be a simple workout but had no idea what the psychiatrist had in mind.

"Stevie, why don't you warm up with a few laps, a half mile or a mile?"

Steve eyed him and hit the track. Samuel, meanwhile, talked with the manager. Asked him if there was a sparring partner available for a bit and they found one. He also clued them in to the fact that he was working with Steve and there would be the possibility that there might be some yelling and release of tension in unpredictable ways. To not worry about it, just let it happen. And if things did get loud, to just have everyone ignore them. The gym wasn't crowded at this hour, but not deserted either.

Steve came back ten minutes later, sweaty. "Okay, sparring time. Here's your partner." Steve knew the man from HPD, a nice fellow; they had sparred a few times.

"Samuel, you don't want me to imagine him as…."

"No, Stevie! God, no! You'd kill the man! Just warm up a bit with him. Two 3-minute rounds."

Steve was good and loosened up after the jog and sparring. He remained wary and honestly afraid— he knew Samuel had something in mind. He took Steve by the arm and led him over to the heavy full size punching bag.

"Okay, Steve, NOW I want you to imagine this is Tommy's father."

Steve stood there, immobile, a ball of frozen tension. It's hard to clench your fists while wearing thick boxing gloves, Steve managed to do it.

Steve's problem was in releasing emotions. That meant some degree of loss of control, and loss of control unnerved Steve, made him feel vulnerable and uncomfortable. He just stood there. Samuel waited. Samuel really wanted him to go at this. Every muscle in Steve's face was tight as a drum, his whole body was rigid.

Eventually Samuel realized a shove was needed. He hated to do it, but it was necessary. "Steve, I'm going to ask you to visualize an image. I'm going to bring a picture into your mind. When it comes up, I just want you to react, let whatever comes to the surface come out. Use the bag." Steve didn't move an inch.

Samuel drew in a breath and actually backed up a step. He was fairly close to Steve, within touching distance. This was cruel, but to not do it was even worse. "Okay, Steve— I want you to remember…… the first time you saw Tommy's back."

Instantly a fist shot out, and in less than a mili-second the other one. Steve went to work pummeling that bag without mercy. Hitting and hitting, punching, pounding, releasing. Samuel let it all happen without comment. A few others around the open gym noticed, you could feel the intensity from all the way across the room, no one said anything nor came near.

He went on and on and on, sweat dripping from his face, but he didn't let up a bit. Samuel was amazed at his staying power. This was good, very good. After about ten minutes of relentless beating, Steve would flag a bit, but almost immediately pick it back up to 100%. Another five minutes and he couldn't keep up that power anymore, but continued to pound away. Slowly, very slowly, after another few minutes he began to be completely drained. Eventually he slid down on the floor next to the bag, still punching with his last bits of strength. He laid on the floor on his back, completely wet with sweat, breath heaving, arms lying at his side, unable to even lift them. After a few minutes, while Samuel just let him be in silence, he slowly opened his eyes and looked at him, exhausted. "Samuel, that was dirty."

"I know, Steve, and I'm sorry. But it needed doing." He helped Steve to a sitting position.

"Yes, it did. Thanks, my friend."

Weak kneed, Steve got up, Samuel unlaced his gloves for him and the man headed to the shower. Samuel drove home, few words were exchanged. It was over, Steve had vented what was bottled up inside him, and he felt about 1000% better.

Tommy was still awake when they got home— he had been worried about Steve. He took one look at the pale, drawn figure and asked anxiously, "You okay?"

Steve grabbed him in a bear hug, "Yes, Tommy, I'm fine. Just wiped out."

And sneaking a look at Samuel, added, "The Monster has been at work, but he's finished. We're done. I'm beat, I'm going to bed."

Tommy looked at Samuel for some reassurance. "He's fine, Tommy. He worked out some deep, painful, uncomfortable emotions, but they are out. He really is fine. Now get yourself to bed."

Samuel took his spot in the hammock on the lanai, reviewing the events of the last few hours. That had been tough on Steve, but necessary and good. It all worked out. He now was confident they'd be okay. He easily drifted into peaceful slumber. He knew he could return to Singapore knowing things were fine with his friend and Tommy.

Chapter 23
New Names

Things were going well. Life was good. Steve learned to balance work with fatherhood, living each part of his life to the fullest. Tommy was learning all kinds of things about a "normal" life, what it means to have family and friends. He spent a fair amount of time each week with his tutor, Professor Carson. The Professor was an excellent teacher for him, and gave him many challenging assignments. They worked together well.

Steve was amazed at how fast and deep the bond between them developed, and was continuing to flourish. *That's God at work. Amazing.*

Tommy was doing well physically. He was close to 100%; his leg and arm were getting stronger and more flexible every day. The skateboarding had worked well. Steve was amazed at the tricks the boy could do on it. He tried once and was barely able to just stand on the unstable thing. That gave Tommy a good laugh, seeing him wobble and struggle to keep his balance just standing.

It had been almost six months since Steve and Tommy had first met. Tommy was well mentally and emotionally. He and Steve seemed to have an intuitive knack for reading each other, providing what was needed when it was needed. A few weeks back he and Steve one day had a long talk out on the beach. Steve knew something was up.

"Hey, what's on your mind?"

Tommy shuffled a bit, kicked some sand with his feet, looked down. Steve waited him out; he'd talk when he was ready. Tommy glanced sideways at Steve, out of the corner of his eye. Steve noticed but didn't comment. He pulled the boy toward him, put his arm around his shoulder, but said nothing. Tommy looked out at the waves, drew in a deep breath and started, "You know, a long time ago when you talked with Judge Tracy about the legal guardianship stuff, you said something about adoption…"

Steve quickly deduced that the boy was wondering if Steve still wanted to adopt him. Over the months they had spent together, they had become closer. Certainly Steve did want to adopt him. He knew that almost from the beginning and that had never changed. Steve smiled inwardly, looked out at the waves himself for a bit. Then he looked at Tommy directly, waited for him to return the eye contact, smiled broadly and said, "So, you ready to be my son? I'm ready to be your dad!"

Tommy was startled by the very direct approach Steve used. He gasped, smiled broadly himself and said, "Yeah!"

Steve gave him a rough bear hug through misty eyes. Laughing, he said, "Well, that's settled, anything else?"

Steve knew— they both knew— that this was a momentous occasion. Steve's making light of it didn't diminish the significance at all, but it did ease tension. As they walked back, Steve said, "So, you know what this means, don't you?"

Tommy was perplexed and cocked his head sideways.

Steve said, "It means I get to call you 'Son'."

Tommy brightened at that prospect. They walked a bit farther and he said, "Then that means I get to call you 'Dad'!"

Steve eyes misted over again and his heart warmed at that idea. Again he pulled Tommy to him for a manly hug as they walked along.   And he raised his eyes heavenward in a quick silent prayer of thanksgiving. And noticed a very slight warmth in the rosary in his pocket. It had been quite a while since he had noticed that at all. This was a momentous occasion, becoming father and son, in name. Practically, they already were, but now it was more formal between them, more solid, more concrete with the names.

Chapter 24
Dirt Bikes and Disobedience

Steve had a friend with a large ranch on the far side of the island. He and Tommy would try to spend a long weekend there every now and then, just relaxing and playing. They'd ride horses, hike, sometimes hunt rabbits. Steve had bought a couple of dirt bikes for trail (and off trail) riding together; they both enjoyed that hobby. His friend traveled extensively and often Steve and Tommy were there alone, the ranch foreman coming in daily to do chores and check on things. That was the case one weekend.

Steve had taken Friday off. It had been a busy week; he hadn't been home as much as he would have liked, the extra day meant a longer weekend with his son. They headed out Friday morning, Tommy excitedly chatting about a thousand different things. The plan was to go biking later.

Steve had to be gone for a few hours that afternoon. There was a surprise going away party for Lisa, who indeed had gotten pregnant and was leaving. Steve didn't much like parties, and his idea was to make an appearance for a little while then leave. He would take her out to lunch alone next week as his goodbye to her.

Normally on his weekends away with Tommy, he didn't let anything interfere; this was an exception. He asked Tommy if he minded very much if he left for it; Tommy told Steve to go ahead.

At the party, Steve sat next to Lisa on the couch. She looked radiant, and to Steve, quite pregnant with a huge belly, though she still had a ways to go before she was full term. Lisa and Steve had a great relationship; she loved teasing him, and would sometimes unexpectedly catch him in something. Now she took his large hand in hers and laid it across her belly, wanting him to feel the baby. He smiled, allowing the action. And suddenly he snapped his hand back in shock, as if he had been burned. The baby KICKED him! Actually kicked him. Hard. He felt it. He looked startled at Lisa, then her stomach, then her, back and forth. Rationally, he knew there was a baby in there, and babies— even unborn babies— move around and kick, he supposed. But to feel such movement startled him considerably. Lisa laughed heartily. "Steve, babies kick."

Still feeling unsettled, he said, "Ummm… yeah." And looked at her stomach in wonder. He never thought much about what it must be like to be pregnant. If he felt that hard a kick from the outside, what was she feeling inside? *Weird, just weird.* He stayed a bit longer and was going to head back to the ranch when he got a call from Doc Epstein who wanted him at the hospital.

Tommy had milled around a while, went to visit the horses. Steve didn't have many rules for him, but at the ranch the rule was no horseback riding or dirt bike riding without him there (unless he had express permission and there were other responsible adults around). Tommy didn't mind the solitude at all.

Generally speaking, he was a very well behaved boy. His experiences and intellect had given him a maturity way beyond his chronological age. Sometimes it was hard for Steve to remember that while way advanced in many ways, he was still an eleven year old boy, getting close to twelve now.

On his way out of the barn, Tommy saw the dirt bikes sitting there. He truly loved riding them. Before he knew it, he had on his elbow and knee pads and helmet and was riding out. He figured just a bit around the property. Tommy had never really disobeyed Steve before, and wasn't thinking about that at all now. He was just enjoying his ride.

A bit around the yard became just a ways down the road. And then up that path. And then over that rise. Pretty soon he was about a mile out, off trail, bouncing along. In the back of his mind, he thought this was fun, but it really was more fun when Steve was along.

Turning to head back, he started down the ridge. It wasn't overly steep; he'd covered it before, several times. But suddenly his front wheel hit a rock or a rut, and he and the bike went careening out of control, sliding down the embankment about thirty feet. He hit a huge boulder at the bottom. While it didn't knock him senseless, it did daze him and had enough force to crack his helmet.

As he recovered, he dreadfully thought of the trouble he would be in. *Why did I do such a dumb thing??* As he got up, he yelped in pain as his arm fell to his side. He had on his leather jacket and wasn't about to maneuver around enough to take that off, the way his arm was hurting, but he felt through the material and thought he could feel a broken bone. *Now what??? What am I going to do?*

He sat back down to think. His arm hurt, his head hurt, he was a mile away from the ranch, and the bike was terribly twisted.

Well, I'm going to give it my best to get things fixed up! He walked back to the ranch, went into the bathroom and a smudged, messy, pale face reflected itself in the mirror.. He cleaned up some, then called a cab and went to see Doc Epstein, hoping he was in. *He should be on a Friday afternoon. I hope he is!*

He walked into Doc's office, surprising him.

"Tommy! Hi! How are you?" Tommy and Doc got along well; Doc wondered what this unannounced visit was all about.

Tommy sat down and hemmed and hawed a bit, looked sheepishly at the floor, only stealing quick glances at the physician. Doc knew something was up.

"What is it, son?"

Now Tommy looked directly at the man. "Doc, I've got a problem, I know you can help me, and I'm really hoping we can keep it between the two of us." This was half a statement, half a question.

Doc was non-committal. "That depends, Tommy. You've got to tell me more before I can tell you if things stay between us or not."

Tommy was tempted to leave, he wanted to leave, just hide or something. He knew that wasn't a feasible solution.

He looked squarely at Doc, drew in a deep breath and said, "You know Dad and I sometimes go out to Ed Parker's ranch." Doc nodded yes.

"And you know we sometimes ride our dirt bikes out there." Another nod.

"Well, dad has a rule that I can't ride without him there."

Doc nodded again, "Okay."

Tommy paused. "Well, I did today."

Doc wondered what was coming, thinking maybe he had crashed but honestly he didn't look like he'd been in an accident. He figured he wrecked the bike or something and wanted Doc's help in putting it together.

"I wiped out."

Doc was a bit more concerned, but still not much, Tommy looked fine, maybe a little pale.

"Doc, I was wearing my elbow and knee pads, and my helmet— that got busted when I hit the rock— but I think I broke my arm," he said, cradling his left wrist.

Now Doc was truly concerned. As he went to the closet for his bag he asked, "You hit a rock hard enough to bust your helmet?"

"Yeah, I was on a hillside and hit a hole or something and went down."

"How far did you fall?"

"I didn't really fall, Doc, more like slid down the hill. It wasn't that steep, maybe thirty feet. There was a huge boulder at the bottom that I hit."

Doc queried, "How did you get here?"

"I walked back to the ranch, maybe a mile, then called a cab. Doc, can we please not tell dad? Just patch me up, I'll be fine."

The medical man came over and started an exam, beginning with Tommy's head. He had a good sized bump on the left side that was very tender. He was concerned about a possible neck injury, as well. The rest of the impromptu neuro exam didn't indicate any concussion, but Doc would do more tests before he'd rule that out for certain. And X-rays.

He then gently helped Tommy get the jacket off. He had a short-sleeved T-shirt on under it. You could easily see the broken bone through the skin. Tommy heaved a sigh. "Awww, Doc... Doc, please, can you just tape it up or something... do you have to tell Dad????"

Doc just looked at him, Tommy knew the answer. "Come on, young man, let's get you over to the ER. Where is your dad, anyway?"

"He's at a surprise going away party for Lisa." Tommy looked totally dejected. And then fear began to creep in. Doc saw the dejection, but not the fear.

Doc said, "I'll call your dad." Tommy quickly said, "Doc, okay… if you have to… but don't tell him… I want to tell him."

The doctor prepared to object, but Tommy was adamant and overruled him. "Doc, let me tell him. If you call him and tell him you've got me in the ER, he'll panic. Just get him here, and then I'll tell him." Now Doc was beginning to see some fear in Tommy.

He said gently, "Okay, Tommy, I can do that. But you don't have to be afraid. Steve will be glad you're okay. Maybe he'll be mad, but he'll get over it."

Tommy didn't look convinced.

They headed over to the ER, Doc ordered head and arm X-rays, Tommy rested on a gurney. He called Steve. "Steve, Epstein over at Queens. I need you to come over here."

A pause as the doctor listened. "No, it's not a rush, but I do need you here. Soon."

Steve objected again, saying he was spending the weekend with Tommy at the ranch. "Steve, just come."

Huffing, O'Shaughnessy replied, "Okay, Doc, I'm on the other side of the island, it'll be about an hour. It better be important!" He was just getting ready to leave Lisa's party.

Doc got the films back, there was no serious head injury beyond the contusion. He was going to sedate Tommy and set the arm. Tommy wouldn't let him. "No, I want to talk to Dad first, Doc. I want to tell him myself."

Doc sighed, stubborn, just like his dad. "Okay, let me give you something to ease the pain a bit."

"No, Doc, that will make my thinking fuzzy, and I want to be clear headed when I talk to dad."

Doc observed Tommy. There was more wrong here than a bump on the head and a broken arm. "Tommy, what's wrong?" he asked gently.

Tommy's lip quivered as tears trickled down his cheeks, as he whispered, "I blew it Doc, I blew it."

"What do you mean, Tommy?"

"I blew it Doc, I just blew it. The best thing that ever happened to me and I blew it. I'm so stupid!"

"Tommy, explain this to me. I'm confused."

Tommy just closed his eyes as the tears rolled out. Doc checked his vital signs again. His blood pressure was up when he first came in, understandably; now it was considerably higher. He was really upset about something.

Sure, Steve would be upset; he might even lose his temper and holler. But Tommy could handle all that. He knew Tommy and Steve well. It might not be a pleasant scene, but with all they've been through together, certainly something they'd deal with. Something more was wrong here.

Doc mentally ran through any other physical things he might have missed that could possibly be contributing to Tommy's apprehension, but couldn't come up with anything. He tried again to talk to him, "Tell me about it, Tommy."

All Tommy would say was, "I blew it, I just blew it, Doc. I'm so stupid."

Doc sat with him as they waited. He had his patient's arm on an ice pack off and on. Tommy lay desolately with his eyes shut most of the time, tears escaping now and then. Waiting.

Tommy's thinking was very skewed, unusual for him. Normally he was level headed and logical. But now the idea that had worked its way into Tommy's mind was that Steve would be disappointed in him. He had intentionally disobeyed him, and that would disappoint Steve. *How could Steve want to continue being my father when he had a kid who was so stupid, one who he was disappointed in, on who couldn't be trusted? Steve values integrity and honesty. He will tolerate mistakes (though he doesn't like them), but dishonesty, deceit, I've so screwed up! All that Steve won't put up with. He's not going to want me anymore as a son. I blew it, just for a few minutes of fun on a stupid dirt bike. What am I going to do now? What a mess. I threw away the one most valuable thing in my life, and now I'm back alone, on my own, who knows what else… There was NO way Steve would live with me after this.* And the tears came again.

    Finally, Doc convinced him to share, and Tommy poured out his thoughts and feelings. Doc was aghast! No way would Steve react the way Tommy expected. Yes, he'd be ticked, disappointed, and who knows what else, but Steve loved Tommy. There was nothing that could get in the way of that.

    Doc tried to explain this to Tommy, but he simply refused to hear it. Doc tried repeatedly, reasoned, used logic, all to no avail. No wonder the kid's blood pressure was sky high. He literally thought his life as he knew it, his wonderful life was over, and it would be back to a horrid existence.

    "Tommy, come on…think about this! Steve loves you."

    "Not anymore, Doc." And he refused (or was unable) to hear what Doc was saying.

    Doc wondered if pain was making Tommy so loopy, so unreasonable. He didn't think so. He knew Tommy's head and arm hurt, but this boy knew how to handle physical pain. And while he hurt, the pain wasn't that intense. Doc was baffled at the boy's thinking.

    Doc got up to leave, to call and find out how much longer before Steve got here. Tommy anxiously asked, "Doc, you're not going to tell him, are you?"

    "No, Tommy, I'm just going to find out where he is…" And headed to the hallway, just as Steve was heading down the corridor to where the nurse had informed him Doc was.

    "Okay, Doc, what's so blasted important that I need to be here?"

    "Steve, settle down! I've got a patient here who needs to see you and talk to you." Doc was at a loss for words, didn't know how to continue. He wasn't going to tell Steve but did want to warn him. He knew Tommy was just on the other side of the curtain and could hear everything.

"Steve, look, this patient is REALLY upset. You need to be helpful and reassuring and calm. Don't fly off the handle!"

Steve looked at the physician. "Doc, you're not making any sense. Who? What? Why? What's going on? What are you mumbling about?"

Doc tried again, "Steve…"

Then not knowing what else to say, how to approach it, simply said, "Steve, it's Tommy."

Steve's eyes widened, he shot Doc a scathing look for not telling him right away, ripped aside the curtain and rushed to Tommy's side in fear.

His initial panic subsided a bit as he saw that Tommy was conscious, no obvious blood, saw the arm on the ice pack. He looked "okay". "What's going on here? What happened? Tommy, are you all right?"

Tommy just started to cry, unable to speak. Doc was going to explain what he understood, Tommy stopped him, asked to be left alone with Steve. Steve's panic was returning. What was wrong here? Obviously something physical, but not life threatening. But Tommy was very upset; Steve could see and feel that. He was giving off waves of fear.

Steve got up close, took his son's good hand, got right next to his face, "Hey, Tommy, take it easy. It's going to be okay. What's wrong, son? What happened?"

And that tenderness just made Tommy more upset, as he realized that kind of love was soon going to be a thing of the past. They sat together minutes longer, Steve trying to gently reassure, Tommy trying to get up the nerve to tell Steve.

Finally he decided he just had to get it out. "Steve." He said "Steve," not "Dad," a point which Steve immediately noticed and worried him.

Indicating the end of the gurney, the boy asked, "Can you please move over there?" He figured it would be easier if he wasn't so close. That request also worried Steve.

He took a deep breath, tried hard to overcome sobbing tears, and said, "Steve, I blatantly disobeyed you. I took the dirt bike out by myself and wiped out. I know you won't tolerate dishonesty or that kind of disrespect and disobedience, so …" And he faltered.

"So, I understand that you won't want me to….be… your…. son… anymore. I'll pack my things and leave. This was the stupidest thing I have ever done, throwing away the one good thing in my life— you— your respect— your love, your trust. I am so sorry, but I know I can't undo it. I know what you think."

Steve was stunned, his mind was reeling. *What???? What is he talking about???*

He quickly moved back to Tommy's head. The boy turned away. Doc had been right outside, listening, he came in and explained to Steve Tommy's thinking. And that Tommy refused any pain meds until after he talked with Steve, so he could be clear-headed. Steve was horrified! At all of it.

"Tommy! You're my son! Nothing is ever going to change that. EVER! Do you hear me???" Tommy hadn't been looking at him, and didn't look now, or respond.

Steve took his chin in his hand gently, "Tommy, look at me."

Finally, just a bit, Tommy looked up and saw Steve's pain filled eyes. He couldn't speak, his lip quivered and tears rolled down his cheeks. And Steve's as well. Finally Tommy said, "Steve, I'm so sorry. I was so stupid."

Steve realized Tommy still thought things were "over" between them. "Tommy, Listen to me. I'm not Steve. I'm your dad. I was three months ago, I was last week, I was this morning, I am now, I will be in an hour, and tonight, and tomorrow and next week, and next year. I'll be your dad forever. That has not and will not change. No matter what. Tommy, you're my son. No matter what you have done or failed to do. Do you understand that?"

Tommy shook his head back and forth. "But, Steve, I've disappointed you, I've let you down. You can't still want me around."

Steve shook his head. *Good God, help him to understand.* "Oh, Tommy! I want you around, more than anything. You have no idea how empty my life would be if you weren't in it. Okay, so maybe, maybe, I'll be disappointed, maybe you've let me down. You've disobeyed. My love for you is not dependent on how you act. I love you. Period. No matter what. You're my son! So if we have some problems, we'll work through them. But we're family. Just because you're not perfect, maybe you screwed up, that doesn't mean I don't want you or that I don't love you! Tommy, how could you even think that?"

Slowly, ever so slowly, Tommy began to think that maybe, just maybe, he had a slim chance of recovering maybe just a part of what he/they had. As Steve talked more with him, thoughts ran through his mind. *Geez, he's devastated! He really expected me to toss him out like bad garbage for screwing up. Where is that coming from? Okay, damage control— help him to see that everything will be okay, I need to get him back on track, reassure him.*

Doc was beginning to be concerned about his patient; this was taking a pretty good toll on Tommy. Steve noticed Doc's concern and deduced the reasoning behind it. He kept trying, and put on his authoritative voice, "Tommy, listen to me, please. Doc is going to fix you up here in a bit. Then we're going to go home— home— to our home. We will work out the problems, the disobedience, whatever. But we will go on as a family. You and me. Father and son. I want you to understand that? Do you understand?"

Tommy eyed him, "But how can you say those things? After what I've done?'

Steve just vehemently shook his head. "What you've done makes no difference in my love for you. None. You're my son, no matter what."

"Do you understand that?"

Tommy answered, "No. I cannot understand how you can love me after what I did."

Steve decided to try another tack, "Okay, Tommy, you don't understand. That's okay. Let me ask a different question: can you believe and accept my love? In spite of what you did?" Tommy had to think about that. He was tired. His head was hurting. His arm was throbbing. He was totally played out. Steve was aware of all this.

Tommy looked at Steve. *Here is Steve, telling me he still loves me, wants things to go on as before. Well, I was a fool to disobey. I'd be more of a fool to turn down his love. He really does mean it. I can tell.*

Crying even more tears, he nodded.

This caused Steve (and Doc) to shed a few tears as well.

Steve commanded, "Okay, Doc, get moving with him!" Tommy already had an IV in, Doc pumped some morphine into it and got ready to set the arm as soon as the medication took effect. Within two minutes Tommy had drifted off and Doc began his work. The break was a simple one, that could be set without much difficulty. Doc and Steve talked quietly as he worked, and Tommy slept. They were trying to sort out Tommy's bizarre reaction, without much success.

Doc finished, had another X-ray taken to make sure the bone was properly set. "Steve, normally I'd want to keep him overnight for observation. But I think it would be much better for him if you took him home tonight. Being in his own home will be good."

Steve agreed. "Thanks, Doc."

He carried the still sleeping Tommy out to the car and took him home. Then up to bed. He sat in his room a long time with him.

Then he went out and placed a long distance call to Singapore to Samuel . Steve explained what had happened. His friend immediately had answers for him, "Steve, it's simple. I expected something like this. It's a good thing."

Steve was baffled! "Samuel, what are you talking about?"

"Okay, Stevie, it's like this. Tommy's subconscious was at work. He didn't really do any of this consciously. What he wanted to know, what he needed to know, subconsciously, was that you loved him, no matter what. So his subconscious did something that he considered terrible, being disobedient and dishonest with you. The thinking, the subconscious thinking, is that if you can still love him despite that terrible thing, you must really love him. It was a test. And you passed, Stevie. I expect over the next few days, Tommy's conscious and subconscious will meld and it will all be fine. I think the point has been made, it shouldn't happen again. Doesn't mean he'll never screw up or disobey you, but I think this incident was a huge test. Follow what I'm saying?"

As Samuel explained, Steve was thinking about what he was saying. It did all make perfect sense the way he clarified it. "Okay, Samuel, yeah, you make sense. Is there anything I need to be aware of, to do?"

"No, just handle it matter-of-factly. Sounds like Tommy's had plenty of suffering for his misbehavior. I wouldn't spend much time on talking about it."

Steve gave Samuel heartfelt thanks and felt much better about the whole thing. He shivered at how bad Tommy must have felt, believing he wouldn't be wanted any more. Steve sat for a long time on the lanai thinking into the night.

After waking early, jogging, and getting cleaned up, he made Tommy's favorite breakfast, and went to his room to get him. "Hey, wake up sleepyhead! How're you feeling?" Steve handed him a couple of pain pills from the bottle Doc had given him last night and a glass of water, knowing Tommy would be hurting.

Tommy took them, and looked at his dad carefully. Steve smiled. "C'mon, breakfast is ready."

"Thanks. My favorite breakfast." Tommy was quiet as he ate.

When they were finished, Steve decided they needed to talk. "Tommy, you screwed up. You disobeyed me. You knew why I had that rule and you went ahead and broke it anyway. That was wrong. You know it. You paid the consequences— with a broken arm, clonked head, and also you paid plenty in terms of emotional upset. But I want you to know that it has nothing to do with my love for you. That is stable, and will always remain stable, no matter what. I think you have learned a lesson here. I'm not worried about you disobeying again in regards to that. If you do— when you do— in other ways, we'll deal with it. I don't expect you to be perfect, I'm not perfect. But we can still love each other— we do love each other, in spite of imperfections. So, case closed, okay?" Steve grinned.

Tommy looked long and hard at Steve; slowly he broke into a grin, accepting what Steve was offering. "Okay, Dad!"

And Steve mussed his hair, telling him to finish eating.

Today he especially wanted to make it to Mass. He hadn't made the six a.m. Mass, but there was a nine a.m. one he could get to at another parish not too far away. He needed to pray about some things. And while he could pray anywhere, he liked doing it in a dark, cool empty church best.

After Mass, he stayed and prayed. He thought about what had happened, mostly about Tommy's reaction. He was truly startled at his belief that Steve would no longer love him because of what he did. And suddenly he had a revelation. His eyes were drawn towards the cross, and Christ upon it.

Somehow Steve knew intellectually that God loved him. Doc had always said so, it was just one of those things. God loves you. He fondly recalled that time months back when he felt immersed completely in God's love, how wonderful that felt.

He'd never forget it. But until this moment, he didn't really know that meant no matter what! No matter what he did, what he had done, what he would do, he would not lose God's love. No matter what. Just like his love for Tommy. He'd love Tommy no matter what he did (or didn't do). That was constant, unconditional. *How simple, how clear, why did I never see this before?*

He also realized that was what Confession was all about. Telling someone —God — you're sorry for what you did and you don't want to do it again. This is exactly what happened with Tommy. He made a mistake, he was sorry, he told Steve, who forgave him, with no strings attached. That was how Confession worked. And Steve knew that, intellectually. He recalled the good feeling he had after making that hard Confession after not going for fifteen years. But thinking about it now, with Tommy, again, so simple, so easy, so clear. Another thing he hadn't gotten until now, really gotten.

The Gospel reading at Mass that day was from Mark. "Taking a child he placed it in their midst, and putting his arms around it he said to them, 'Whoever receives one child such as this in my name, receives me; and whoever receives me, receives not me but the One who sent me.'"

It struck Steve strongly that the Lord was telling him that making Tommy a part of his life was exactly that. As the man pondered the verse and its meaning another one came unbidden into his mind. It was one he'd heard many times, but wasn't sure where it was in the Bible. "This is my Son, my beloved, with whom I am well pleased."

And suddenly, as clear as day he had the feeling of being in direct communication with God who was telling him, "You are my son, and I am well pleased with you." It wasn't any voice he heard, but the words were forcefully present inside his mind.

Steve was baffled. More came to him: "For what you've done, for taking care of my little Tommy, I am well pleased with you."

Steve objected, and it was almost like a bewildering supernatural conversation.

"Lord, I didn't do much. It was just there and needed to be done. I'm not any special saint or anything."

"You did exactly as I wished, my son. You didn't run away from the challenge I placed before you."

"God, I'm back to the idea that I just did what needed doing. Honestly, Lord, thoughts of you were not very much in my mind."

"That matters little, my son. You served me. You received Tommy into your home and life and heart, you also received Me in doing that. You are my son and I am well pleased with you."

Steve argued no more, just sat and basked in the love he felt pouring out to him from God.

He said a quick prayer of thanksgiving and was happy and anxious to get back to Tommy. The boy was bringing so much into his life, so many unexpected things. On his way home he smiled as he thought that must be how God feels— happy and excited to be with us. Life was good.

And Steve and Tommy lived happily ever after.

For a while. Everyone's life has its ups and downs. It was three years before they had a significant "down".

Chapter 25
Pressure

Things had been going well for Steve and Tommy. He had made lots of friends, was doing exceptionally well with his education, and the relationship with his dad was phenomenal.

He was spending three days a week at a school for gifted students, and two days a week with his beloved Professor Carlson. He had one instructor he especially liked, Mr. Benson; but this man also pushed him, quite hard. He knew Tommy had exceptional capabilities and did everything he thought was best to help him to live up to his full potential. And sometimes this led to heavy pressure on the fourteen year old boy. It was also easy for folks to forget that he was a fourteen year old boy. With his intellect and maturity, often he acted much older. But he had yet to hit any kind of adolescent growth spurt; he remained smaller and child-like physically.

One of Tommy's favorite pastimes was chess and he belonged to the school's chess club. Acting upon the advice of the club's coach, Harvey Dittman, Tommy had entered some chess tournaments.

A state-wide science fair was scheduled in about six weeks that he was signed up for. Mr. Benson, his science teacher, was very impressed with Tommy's grasp of astronomy and had strongly encouraged him to enter a project in that area. This sounded good to Tommy, but over the planning and development stages, his fairly simple project had grown to a major undertaking, requiring lots of hours of research and work.

There was an important chess match coming up a week before the science fair. Competition was expected to be steep, and Mr. Dittman was drilling Tommy sometimes several hours daily with strategies, moves, or studying techniques. The contest was scheduled for the last weekend of the month. He was looking forward to it, but also a bit nervous. He liked playing chess for the fun of it, the challenge. Tommy liked winning, but all this was getting overwhelming for him.

Tommy had stopped for now his time with Professor Carlson and was just working on school and the astronomy project and studying and practicing chess.

Between those things, there were few hours left for relaxing or "down time". It was getting to Tommy. Steve had been really busy with work. Keo had been injured with a badly broken leg, and had already been out for almost three weeks, leaving them a man short at work. Normally Steve kept a pretty close eye on Tommy and his school work and activities— he enjoyed it and truly was interested.

There had been plenty of nights lately when Steve got home late. Sometimes Tommy would still be burning the midnight oil, and his dad would admonish him to get to bed and get some sleep.

At school, there was an older brother of a classmate that Tommy had run into a few times. He had graduated a few years back from public school, not this private academy for gifted students, and he hung around the school parking lot a fair amount. Tommy always felt a bit uneasy around him. Eddie, the classmate, knew Tommy was stressed out, not having enough time to get everything done that he wanted to, and was being pressured into. Tommy would often fall asleep at night while reading some text or chess manual. Eddie had told him his brother could help, and Larry talked a bit with Tommy. He said he had some stuff that would give him more energy, allow him to get more work done, and work longer without getting tired.

"Drugs, Larry?"

"Hey, man, not 'drugs'. Just a little something to keep you going when you're beat. No big deal. Not like pot or bad drugs or anything. These are doctor prescribed pills."

Tommy turned away, "No, thanks."

A few afternoons later, as the chess tournament and the science fair dates loomed closer, Larry again approached Tommy. "Hey, man, you look beat. Look, just try one of these. It's not going to hurt you. I'll bet you're falling asleep at night before you get everything done you want to get done. Hey, you need to work more on your stuff to win; you know everyone's counting on you to win. Especially your dad."

Tommy walked away, but he was tempted. He knew Larry was offering him drugs— uppers— but the way he talked, it didn't sound so bad. And they were counting on him— his dad, Mr. Benson, Mr. Dittman, the chess club, the whole school, really, in one way. If he could just get another few hours in each night… But he knew taking drugs was wrong and he wasn't going to do that.

The next day, after school, there was Larry again. "Look, Tommy. Here, you can have these; I'm giving them to you. I want you to be the winner as much as anyone else, so I'm just giving these to you. Use them; they'll help you come out on top. It's no big deal, Tommy." And with that, he stuffed a small bottle of pills into Tommy's jacket pocket, then turned and left.

That night at home, Steve was there early for a change. They had a nice supper together. It was still over three weeks until the chess match and almost a month until the science fair. Steve asked about his progress, if he needed/wanted any help. Tommy knew his dad was still shorthanded at work, and busy. And that he was home early that night and offering his help because it was the "right" thing to do.

"Naw, dad, I'm good." Steve eyed his son carefully. There was some undercurrent there that didn't quite sit right with him, but he couldn't put his finger on it. Tommy knew he was being scrutinized. "Dad, really, it's all coming together." Then he made excuses to head to his room to work. Steve watched him go.

A few hours later, Steve went to his son's room to talk a bit. Tommy was hard at work detailing some reports for the astronomy project. "Working hard?"

"Yeah, Dad, but I'm getting there."

"You okay if I head back in to the office tonight?"

"Fine, Dad, I'll work a while longer."

"Okay, but get to bed at a reasonable hour. You need your rest, too."

"Yeah. I will."

By eleven, Tommy was bushed. But he knew there was so much more that needed doing. With the new angles Mr. Benson wanted with the astronomy display, there was a lot more extra work to organize and finish. The teen glanced at his jacket pocket, then turned away.

Ten minutes later he went over and took out the bottle of pills, opened it, and looked at them. He rationalized in his mind that taking just one of these would be okay. He also knew he was lying to himself, but he popped the upper anyway.

And it did act just as Larry said it would. He felt good, he had energy, and he was able to work much longer. At three a.m. he finally went to bed.

The next day at school, Larry was there. He asked how he was doing. Tommy didn't even talk with him. As the young scholar walked away, Larry grinned.

That night Tommy took another one when his energy began to flag.

And the next night as well. And then at two a.m., when it seemed to be wearing off, he popped another.

Over the next week, he took two or three each night. Steve was home some of those nights, but didn't notice. Tommy kept in his room pretty much, claiming he had to devote his energy to his work. Steve sensed that he was almost obsessed, but it was two major things back to back. Standing in the bedroom doorway, he asked, "Hey, Tommy, whaddya say we take tomorrow afternoon off and go sailing?"

Tommy barely looked up from his typing. "Dad, I'd love to, but I need to get this done. We can go after the chess competition and the science fair."

Steve scrutinized his son, and Tommy was aware of it. "Tommy, are you doing too much?"

"Dad, it is a lot, and these two things came up one right after the other— I hadn't expected that, but I want to do them both. I really want to do well and win. When they're done, it will ease up." He said all this without making direct eye contact.

Tommy continued taking the pills, up to three or four each night, and often two or three during the day. Larry had graciously replenished his supply, at no cost. He knew (subconsciously) that the pusher was getting him hooked.

Tommy sought out Larry a few days later. "Larry, your pills are working, but I can't sleep at all now. I feel wrung out. I mean, I've got energy to work, but I can't… turn off…. I guess is how I'd put it."

"Common problem, buddy. Here, take one of these when you want to sleep. Works really well."

Tommy knew he was just getting in deeper and deeper, and hated it. He figured that as soon as all this was done, he'd quit.

That night, about three a.m., he took one of the downers and was asleep in minutes. This stuff worked, he wasn't really surprised.

Tommy was beginning to feel haggard, exhausted, and weary. When he took the uppers, he'd perk up, but it was a false feeling. He'd snap at people, and his dad; he was moody and irritable. Everyone chalked it up to pressure from the upcoming events. Steve had a talk with him one night, suggesting maybe he skip one or the other, if it was getting to be too much. Tommy lashed back saying with all the work he had put into them, no way. And then apologized for his outburst and worked hard for the rest of supper to be sociable.

The chess tournament came. Father and son drove over together. Tommy was tense and nervous. Steve encouraged him to relax and just have fun. "C'mon, Tommy, doesn't really make any difference if you win or not. Just have fun." Tommy didn't reply. It bothered Steve that he was so wound up; nothing he said seemed to make much difference.

As Tommy played through the elimination rounds, he did well and made it to the final four contestants. It had been a long day, with three tough matches for him so far. Tommy found himself taking an upper every few hours to stay on top of things. He lost his next match and was quite irritated with himself. He received hearty congratulations all around from parents, competitors, teachers, press, and so on. Coming in fourth out of over 200 highly skilled and accomplished players was a significant accomplishment.

His dad suggested they go out for a celebratory dinner. Tommy declined, saying he was tired and just wanted to get home and go to bed. Steve's radar had been tuning in to him more and more over the last week, and he didn't really like what he saw. But again, he assumed it was just stress and fatigue.

Tommy went home and headed straight to his room, took three downers (one or two didn't do the trick anymore), hid his pills carefully as he always did, and flopped onto the bed, clothes and all. Steve made a sandwich and brought it in to him, finding the lad sound asleep. He watched him a while. Slow easy breathing, some twitching now and then. He looked so young and vulnerable, tired, worn, drawn, unhealthy. Steve didn't like him feeling so pressured. Life is full of pressure, but there was something about this that bothered him.

Steve purposely stayed home the next morning instead of heading off early to the office. It was Sunday anyway, and Steve usually didn't work on Sundays. He was worried about Tommy and told him so. His son had been cranky, irritable, just not himself the last few weeks.

"Dad, I'm okay. Just tired. I'm sorry; I know I've been touchy lately. I just need to get through this week, get my project finished, then things will ease up."

"That's all there is, Tommy? Nothing else bothering you?"

"No, Dad. I just want to do well at the science fair. Mr. Benson has really helped me a lot and I want to do well. I need to finish some diagrams this afternoon, then get the rest of the research done and written up by Tuesday or Wednesday."

"Tommy, I think a break would do you good. No one can carry on full speed for a long time. Let's do something together today."

"Dad, I'd really like to. But I can't, really. I wouldn't enjoy myself with stuff undone hanging over my head. After this is over, I promise."

Steve wasn't so sure that Tommy was being 100% honest with him, but sighed and headed out for a jog. Later he went to Mass with Tommy, then planned to spend the day at home, painting and doing some chores around the house. He didn't like what was happening with Tommy, but decided to give it the week. Science fair was Saturday.

And the week passed. Tommy was taking quite a few pills now to stay awake and alert, and then to sleep. Larry had happily kept him supplied with as much as he needed.

Friday he brought his project to the convention center and set it all up. He had a second set of notes that he planned to continue to study. The event involved both your project/display itself and an oral presentation. There was a panel of judges who would interview you and ask questions.

For the second Saturday in a row, Steve and Tommy were off to an event. And again, Tommy was edgy and anxious. Steve tried to calm and reassure him with little success. When they got to the center, Tommy took off. He made a stop in the men's room and took three uppers. He thought about taking even more, but figured he'd start with that and then see. He could always pop a few more easily. The amount of drugs he was taking bothered him, but he pushed the thought from his mind. He refused to think about it directly. And he didn't think of them as drugs. He thought of them as prescription medications.

He went to his display and waited. Observers weren't allowed in until after the competition. Steve waited outside, thinking about Tommy.

After over an hour's wait, it was Tommy's turn. As the judges were studying the entry just before his, he swallowed another couple pills. His turn came, and he did an admirable job of presenting his data, project and information. He was able to answer the judges' questions well, despite being jittery. It would be another hour or two before they would be finished, he didn't want to go back out to his dad, so he just waited around in the auditorium.

All contestants and guests were ushered into the auditorium for the awards portion of the event. There were almost 300 entries. Tommy's project got an Honorable Mention, as well as Second Place for Most Detailed, and a Third Place for Most Unique. This was very good placing. Steve was most proud of him, as were many others. Doc was there, and Marco, some friends and teachers from school. There were many congratulations and photo snaps.

After most of it died down, Tommy asked his dad if they could leave instead of attend the afternoon sessions and presentations. Steve was fine with that.

Again he would have liked to take him out to eat for a celebratory dinner, but instead asked tentatively, "Home?"

Tommy just nodded. He was barely able to hold back tears. He knew he was royally screwed up, and knew he had to face and his dad and the music, but was tired, and scared and ashamed and a thousand other things. Steve knew something was up, but was also willing to wait it out, he knew Tommy would bring it up.

Chapter 26
Dealing with It

They went into the house, and Tommy flopped on the couch. Steve sat next to him. He wouldn't look at his dad. Steve put his hand on his son's arm and gently asked, "What's up?"

Tommy jerked away, bounced up, and shook his head. He rested it against the lanai door frame. In a weary, resigned voice, he sighed, "Oh… Dad…"

Steve got up, went to him, laid a hand on his shoulder, but said nothing.

Tommy finally said, "Let's go outside….", turned and headed out the lanai door down to the secluded beach. He went to a rock where he and his dad had had many talks over the last few years, and plunked down, burying his head in his hands.

Again, Steve made physical contact but remained silent.

Tommy began to cry, heavy sobs. Now Steve spoke, "Tommy, what is it? I'm here for you. Whatever it is, we'll handle it. It'll be okay."

More crying. "Tommy, I love you."

And that just made it worse for the boy. Steve just sat with him. Finally the exhausted, chemically battered whiz kid began to talk, "Dad, I've made such a mess of things. And what I've done is going to hurt you. That's what makes this so bad. I don't care about me or what happens to me. I'm just so sorry it's going to hurt you. You're going to be so disappointed in me, I don't know how you can ever care about me again."

Steve had become aware over the last few hours that Tommy was very distressed. He wasn't sure why, what was going on. So he chose to hit the basics. "Tommy, I love you. Do you know that? I love you no matter what. That's not going to change. Do you understand and believe that?"

Tommy cried harder as his dad hugged him fiercely. After a minute Steve took his son's chin in his hand and brought his head up to try to force eye contact. Tommy's eyes remained downcast. "Son, look at me. I love you. Nothing will change that. Look at me."

He didn't comply with the request, but kept his head tucked down and his forehead resting on Steve's chest. Steve let him cry it out without comment. This wasn't the first time Tommy had ever shed tears, but he seemed unusually upset today. Eventually the sobs subsided. Tommy took about a half dozen deep slow breaths. Steve knew he was trying to gather enough nerve to speak. And then Tommy lifted his head and looked him in the eye. Steve was aware of the courage it took to do that, look directly at him.

Slowly Tommy spoke in a quavering, faltering subdued voice, "Dad, I've screwed up. It's all my fault, my doing, no one else's. Dad, I'm on drugs. Uppers and downers. I'm sorry. I'm sorry I ever took that first one. I know I've disappointed you. I love you. I'm sorry to have let you down. I want to quit. I don't want to be like this. I need help, Dad. Please help me."

Steve's mind was reeling as he held his once again sniffling son. Several things had passed through his mind over the last hour, possibilities of what might be amiss. But the idea of his son taking drugs had never entered his thoughts. He was flabbergasted. But looking back, he could see it. Symptoms he had attributed to stress, the irritability, edginess, were all side effects from the drugs.

The father quietly asked, "For how long, Tommy?"

"About a month." That made sense to Steve. His mind was working

"Are you taking anything besides uppers and downers?" Tommy shook his head no.

"How much are you taking?" Tommy looked down and gulped.

"A lot, Dad. I started out with only one. The guy said it would give me more energy to concentrate and work longer on my stuff. And he was right. It did. But after a few days one didn't do much, so I started taking more." Tommy paused and repeated himself. "A lot, Dad. I've probably had already a dozen uppers today."

Steve was stunned. It was only mid-afternoon. Steve's mental gears started as soon as Tommy confessed. He was going to waste no time, and shepherded his son towards the house. "Tommy, we're going to Doc's. Now. And give me the pills— all of them."

Steve called Doc, who was at home. The detective knew the physician would want blood samples and more— who knows what all. "Doc, it's Steve. Can you meet Tommy and me at Queen's in ten minutes? We've got a problem and need your help."

"Sure, Steve. What's up?"

He tersely replied, "I'll explain when we see you, Doc."

As he drove, Steve glanced at his son, who was shaking, either from the drugs or the tension, or both. "Tommy, where'd you get them?"

Tommy confessed without hesitation, "Larry Anderson. He's the older brother of a kid at school."

"How'd you pay for them?" Wondering if his son had also been stealing, though he had found nothing missing from his wallet or belongings.

"I didn't. He just gave them to me. And more when I needed more. I thought it was weird he didn't want me to pay."

Lips compressed into a thin line, Steve's mind raced. *Yeah, weird. Not! Get the kid hooked hard, then you can rake him over the coals and charge anything you want.*

He looked again at Tommy. What he saw was a small, young scared, shivering and shaking, sad, lost boy. "Hey, Tommy. I love you. We'll get through this." And guilt began to build in Steve. He knew his son started drugs due to pressure. Pressure from school, teachers, HIM, from lots of people to excel, to be the best, to achieve. Having high standards and goals is good, but needs to stay in balance. And he was feeling guilty because he didn't see what was happening. He was too busy with work to even notice Tommy's distress. And willing to let it slide way too easily when Tommy brushed off his attempts to take a break and go out sailing or something. Damn, this was his fault.

"How're you feeling?"

Tommy shrugged. "You mean physically, or inside my head?"

"Both."

"I feel stupid, really stupid for getting into this. I'm scared. I'm upset that I've hurt you. I'm cold. I feel wired, coiled up, like I'm ready to explode. I really would like to take a couple of downers and just climb into bed." He braved a look at his dad with that last comment— that really was what he wanted to do. His glance was met with a stern glare from his dad— no way.

As Steve parked at the hospital, a sense of dread began to well up in Tommy. His dad's intuition told him his son was feeling uneasy, took him by the arm, and hustled him up to Doc's office. Tommy sat down on the couch, at the very end. Doc looked at him, then Steve, waiting expectantly for an explanation. Steve looked at Tommy, then Doc, then proceeded to relate the whole story. Tommy put his head down; he didn't want to look at Doc. The medical man took his bag and sat down next to the boy and began an examination. It had been almost three hours since Tommy had taken anything, and his body was beginning to crave a hit. Doc drew blood, and asked questions. The replies were short, usually one-word answers. The boy was beginning to feel ill, and he was irritated with the exam, the questions. Again, more than anything he wanted some downers and to crash. He appealed to Doc for that purpose. And was met with the same response he got from his dad.

"Steve, let's get him admitted."

Tommy jumped up. "NO! Look— Doc— Dad... I know I need help. And I'll take your help. I know I need to get off these damn pills. And I want to. But not here. Isn't there some way, some place, we can do that— not here— not at the hospital? At home? I can get off them just as easily at home. Dad, Doc, if I'm admitted here, this is all going to be public record. And I don't care for my sake, but what will it do to dad? Word gets out that the son of the head of O'Shaughnessy Investigations is a druggie? The newspapers would love it. He'd never get over it. It would damage his career and the company. Not the hospital, please. I'll do whatever you want, but can't we keep this under wraps? Please?"

Steve and Doc looked at each other— they had not thought about this. Steve asked, "Doc? We'll do whatever needs doing, including hospitalization if necessary, but maybe Tommy's got a point."

Doc looked at Tommy, then addressed Steve, "Okay, coming off drugs is not a pretty picture. We're going to do this cold turkey. I think I can consider a location other than here, and keeping this quiet." He paused as he thought. "Let's use my beach house. It's secluded, private. Helen will need to know, she can help. You and I, Steve. We'll need more help than that, we don't know how long this will take, could be a couple weeks at least. He'll need 24/7 supervision. Can we ask Marco?"

It was all decided and arranged. It seemed with each passing minute Tommy was growing more agitated, though he tried to hide it. Doc noticed and said, "Let's go." They all went in Steve's car to Doc's beach house. Doc and a sullen Tommy sat in the back seat. He tried again to plead with Doc, "Doc, give me just a downer. Then I can sleep and will feel a lot better." Doc simply said, "No." Tommy mumbled a nasty remark, too quietly to be heard.

The rest of the drive was quiet, each occupant of the car immersed in his own thoughts. They got to the house and went in.

"Steve, Tommy's not going to be himself as he goes through withdrawal. He's going to be angry, belligerent, sneaky, and a whole lot more. Not a very pretty sight. If you want, we can handle this without you."

"No, Doc. I'll stay. It's my fault he's in this mess, anyway."

Doc whirled around, "What do you mean by that?"

"Doc, I should have noticed something was up. And I'm the one who pressured him to do well, to do better, to do more."

Doc came nose-to-nose with Steve. "O'Shaughnessy, get that nonsense out of your head now. This is not your fault. You're far from perfect, but this is not your fault. Get over it or get out. I'm not going to let you stay here if you're wallowing in that kind of garbage."

Tommy heard this conversation, and filed it away in his head. He knew it wasn't his dad's fault, but right now he was too absorbed in his own misery to address the issue.

Doc ushered Tommy to one of the guest bedrooms, then got out a set of pajamas. "Tommy, do you want to shower and then try to get some sleep? Or are you hungry? Thirsty?" He took his pulse, which was racing. Tommy just shook his head and lay down on the bed, grabbed the bedspread and curled up. Another plea, "Doc, just one downer, please?"

Doc shook his head, "The answer is no, and it will be no every time you ask. Forget it, Tommy. You're going to kick this 100%. Until your body gets over it and adjusts, you'll feel miserable. But it needs doing, and we'll be here to help." Tommy rolled over, feeling surly.

Steve called Marco and asked him to come to Doc's. Doc called his wife, Helen, with the same request. Doc was trying to think of all that needed doing, how best to handle things. As hard as it was for him to do it, he figured that it would be best to barricade the bedroom window. He expected there to be times when Tommy would need to be locked in and would do anything to get away. He decided to ask Marco to do that, he knew it would break Steve's heart when he realized it.

The four adults had a meeting. Like Steve and Doc, Marco and Helen were shocked at what had happened and were more than willing to do whatever they could to help. Doc stated that there would need to be at least one (awake and aware) person with Tommy 24/7. And during the worst of times, two people. They may need more help, and decided to recruit Bobby if need be. Keo wouldn't be able to help with his bad leg. Steve and Doc both had other friends they could recruit in confidence if they needed more help. Doc was pretty confident that medically it was okay not to be in the hospital, that Tommy could detox and withdraw here, under supervision. But if he ever thought hospitalization was indicated, they'd go. The story they would circulate was that Tommy had been ill, and was staying at Doc's while recovering.

Meanwhile, in the bedroom, Tommy was miserable. He was hot, then cold. Clammy, crampy, very restless. Sweaty, then chilled. He thought to himself, all I need is a downer, then I'll be fine. He just couldn't get comfortable.

Steve was pretty good at helping Tommy relax, knew trigger points on his body where gentle massage would usually calm him down. He went in to try to help him unwind. He took his son's hand and began to rub. The boy jerked away. Steve was not deterred— he reached for his upper back and neck and kneaded gently. This time Tommy didn't break away, but Steve's ministrations had no effect. The muscles were tight, tighter than Steve had ever felt them before. He whispered quietly to him. Tommy didn't respond at all. Steve kept at it. Sometimes for a few seconds he'd seem to relax a bit, then tense up again. He begged, "Dad, please can you get me just one downer?"

Steve answered sadly, "No."

Tommy moved away from Steve and wrapped the covers tighter around him, his back to his dad in rejection. "Some friend you are." Steve was going to reply but just let it pass. He stayed in the bedroom a few minutes longer watching his son, and offering up a silent prayer. He didn't think he was sleeping, but at least he was quiet and seemed somewhat calm; for now, anyway.

Steve went back into the living room and joined the quiet discussion. They looked at him for a report. He shrugged, "He's quiet, shoulders and neck are very tense. He's pretty insistent on getting one of us to get him some pills. Doc, this is going to be hard, isn't it?" Doc nodded affirmatively.

They set up a schedule for the next few days. Steve, of course, wanted to stay the whole time. Doc and Marco convinced him that wasn't best. First, he'd need his own rest. And this could drag on a few weeks; he'd have to put in some time at the office. Doc and Helen would stay the remainder of the weekend, through to Monday morning. They'd rotate from there on out.

The next week was hard for all of them. Tommy went from being totally withdrawn to angry and belligerent, hostile and abusive. Doc threatened to restrain him if need be (and had restraints on hand, just in case). The boy acted in ways he normally never did, cursing and swearing, pressuring anyone who was there to get him some drugs. He cried and cajoled, begged and pleaded. Physically he would be sick and vomiting, and went through just about every symptom in the book: chills, fever, cramps, racing metabolism, lethargy, spasms, irrationality, and more.

Doc kept a close watch on his physical condition, checking him frequently. He was doing okay; Doc knew that given time, he'd recover, but it couldn't be too soon for him.

One day was Marco's turn to be with him. Doc got back about six and asked how it had gone. Marco shrugged, "So-so."

Doc was concerned about the toll this was taking on Tommy's body. He asked Marco to stay a bit, he might need his help. "Did he eat anything?" Marco said no. "Drink much?" Another negative answer. Doc went over to examine him. Tommy was sullen and hostile, but Doc managed to check a pulse and blood pressure and his eyes. His questions to the lad were left unanswered.

"Tommy, you're getting dehydrated and weak. You need to eat and drink." Doc had said the same thing yesterday. He knew his next course of action was not going to be well liked, but necessary.

"Tommy, I'm going to start a sugar water IV in you. It will get you hydrated and get some calories into you. You'll feel a little better with it."

Tommy glared at him. "No."

"Tommy, come on, cooperate."

Suddenly the boy smirked and smiled wickedly. "OKAY, Doc! I'll cooperate with YOU— if YOU cooperate with ME!" Doc was wary.

"You can start an IV, do anything you want, if you get me some pills."

Doc shook his head, "You know I won't do that, Tommy." Stubbornly and with a determined look, Doc ordered, "But you will get the IV, young man. With or without your cooperation." Doc looked at Marco, so did Tommy. Marco now knew why Doc wanted him to stay— to help if Tommy wasn't cooperative. And it didn't look like he would be.

Doc gave the boy a few seconds to think about it. "So, what's it going to be? Cooperative or not?"

Tommy glowered at him. "Go to hell, you bastard!" Doc was shocked at the language he used, but didn't let it show. Marco gasped.

Matter-of-factly the physician replied, "Okay, have it your way." He took Marco's elbow and ushered him out of the room and shut the door. In the hallway he explained to Marco that he had restraints and described the best way to physically subdue Tommy. As a pre-med student Doc had worked in a psych ward and learned a few tricks in restraining patients. "Marco, I know this is going to be hard for you to do, but we're going to have to do it. And better you than Steve."

"Doc, how long will he need to be restrained? He's going to hate it." And he left unsaid that it would tear Steve's heart if he saw his son that way.

Doc sighed, "A couple days, I want to do at least three or four bags of fluid. And yes, Steve's coming tomorrow and will see him tied down. Not much we can do about that. Once I've got the fluids in him, I'll take the IV out. If he drinks enough, he'll be okay. But I could have to repeat it. Although he may be a bit more cooperative about drinking enough if he knows I'll do the IV again."

After discussing strategy, he looked sadly at Marco. "Ready?"

"No, but let's go."

They reentered the room. Doc asked him once more if he'd let him put the IV in. Tommy's body language was answer enough. Doc gave him a warning, "Tommy, if you don't let me put it in, we'll restrain you and then I'll put it in."

Tommy laughed snidely, carefully eyeing his two wardens, "Like hell you will!"

Doc walked to the dresser, removed the multiple heavy duty restraints. Tommy was over by the wall; Doc and Marco approached him carefully. Marco pleaded, "C'mon, Tommy, don't make us do this…" Tommy now had heightened wariness and took on a defensive posture. As they had planned, Doc tackled his legs, and Marco his upper body. Doc had said quick and dirty. Before he knew what had happened, they had him on the bed and were fastening the restraints. Tommy was howling, screaming and swearing like a mortally wounded animal. Doc had said that his reflexes would either be much sharper or much duller due to his withdrawal. Lucky for the two men, they were dulled. Doc triple-restrained his left arm and hand, where he was going to start the IV. When he did insert the line, Tommy shrieked like he was being stuck with a hot poker. And the vulgarities that spewed from Tommy immobilized Marco who just stood there, mouth hanging open. Doc continued explaining that he'd be using a urinal, which yielded many more obscenities. This was necessary as the patient wouldn't be getting up to use the bathroom, and the color of his urine would give Doc a good indication of how well he was rehydrating.

"Doc, is he okay?"

Doc shook his head affirmatively. "It'll pass." And he knew it would, but it was very hard to take.

The next day Steve was on the slate to be with Tommy. Marco said, "Doc, I want to be here tomorrow morning before Steve comes. Let me take tonight for you." Doc understood that he'd want to prepare his friend before seeing his son like this. And that if he talked to him tonight, Steve would rush over. "Okay, Marco." He instructed him how to start a new bag of solution when that one was empty. "Call me if you have any questions or problems. Our 'guest' is angry, but physically speaking, he's okay, or as okay as can be expected. He may or may not sleep. Tell Steve I'll be by early in the morning, probably around 8. And tell him in no uncertain terms that Tommy is to be left in these restraints until further notice from me."

Marco walked to the door with Doc. He stayed out in the fresh air a while. The offensive sounds from the bedroom had stopped. After a few minutes, Marco went back in and to the bedroom. Tommy's eyes were closed, Marco hoped he was sleeping. But he wasn't. The eyes slowly opened and Marco was taken aback by the venom in them, the hatred and rage. These were things he had never seen in the boy. He knew intellectually that it wasn't Tommy, but the drugs. But the intellectual knowledge didn't stop a shiver from piercing straight through his heart.

Gathering his courage, he was going to try to help. He walked over, gently brushed some hair off Tommy's forehead, and feebly said, "Hey, try to relax, Tommy."

Tommy's eyes shot daggers of hot fury to Marco, who involuntarily took a step back. Continuing to look at Tommy, he just said, "Look, call me if you need anything. I'll be here." His kindness was rewarded with a string of obscenities that Marco didn't think Tommy even knew.

Marco got a sleeping bag and camped out that night in Tommy's room. The suffering boy may have slept some, but was restless most of the night. He was usually quiet, but every time you looked at him he radiated hate. Marco felt badly that he was suffering so much. He was also shocked at the depth of this addiction, how it had taken hold of his young godson. He had seen drug addicts before, but never anything as personal as this. It hurt, and was painful to watch and be a part of. He wanted to be there for Tommy and Steve, and would be, but that motivation didn't lessen the sorrow.

Dawn came, Marco tried to feed his charge some breakfast, which he didn't want. Much less hostile than the night before, his attitude was more defeated this morning. He did drink a half glass of orange juice. He begged Marco to release him, which wasn't going to happen without Doc's okay, no matter what the boy said.

Marco heard Steve's car drive up around six, early, but he had expected that. His friend was surprised to see him instead of Doc, whom he expected. He looked perplexedly at his young associate as the door was opened. Marco stepped outside on the entry porch, "Let's talk, Steve."

Immediately on alert, Steve looked past Marco into the house. As he blocked him from rushing into the house, Marco reassured him, "Tommy's okay, he's inside. I spent the night instead of Doc. I wanted to talk with you this morning before you saw Tommy."

Tersely, Steve asked, "Why?"

Marco took a deep breath. "Steve, when Doc came last night and examined him, he said he was getting dehydrated and wanted to start an IV for fluids and some glucose." Marco looked at Steve, who was getting impatient, "And?"

"And it didn't go over too well. Tommy wanted none of it, Doc said it was necessary."

"Sooooo? Get to the point, Marco!"

"Steve, we had to restrain him to get the IV line started. He's still restrained and will be until Doc says he can stop the IV." He laid his hand on his friend's arm, "Steve, he's pretty angry and …. well… nasty is a mild word. It's not him, Steve, it's the drugs. He's probably going to hate you as well. And try to convince you to untie him. You can't do that, Steve."

Steve was ready to rush past his friend and see his son. Marco knew Steve was acting as he had to, but grabbed his arm before he went in and warned, "Steve, Tommy's under the influence of drugs and withdrawal right now. He's not the son you know." That was a statement Steve didn't want to hear, and in his heart, didn't believe.

He opened the bedroom door and saw his son, sweaty, ragged, in pain and agony, tied to the bed. Tommy was quiet, his eyes drawn to the door when it opened. He quietly and calmly said, "Dad...."

Marco had come in with Steve and watched at the door. Steve rushed over and sat next to his son, looking him over, hating the restraints, the urinal sitting there, all of it. "Hey, Tommy, what goes?"

Tommy shrugged, sneaking a glance at Marco. "I screwed up, Dad. Doc wanted to start an IV because I'm dehydrated and I... well.. I wasn't exactly cooperative. He and Uncle Marc had to tie me down to get the IV in. I'm sorry. And I said some pretty awful things to them."

Tommy seemed completely in control of himself, and remorseful of his earlier actions. Marco knew it was all an act. He moved over to the foot of the bed and crossed his arms. Tommy ignored him, knowing that Marco was seeing through his act.

Tommy lay there a bit, then asked "How are things with you, Dad?" Marco was amazed at how well he was carrying this off. And he saw that Steve was completely taken in. Normally Steve was way too savvy to be hoodwinked, but right now, his emotions were playing havoc with his common sense.

"I'm okay, Tommy. How are you?"

"I dunno, dad. Okay. Better, I think. Doc said that if I had some fluid and calories in me, I'd feel better. And he's right. I do." He moved a bit and moaned.

Steve asked, "What's' wrong?"

Tommy sighed, "Nothing, really. I'm just kind of sore and stiff from being in one position too long."

Marco thought to himself that Tommy was playing this game really well; he had not asked Steve to untie him.

Steve, without thinking said, "Here, let me untie you so you can move around. You won't pull out the IV or anything, will you?"

Tommy modestly shook his head no. Marco grabbed Steve and pulled him out of the room and shut the door. "Steve, you can't do that. Tommy's playing games with you! You can't trust him."

Steve was incensed with Marco, and ranted, "You think I don't know my own son? You've got him in there hog tied like some animal and now you're telling me I'm supposed to let you continue that kind of treatment. Aitkins, you're pushing way beyond your right!"

Marco met him face to face, and returned the volley with as much force, "No, the kid in there is not your son. Not right now, anyway. He's a sneaking, drug addicted kid whose actions are motivated by one thing and that's getting a fix. You don't know him, and he's hog tied for his own good, and he's staying that way until Doc says otherwise!"

Steve didn't reply, but gave Marco a good shove. Marco stood his ground and shoved back. "No!" Steve was ready to use more force on his friend, but instead locked his gaze on Marco's. The long-time loyalty of his kainkaina penetrated his mind. Marco was wrong, he was sure of it. But his friend was so adamant.

Marco pleaded, "Steve, look. Doc's coming out this morning, early he said. He should be here in an hour or so. Please, let's wait for him. See what he says."

Unpleased with the situation, Steve curtly replied, "Okay," and turned and went back in the bedroom. Tommy looked at him pitifully. The father almost rescinded his word to Marco, who looked at him shaking his head no almost imperceptibly. Tommy caught all this. Steve said, "Hey, son, look, Marco thinks we should wait for Doc to get here before we do anything. He'll be here soon." And went over and stroked his son's forehead. Tommy tensed up at the edict and the touch, but tried valiantly to keep his calm façade. Quietly he said, "Okay, Dad." Then turned a bit and moaned again. He really wanted to get loose before Doc got back; he knew the nasty old guy would never let him go. He wanted to get loose and then he'd hightail it out of there. He knew he'd be able to get away if he had a chance. Then he could find Anderson— or anybody— and get what he really needed. To hell with Doc and his withdrawal!

Steve began to reach for the wrist restraint and Marco grasped his hand mid-air, but didn't say anything. Steve looked at Tommy, then Marco, and back to Tommy. The boy looked so sad, so down. Loosening one arm couldn't hurt. But Marco gripped tighter, not to physically impede Steve, but as a reminder to what he had agreed in the hallway. Steve withdrew his hand and reached to rub his son's shoulders.

At that point Tommy knew he had lost the battle. He was livid. And he let it be known to Marco and his Dad. Steve staggered backward at the toxins spewing from his son's mouth, and the strength of the intangible waves of loathing and fury emanating from Tommy. He blinked, stunned into speechlessness. Marco took him, pulled him out of the room and shut the door. He escorted him outside onto the lanai, closing the door behind them. You could still hear Tommy seething. Marco sat Steve down and got close to him. "Steve, that's not Tommy. It's the drugs, the withdrawal."

Steve shook his head, looking at his friend, but not really seeing anything, "My God, Marco...."

Marco reassured him, "Steve, he will come out of it. Doc said so. Others have done it." His friend and boss was in a state of shock. "Look, Steve, why don't you forget today. Leave. Go home. Paint. Go for a run. Go to work. Anything but being here. Doc or I will take your turn. You come when he's better."

Steve just shook his head no. He looked wistfully inside towards the bedroom. "I need a few minutes, Marco. Just stay here with me." And the two sat in silence a while.

Then Steve swallowed, took a deep breath, and said, "Okay, God help me. And Tommy. I'm going back in there. I'm not going to abandon him. But I also know you're right. I'm not going to untie him." When he said "God help me," that wasn't just a phrase he was using, he truly meant it as a prayer.

The two went back into the bedroom. Tommy lay shivering now. Steve covered him with a blanket, offered him a drink of water or juice. Tommy swore at him. Steve only winced a bit, sat on the bed next to his son, who as much as possible under restraints moved away. "Sorry, buddy. I'm sticking with Doc and Marco on this one. I love you, and I'm here for you, but I will not listen to your demands, nor give in to them. That kind of garbage is not you, but the drugs. We've been through tough times before, my son, and we'll weather this as well." Tommy spat at him. Steve simply wiped it off, then he got a damp washcloth and began to bathe his son's fevered face.

Tommy went back to sympathy/pity mode. Begging and crying, whimpering and sobbing. Marco knew it was torture for Steve, but he didn't relent at all. From somewhere when they were out on the lanai, he had gathered an inner strength. Perhaps his prayer had fortified him, but he was solid now.

Doc came, and came into the bedroom. He took a look at Steve and Marco. "Tough morning?"

In unison they replied, "Yes." Doc then looked at Tommy and examined him. Tommy remained quiet, cooperative. He (supposedly) sheepishly asked, "Doc, I'll stay still. Please undo me." Doc knew it was fake, he had felt the tension the second he touched Tommy's wrist to take his pulse. Plus you could see it streaming off him.

"Sorry, Tommy, not yet. Maybe tomorrow." With that pronouncement came another round of epitaphs that would embarrass a Marine. Doc ignored it, the three left the room.

Over the next two days Doc kept hydrating him with the IV fluids, and finally decided to remove the IV and restraints. Steve had been with him part of that time, Bobby, Doc and Marco also each taking a turn. Tommy had given up his hostility, for now anyway. Doc had warned all the caretakers that he was still in a very precarious state and likely to have times when his craving for a drug would be overwhelming, that he'd try anything to get some, or get away.

But for now he had a defeatist, resigned attitude. Doc talked softly to him as he removed the IV, then the restraints. Steve was there. Tommy simply said, "Thanks." Then he stretched and rolled over, hugging the covers to him. His attitude towards his dad was one of abandonment. Steve rubbed his shoulders a while, Tommy didn't jerk away, nor did he acknowledge it, except Steve was aware of a degree of relaxing of the muscles. Doc brought in some orange juice and toast. He drank some of the juice, left the toast untouched.

The next day, Marco and Steve were in the living room talking. Tommy had gotten out of bed and went to the door. It was unlocked— it hadn't been before, the many times he tried it. He peeked out, unnoticed, and surveyed the situation. Immediately he began planning an escape strategy. The quickest route was to get down the hall, around the corner and out the front door. His options were to try escape now or wait and see if Dad and Marco might move someplace where he'd be less likely to be seen. Tommy's thinking was still obscured by the drugs. The adults had forgotten to lock the door, but there was no way he'd make it around them. If he had been alert, he probably could have slipped into another bedroom and snuck out a window there.

But Tommy tried to stealthily sneak down the hall. As soon as he turned the corner, he bolted for the door and actually made it out and maybe a few dozen yards down the drive before being tackled by Marco. He fought like a banshee and it took all Steve and Marco had to get him back in, kicking and screaming. He managed to land a solid blow on Steve's face, giving him what would be a nasty black eye.

They got into the bedroom and released him. Steve was getting mad. He was lacking sleep, his emotions had been doing flip-flops since this started, and he was just fed up with all this.

He laid into his son, "Dang it, Tommy! That's ENOUGH! Too bad you're so miserable, but this is something you're just going to have to go through. Now stop your fighting and cooperate with us. We're trying to help you!"

Tommy sneered at his Dad, "Go to hell!"

Steve took a step over, looked like he was ready to belt him one. Tommy stood his ground, defiantly staring at his dad. And instead of slapping him, Steve grabbed him in a bear hug and embraced his son, "It's going to be okay, Tommy. I love you."

Tommy melted into the hug, his body heaving with sobs. Steve held him until he fell asleep, and then gently lowered him to the bed. Before he exited the room, he laid a hand on his son's head. *God, help this all to be over soon. I don't think any of us can take much more.*

Chapter 27
Beginning to Get Better

Going into the kitchen and looking at the clock, Steve was surprised to find he had been in Tommy's room over an hour. Marco had gone to work, and had left a note for him.

Bobby was the relief that night. He came by about six and had a huge pizza, along with breadsticks and salad. It smelled delicious. Steve took a serving in to Tommy. Surprisingly, he ate almost a whole slice. "Thanks, that was good." He then went back to sleep. Doc had said that all this sleeping at this point was normal; his body had been through the wringer and needed the sleep to recover.

Over the next two days Tommy got better. And began to eat and drink small amounts. It had been two weeks; the boy began to settle down consistently. His sleep seemed somewhat restful as opposed to the agitated tossing and turning he had been doing. His appetite was poor, but better than non-existent; he'd at least try things brought to him. He didn't have any more obscene outbursts or try to escape (though they still kept him locked in the room). He'd talk with his "babysitters" as he referred to his caretakers a little, more than just the mono-syllabic answers or "no" answers he had been giving.

Doc said he was improving. You could see it, though he still looked quite thin and haggard..

At the two and a half week mark, one morning he was lying in bed. Doc was with him, Steve walked in. Tommy looked tired, but somehow improved. His eyes were clearer. "Hey, son, you're looking better. How goes it?"

Tommy looked at him and Doc, truly looked, not just a dull stare. "Dad, Doc, thanks. You guys have been great. I know I've been terrible to you, I'm sorry. But I really want to thank you for all you've done."

That coherency got a big smile out of both of them. In unison they replied, "You're welcome."

Tommy continued, "Dad, can I ask a favor, please?"

Anxious to please his son, but wary, Steve cocked his head asking what.

Tommy looked at Doc. "Dad, Doc's been great, really he has. And he's given his house and all, and his pajamas. But… Dad… he's a really lousy cook. Can you make me something good to eat?"

Steve laughed heartily. He was so happy to see Tommy joke— you could tell he was feeling better. And he wanted to eat— he had had no appetite at all the last weeks and was looking mighty thin. "You bet, son! Anything in particular?"

"Anything, Dad. Everything you make is good."

Steve headed to the kitchen. Tommy looked at Doc, grinned, "No offense, Doc, but it's the truth."

Doc smiled. "Why do you think I keep Helen around?"

Tommy stretched, "Doc, okay if I get up and take a shower and get dressed? I'm sick of being in bed."

"Sounds great, Tommy. But you're weak, weaker than you may think. Take it easy, and I'll be right there to help if you need it."

Tommy thought Doc was overly cautious, but that was okay. He did feel weak in the shower and sat on the floor in it, assuring Doc he was okay and wanted to stay there, letting the warm water spray massage his body, just while he sat down. After a long shower, he got dressed, with Doc's help, and smelled good things from the kitchen. He knew his dad would be bringing a tray in to the bedroom, but right now he just wanted out of that room where things had been so wretched for him. "Doc, I want to eat in the kitchen." Doc understood and slowly he helped him make his way there. Tommy sat at the dinette table and his dad served him a beautiful looking plate of pineapple and coconut crepes with fresh orange juice glaze. It looked delicious and Tommy began to eat. Steve was surprised and grateful to see him up and dressed but he also saw how that little exertion almost wiped him out. After less than a half dozen bites he was ready to fall asleep and drop head first into his plate. They were going to help him back to his room. Tommy gently resisted, "Please, can I go anyplace but back there? I just….. that room… I can sleep on the couch, on the lanai, anyplace. Handcuff me to the railing if you want."

They understood, and Doc took him to the other guest bedroom. Tommy lay on the bed and was asleep, a sound peaceful restful sleep, in minutes. Doc quietly said to Steve, "I think the worst is over." And they silently exited back into the main living area.

Steve asked Doc, "What next? Just time? Or can we expect more …. drama? Is he completely withdrawn now?"

"We'll have to play it by ear, Steve. Most likely he'll still, for a while, a few weeks maybe, every now and then crave drugs. He's not completely out of the woods yet. I'll want him to stay here, and continue being watched another few weeks. And we'll have to cover with him, or someone will, ways of dealing with stress and pressure, so when he runs into problems again he deals with it in a less destructive way. Talking with Samuel Goldberg might be a good idea."

"I'll call him."

That night was Marco's turn to stay with Tommy. The boy woke about four a.m., and went out to visit with his Uncle Marc. They talked some, Marco was pleased with the way his godson looked and acted— much better than two days ago. They fixed an early breakfast together, and Tommy asked if it was okay if he went outside— he hadn't been out since he'd come to Doc's. That was fine with Marco and the two of them went out to the beach and watched a beautiful sunrise. Tommy was still very weak and tired easily, so after they walked the short distance back up to the house, Tommy went back to bed for a nap.

Steve came back again the next night— it was his turn for night duty. He didn't think of it that way, if it were up to him, he would spend all his time with Tommy until he was recovered, the others made him balance things. Tommy was up in the living room, dressed. He looked at his dad, "Dad, what happened to your eye? Were you in a fight or something?"

Steve looked carefully at Tommy. It was apparent that the boy truly was unaware that he had punched his dad. Steve laughed, "Yeah, you could say I was in a fight." Marco looked at his friend out of the corner of his eye. Tommy noticed the glance and thought about it as his dad and Marco talked shop. He got up, went to his dad, studied the black eye carefully.

"Dad, I didn't do that to you, did I?"

Steve never lied to his son, but didn't want him feeling bad. He replied, "Not the Tommy I know. There was this kid strung out on drugs who didn't know what he was doing and couldn't control himself." Tommy slumped down on the couch, horrified with himself.

He shook his head sadly, "Dad…."

Steve sat next to him, "Tommy, you were in full blown withdrawal, you really didn't have control of yourself."

The black eye stared at Tommy, "Dad, I'm so sorry….."

"No problem, buddy." He slapped his son on the back.

Tommy looked at Marco, then his dad again, as things began to sink in. He thought now about the boarded up bedroom window, the locks. Hesitatingly, he asked, "Dad, what else did I do?"

Steve wanted to save his son any further pain, trying to skirt the issue, "Nothing that was any big deal."

Tommy looked at him knew there was more. "Tell me, Dad. Please."

Steve sighed, looked down. "Well, let's just say if you ever join the military, you won't need any lessons on … language… sometimes used by soldiers. I had no idea you knew words like that. And you were pretty angry with me and Marco and Doc, all of us, because we wouldn't get you drugs. Let's just say we got some pretty intense verbal lashings from you."

"What'd I'd say, Dad? I don't remember."

"I'm not going to repeat it, Tommy. It doesn't make any difference. It wasn't you, it was the influence of the drugs. End of discussion."

He could see in his dad's face that he had been hurt by whatever he had said. And probably others as well. Again he apologized to his dad, and Marco, then later to Doc, and Bobby.

"Dad, will you forgive me for the pain I've caused you? Not just in becoming addicted, but also whatever I said or did the last few weeks?"

Steve hugged his son, "Yes, Tommy, all is forgiven. I love you, son."

Over the next four days, he slowly regained some strength, and his old personality. A few mental scars from his ordeal were still there, probably always would be. He began to badger Doc about going home. Doc was beginning to sway in that direction. They had arranged for some of his friends to visit, which helped his boredom.

Take My Hand

One day when Steve arrived, he heard Tommy singing, a sound he hadn't heard in quite a while. He loved his melodic voice, and the fervor, the emotion he put into his singing. The song was from Peter, Paul and Mary, "Day is Done". Steve liked the lyrics, he wondered what they meant to Tommy (if anything):

> Tell me why you're crying, my son
> I know you're frightened, like everyone
> Is it the thunder in the distance you fear?
> Will it help if I stay very near?
> I   am   here.
>
> And if you take my hand my son
> All will be well when the day is done.
> And if you take my hand my son
> All will be well when the day is done.
> Day is done, Day is done
> Day is done, Day is done

Steve had talked years earlier with Tommy about using his voice, singing for the church choir, or entering talent shows, that kind of thing. Tommy wasn't interested, Steve didn't push it. The boy was content just to sing as he went about his day. Steve very much enjoyed it as 'background noise"; sometimes in jest he'd refer to Tommy as his "lark". Steve knew that music was an important thing. It can affect us, our moods, our feelings, even our thinking. Uplifting music can energize us, soothing music can calm us. And lyrics can program our minds, even if we seem to be paying no attention to them. Steve and Tommy pretty much enjoyed the same kinds of music; usually there was something quietly in the background. Steve had made sure there was good calming music playing during much of Tommy's withdrawal.

Samuel paid a visit. He and Tommy sat outside in the sun on the beach many hours talking. Tommy freely opened up to the psychiatrist, talking about how he had gotten to the point he did, what he might do differently to deal with building stress and pressure.

The school year was over now, but arrangements were made for Tommy to finish up his work and take his finals when he was feeling better. He and Doc and his dad also had some long talks on handling stress and pressure from exams as well, and other things. Tommy, Doc, Marco and Samuel all thought he had a pretty good handle on it and that he wouldn't turn to drugs again to solve problems.

Tommy was wondering about the drug pusher. "Dad, did you ever go after Larry Anderson?"

Steve sighed, "Yes. He was found a few weeks back dead in an alley from stab wounds. Looks like someone was after drugs he had and killed him for them. Not an unexpected thing when you're dealing drugs."

There was one more thing on Tommy's mind. "Dad, I remember, just a bit, something you said to Doc when we first got here. Something about this being your fault." He looked at his dad, whose gaze was downward.

Tommy realized he was right in his judgment of that conversation, that his dad felt terribly guilty. He tried to set him straight and said determinedly, "Dad, none of this is your fault. You did not push me too hard. No one did. I let it happen, I let myself get in too deep, to overdo it. I'm at fault, no one else, certainly not you. You never gave me any pills; you never popped them into my mouth. ME. I did it. Not you. You tried to figure out what was wrong, you knew something was, and I hid from you. I weaseled out of your attempts to talk or be together. Not your fault, Dad. Don't blame yourself."

One part of Steve knew his son was right. But a much bigger part felt guilty. He also knew that guilt could tear a person or family apart terribly. "Oh, God, Tommy, I'm sorry I wasn't a better father for you the last month. You're right. I do feel guilty.

I should have seen the signs. I did see them, but I was blinded. I let myself be blinded. I chose not to face it head-on. I didn't know what was wrong, I knew something was, but I didn't doggedly hang in there until I found out. I let it go. I let you down."

"Dad, no, I don't see it that way at all...." Steve interrupted him, hugged his son, placing his arm around the boy's shoulders.. "C'mon, let's walk a bit."

They walked slowly along the beach in silence. Finally Steve said, "Okay. I think we both made mistakes. Let's forgive each other, and ourselves, and move on. No more talk, no more blaming ourselves." He smiled as he stopped and faced Tommy, looking at him as he suggested this. Tommy was going to reply with something, but changed his mind, and smiled, and nodded yes as he gave his dad a big hug. And they walked back, each having a peaceful heart.

Steve made a mental note to get to Confession. Since that "first" time some years back, he sometimes went, but pretty sporadically. When he did go, he felt good afterwards, but maybe a few times a year was it. But there was something about Confession relieving guilt. Steve had learned a lot about guilt. In its place, some guilt can serve as a compass as to what is right and wrong. But then once you know what's wrong, either fix it, if you can, or let it go, if you can't. History is history, you can't back up life. You can only move on. And way too many people let guilt handicap them. He learned that people usually did the best they could at any given time. And so they often needed to forgive themselves for real or imagined offenses. Not always an easy thing to do, but very helpful for good mental health.

One clear breezy morning after Mass, Steve again stayed in the pew, this time thinking about another "religious" thing. Something Doc had taught him was beginning to fall into place— The Communion of Saints. During the Creed, Catholics pray, and he prayed it along with everyone else, "We believe.... In the

Communion of Saints…" Steve never really understood what that meant. He still didn't, but had a sneaking suspicion that at least part of the doctrine meant that Doc was up there in heaven watching out for him, steering him into things like Confession. He sure wouldn't have done that on his own. It made him chuckle to think of Doc up there keeping an eye on him. And it warmed his heart.

Doc, are you up there looking out for me? Are you… interceding… in some way? Doing things from up there? Is that how it works? Well, if you are, thanks. And if it's you, God, or someone else, thanks to you, too!

He wasn't quite sure if he was "asking" Doc or God. He just had a feeling that Doc was doing things to help him out, guide him, and direct him. He looked up to the church ceiling. At that action, he laughed at himself, wondering what he expected to see.

He didn't really expect anything, but on the other hand, so many supernatural things had been happening to him, he wouldn't have been surprised. But there was no smell of roses or flowers, no flashing lights, floating angels, no statue changed expression, no door that slammed, the rosary in his pocket wasn't warm. He had been hoping for some kind of sign and was disappointed in not getting any.

Again he laughed at himself. *Yeah, Doc, that would be just like you. Letting me figure it out for myself. You're up there, I can tell, chuckling at my predicaments here, and not sending me any sign or confirmation, just letting me fumble along.* Then, as Steve thought more seriously, he reflected on the many small signs and miracles he had been given over the last months. Few people ever get any as directly as he had. Many people, he supposed, had miracles in their lives but never realized it. But he had been the recipient of some very special gifts: the rosary that had changed color and sometimes warmed, the smell of roses on several occasions, that heavenly taste he still experienced a little bit at Holy Communion, the overwhelming powerful feeling of God's personal intimate love and approval of him. *Thank you, Lord, for so very much! Help me to remain a faithful, humble servant of yours.*

During the years Steve lived with Doc, he went to Mass every Sunday, and Confession a few times each month. Doc helped him prepare for his Confirmation. Steve chose the name Michael as a Confirmation name; at the time he liked the idea of Michael being a warrior, a defender. The holy cards and statues all had him pictured as big and strong with a mighty sword, looking impressive. He had a revelation that he was a defender— he had always wanted to be and realized he was. *I want to defend Tommy, from bad and evil things happening to him. That is what I've been doing, and a big part of what this is all about. When I was young I had no defender. That was wrong, and I want to be "Michael" for Tommy. I am Michael.*

The day came when Doc let Tommy go home. He was overjoyed, so was everyone. Steve hadn't been home much over the last few weeks, he spent most of his time at work or Doc's. When he was home, the house seemed empty. It would be good to be back there with Tommy. Steve had arranged for two days off. He really wanted to take more, but didn't want to appear to be hovering to Tommy. And he did want to do some mini-vacations and one-day excursions, but that would be better later, when Tommy was stronger. Both father and son enjoyed their first day back home… lazy, calm, peaceful.

Life was good. And Steve and Tommy lived happily ever after. Life was fairly uneventful for several years.

Chapter 28
Tommy Grows Up

Tommy had been Steve's son now for almost six years; he was nearing seventeen, They had been through much during that time. Like when Tommy disobeyed Steve and went dirt bike riding alone, ending up with a broken arm. And they weathered Tommy's drug addiction. Both father and son had grown, as individuals and as a family.

Summer was just starting. Steve had cut back some with his work when he adopted Tommy— he still put in well over forty hours most weeks, but also made spending time with Tommy a priority. And he enjoyed being with him. Tommy was growing up, becoming a very nice young man.

The two were making supper one night, Steve working slowly, studying his son. People, including Steve, were amazed at how much alike they looked despite no biological connection. Tommy had dark hair, like Steve. For a while he had let it grow long, long enough for a pony tail, but decided he didn't like that and choose a hair style similar to his dad's. While he wasn't lanky like Steve, he was lean and slender, almost willowy. His features were attractive, he had a solid face, though his jaw was not as square as his dad's. His eyes twinkled brightly. He had recently just hit the six foot mark in height. Steve chuckled inside as he thought about how young Tommy looked. He barely had even any peach fuzz over his lip. That was fine by Steve.

Personality-wise, Tommy was sensitive. His intuition was usually pretty keen and on target. Tommy was generous, always wanting to help others, and he had a gentle demeanor that naturally led others to trust him. Seeing the big picture was something he was good at, a trait that helped to make him a natural leader. Friends were easily made for Tommy— he had many. But he was also rather reserved and guarded about parts of his life, and few knew him really well.

While he wasn't a great athlete, he was comfortable with his body and enjoyed sports. He had tried swimming, diving, track, golf, tennis, surfing and more. Tommy did fine in them, but just didn't really want to devote the time and energy to them to be at the top. He enjoyed playing handball with his dad now and then, sometimes even winning. One activity he did participate in consistently was martial arts. He and his dad usually met two mornings a week at six a.m. with Steve's long-time master for sessions. Tommy had worked up to a brown belt. Sometimes Master Fen would pair him with his dad for sparring. Once in a great while he would be able to pull one over on his dad, which gave him great pleasure. Usually his dad whomped him. The teacher would sometimes handicap Steve, pinning an arm behind him, or adding weights to his ankles. Tommy enjoyed those rounds best. All in all, Tommy was quite attractive and handsome.

They shared their evening meal together on the lanai. Small talk included Tommy's plans for the summer. He was going to be doing research for Professor Carlson for a book, plus various chauffeuring and errands for the elderly gentleman. The professor was declining some physically and unable to drive much anymore or do certain jobs that needed doing. So it worked well for Tommy to be his assistant in several areas.

In the fall, he'd be a student at the University Of Hawaii Institute Of Astronomy and had been able to land a spot for his first semester at the Mauna Kea Observatory which was situated on the Big Island of Hawaii. He was the youngest student, but with his exceptional intellect he had already done some advanced placement tests, and taken some college courses and done well. He'd be living in a small dorm. Steve knew he was ready for the challenge and excited about it. Tommy was mature socially and mentally for his age, he expected him to do fine despite being only seventeen. He was going to miss him, though. The Big Island was not that far away, but also not just a quick drive. And a long distance phone call. Tommy was a bit nervous and admitted it.

After they cleaned up from supper, Tommy asked, "Dad, can we talk some?"

Steve gave Tommy his full attention. "Sure, son. What's on your mind?"

Tommy cocked his head towards the beach, "Out on our rock?" The large boulder had been privy to many serious discussions over the years; it was a secluded place where there would be no interruptions.

"Sure."

Together they walked out. Steve didn't think anything was amiss with Tommy, he was pretty good at reading his moods and his son didn't seem upset or tense at all. Steve was patient as they watched the waves. Tommy looked sideways at his dad and grinned.

With a perplexed look on his face Steve asked, "What?"

"I need your advice, Dad."

Steve waited a minute, and his son was not forthcoming with any other information. Finally he said, "On?"

Again Tommy looked at his dad and chuckled. "Women!"

Steve raised his eyebrows and chuckled, "Ahhhhh!"

Tommy still didn't say anything. Steve took an accurate guess, "Megan?"

With a wide smile, Tommy nodded. Father and son had had some long talks about women, girls, sex, respect, expectations; they had covered all the important basics. Steve was pretty confident Tommy was on a solid base with all that. Doc Burns had drilled into Steve respect for women. Everything from holding doors open to being considerate and never taking advantage of women. Steve took on the job of imparting those same values to Tommy and did well instilling a proper attitude into his son.

Tommy didn't date much, but he enjoyed time with friends, both male and female. He'd go to parties and sometimes movies or other things with girls, and/or friends. Socially he was fine, moderately popular. About four months ago he began dating a girl from his school. Megan was only fifteen, but mature for her age, and smart. She'd be a junior next year. Steve had met her on several occasions and liked her. Some of Tommy's friends almost seemed afraid of Steve, but she wasn't intimidated by him, or his job and position; she was courteous and respectful. Tommy had invited her out to the house a few times as well.

"What exactly are you thinking about, Tommy?"

"You've never gotten married, Dad. But you've been in love, right?"

Steve nodded, remembering. "Tell me about it, Dad."

Steve looked at Tommy and smiled. "Susan was my first love. I was in the Navy. I had had girlfriends now and then, but no one serious like her. She was wonderful; I loved her and wanted to marry her. And she loved me, too, I think. In one way."

"So what happened? Why didn't you get married?"

Steve sighed. "She was dishonest with me. She was engaged to another man, committed to him. He was in Europe, she was here in Hawaii. It was very hard to deal with the deception and all."

He wasn't forthcoming with any more information, so Tommy asked, "There was another one, wasn't there, Dad?"

"Yes, Tommy." Steve smiled again, in remembrance. "I met Andrea working on a case. We began dating, fell in love and planned to get married. She ended up getting murdered. I'm not proud to say if Marco hadn't stopped me I may well have killed the guy when I caught up to him." His face took on a sadness for a moment.

The two sat in silence for a while, Steve reminiscing, Tommy pondering. Then Steve looked at his son, "So… why all the questions?"

"I'm trying to figure out love. I mean, I know you can take a lifetime and still not get it all, but I'm trying to sort things out."

Steve waited good-naturedly for him to continue. "Dad, I'm not saying I love her or anything. I like her, I really like her. I enjoy being with her. And I have thought about her as a wife. I could see myself spending the rest of my life with her. Not saying I want to get married soon or anything, just that I could see that as a possibility. Maybe I do love her, I really don't know."

He was quiet a bit, then continued. "The thing is, I'll be leaving in a few months. She'll only be a junior in school. I don't really want her to be committed to me, to me alone and not to be able to go out and have fun with other people. And really, the same for me. I just don't think it's a good idea for us to bind ourselves to each other, committing not to ever see anyone else. But I really like her. I'm not really sure how to say that to her. I want her to know how much I like her, but that I want her to be 'free', so-to-speak, while I'm gone. Understand?"

Steve nodded, "Ummmhummm, yeah. That sounds like a good plan, Tommy. If you're right for each other, it will work out." He didn't want to say too much, preferring his son to work it out himself; it taught him more that way.

They sat in silence a while longer. Then Tommy said, "You know, Dad, there's something that really bugs me. I even went to see Dr. Epstein about it a few months back." This was news to Steve; Doc had said nothing to him. He was concerned, but waited for his son to continue.

Tommy looked at him and said in a defeated voice, "Dad, I'm almost seventeen. I look like I'm about thirteen. Did you know that I've been pulled over twice by HPD when I've used Professor Carlson's car? They thought I was some underage driver out joyriding!" Steve hadn't heard about that.

"I went to see Dr. Epstein about …. maturity. Like why don't I have a beard yet. I mean, you get a five o'clock shadow by noon, I don't even shave yet! There's nothing on my face! He said there's nothing wrong, even that it was good for a person not to mature too early. You know what they call me at school?"

Steve was having a hard time holding in his amused reaction. This was serious for Tommy, he didn't want to make light of it. So in reply, he just shook his head no.

Turning red with embarrassment, Tommy confessed, "Baby Face! BABYFACE, Dad! It's embarrassing."

Steve tried to help, "It'll happen, Tommy. All in good time."

"Can't be too soon for me, Dad! Dad, the other day I took a message for the Professor, and the guy on the phone said, 'Thanks, Miss' when he was done. A lot of the time people on the phone think I'm a girl!"

"You know, Tommy, you might want to talk with Marco. He looks younger than he is. Did I ever tell you about one of the first times he went undercover?"

Tommy shook his head. Steve snickered as he related the tale. "We were handling a case that had to do with a man's high school son and a cult. Marco went undercover into the high school as a student. He had a hard time convincing both students and teachers there that he really was a senior— they all thought he was a freshman. He was twenty-three. Talk with him; I think he might understand where you're at pretty well."

The pair chatted a bit more in general about relationships, school, summer, and more, then headed back in. It had been a good talk.

A few weeks later they had a Sunday sailing outing planned with Marco. A few days before, Tommy asked if it was okay if he invited Megan. That was fine with Steve, he told Marco to bring a date as well. And Steve invited a friend himself. They were all looking forward to it.

Sunday dawned bright and sunny. Steve's date had canceled— her mother had suddenly become seriously ill and had been hospitalized in Chicago and she flew to the mainland to see her. So the five of them gathered at the boat and took off on a fairly calm, sparkling ocean. Steve and Tommy and Marco had been sailing together frequently, all three of them together and also as pairs. They worked efficiently as a team. About forty-five minutes out, Tommy went over to his dad, Marco was there talking with him, the girls were at the front of the boat. The boy said, "Dad, it's hot out today."

Steve looked at him, thinking that was kind of a funny thing to say, it was the way he said it that alerted him. He looked at Tommy and said, "Yeeessss… and?"

Tommy looked down, and then looked at Marco and back at his dad, both of whom were shirtless. He sighed, "Meg's never seen me without a shirt." Now Steve understood. It wasn't so hot that you needed to be without a shirt, but warm enough that you could easily be without one. But Tommy was concerned about Megan's reaction to seeing his body, which was full of hideous scars. It was pretty ugly, and Tommy figured she'd be disgusted. He always wore a T-shirt, even when swimming or surfing. Exceptions were when they were in private, alone on the boat, or at a private pool, and only with folks who knew him well, like his dad, Marco, Doc. That was a part of him that he kept private, except for a few select friends. Tommy was a bit concerned about Marco's date as well, but cared less about her and her reaction.

Steve was a "fixer". He liked to fix people's problems, but had learned that often it is best to let them fix their own. So he simply said, "Oh." He could sense Tommy's internal struggle. The boy looked at his dad, decisively pulled his shirt off and headed forward. Steve and Marco watched. Steve said a quick prayer.

The women were looking forward as he approached. "Hey."

They turned, smiling. He moved all the way forward and leaned forward, resting his arms on the front of the boat. Megan's smile faded from her lips, her eyes grew wide with a look of horror. She looked from Tommy's face to his torso, back to his face, then down again. Tommy focused on Megan and said resolutely, "When I was a little kid, before I knew Dad, I got beat up. The scars are from that. They're part of me, my history." Marilyn, Marco's date, didn't say anything, turned and looked back out on the ocean. Megan kept staring at his chest and back, then she looked at his eyes, and back to his body. She gulped and swallowed, then asked, "Does it hurt?" Tommy shook his head no. She reached out very tentatively and touched a scar, tracing her finger along it.

Steve was watching closely. *That took guts, to face this so directly, to actually touch him.* Tommy stood still, not flinching. Steve knew there was no pain, physical pain, but there had to be considerable mental distress for his son, who had suffered so much. The teen spoke to his girlfriend. "I'm okay. It's history." She looked again at him and just nodded, accepting Tommy, and his scars and his history, at least as much as she could for her first exposure to it.

Finally she turned her attention away from his scars and moved to be close to him, side by side, and slid her arm around his waist. She smiled and said, "Hey yourself..." Tommy laughed, smiled widely, put his arm around her shoulder and exhaled.

Steve was impressed again with her bravery. A girl with less mettle would probably have thrown up and turned away. Tommy glanced back at his dad and Marco and gave a thumbs up sign, they smiled back at him, this young lady was a treasure. Marco looked at Steve and wordlessly conveyed the message, "WOW!" Steve agreed.

They landed at a secluded beach for a picnic lunch, some swimming and sunning. Steve didn't have a date, but enjoyed watching his son and Megan. He had some good feelings about this girl and Tommy. Marco's date was reserved — Steve suspected she was pretty repulsed by Tommy, who chose to leave his shirt off. She didn't mean to be, he thought, but seemed the type who couldn't handle things that weren't all perfect and pretty.

When they docked back at the pier and had everything properly stowed away, Marco and Marilyn headed their own way, Steve and Tommy drove Megan home, and Tommy asked if he could stay there for a while. Steve decided to stop at the office and tackle some paperwork, then pick Tommy up in a few hours. It had been a good day.

On the drive home later, he and Tommy talked. Tommy was excited, "You know, Dad, I was really scared today when I took off my shirt. But Megan was awesome! You saw her, Dad! She was able to ... be okay... with me, with the way I look. I half expected her to scream and run away. She's amazing, Dad."

Steve smiled, "Yes, Tommy, she is. I was impressed with her reaction and the way she handled it. She's quite a girl, I think." Tommy grinned broadly at his dad's opinion.

Over the next few weeks Steve saw Megan a few times. He and Tommy went to a special astronomy exhibit at the Science

Museum and Megan came along. And she had come to the house a few more times. Steve continued to be impressed with her—she was mature, self-confident without being arrogant, pleasant, articulate. Tommy's summer work was going well. He was enjoying his time before heading off to college. And he managed to spend a fair amount of it with Megan. She was working part time during the summer at a floral shop.

It didn't escape Steve's keen eye how comfortable Tommy felt around Megan. Truly comfortable. He was at ease with most people, but it seemed with her, there was a degree of openness Steve hadn't seen with any of his son's other friends.

To celebrate Tommy's seventeenth birthday, Steve took him out to an exclusive restaurant. They invited Megan. Together father and son picked her up at her home. They both went in; Steve met her parents for the first time.

"Mr. and Mrs. Danvers, this is my Dad, Steve O'Shaughnessy. Dad, Megan's parents, Mr. and Mrs. Danvers." They shook hands.

"Mr. O'Shaughnessy."

"Make it Steve."

"Great, Steve. Bob and Eleanor." Steve nodded his head cordially. "May I offer you a drink?"

"No, thanks."

Mrs. Danvers suggested ice tea which she had made, Steve accepted. They sat in the spacious living room of the unique home.

"Tommy tells me you're an architect. Did you design this house?"

"Yes, I did. It was fun to work with the slope of the land to design a house to suit it."

"You did an admirable job, it fits beautifully."

Steve continued, "I'd like to compliment you on your daughter, she's a delightful young lady, and I'm impressed with her."

Bob said, "Thank you. She is a gem. Tommy's quite something as well. You adopted him when he was ten, right?"

Steve smiled at the compliment to his son, and said, "Yes, it's been a pleasure being his father." He choose not to pursue the history of their relationship.

Megan came downstairs, ready to go. They all chatted a bit more with small talk, then left. Steve liked Megan's parents. As a seasoned detective, you get a feeling for people pretty quickly and he liked the couple, thought they were good people.

When Steve was together with Megan and Tommy, he could have felt like a third wheel, but never did. It seemed natural and comfortable being with them. He had thought about bringing a date of his own, but that would have been superfluous, unnecessary. And distracting. Steve just wanted to enjoy Tommy and his girlfriend. They had a wonderful evening.

Three weeks later, Steve had a little "Sending Off" party for Tommy, who was leaving the next day. They invited Steve's friends, and Tommy's, classmates, teachers. Keo and Marco more or less took charge and it turned into a full blown luau, but that was fine. All had a good time and wished Tommy good luck.

After all the guests but Megan had left, Tommy and Steve sat and talked with her very late. She had told her parents before they left Steve's that she might be late. Steve assured them he'd make sure she was fine. As the clock hit one a.m., Steve called her folks to let them know she was fine, they were all up late talking, and he'd bring her home later. And they talked another few hours before Steve and Tommy drove her home.

About a month earlier, Tommy had another "woman" talk with his dad out on their rock. "Dad, I need more advice."

Steve waited for his son to continue. Tommy looked at him, was red with embarrassment. "Dad, you know I really like Megan. And you have instilled in me all this stuff about respect and virtue and all that. And I agree with it, I really do. But, sometimes, when we're together….. it gets… really challenging to not go farther than what is right….. I know guys who don't care and go all the way, but I don't want to do that, neither does Megan. But controlling myself sometimes almost seems more than what is possible."

Steve bailed Tommy out from having to explain more. "I know what you mean, Tommy. That's normal."

"So, is there anything I can do, Dad, to…. help…. when it gets hard?"

Steve jerked his head towards his son to see if he had purposely chosen those particular words, realized he hadn't, and then almost spluttered with amusement at his son's unintentional choice of words and unrealized pun. He coughed to mask his chuckle. "Tommy, one of the best things is to avoid time alone together. Go ahead and be together, just not alone, in private places. A walk on the beach is fine, where there are other people. A movie, other people are around. Here, or at her house. The idea is not to be alone together with no one else around. Don't be alone with her in the car. Understand?"

Tommy nodded; he thought that was good advice. That's why it was not odd when he asked Steve to come with him that last night to take Megan home. They drove to her house, and Steve waited in the car while Tommy escorted Megan to the door. He couldn't help but watch as his son embraced the girl, struggling to keep his passion in check. They drove home peacefully, without saying much.

They were scheduled for a mid-afternoon flight the next day, Saturday, to the Big Island. Steve was going to help Tommy get settled in, then return home the following day. School started Monday for him.

It was a bittersweet parting for both of them, But especially Steve. He loved Tommy dearly and the boy had brought so much into his life, had given Steve so much, had helped him grow. And still would. But a part of that life together as father and son was over now. Tommy was growing up and moving on; this was good, expected.

The moment had come. Both had been quiet and subdued as they organized the small dorm room and put away Tommy's things. Steve looked at Tommy, and the tears spilled. And Tommy looked at his dad, and his tears fell. They embraced in a hearty hug. "I love you, Tommy. The day you came into my life it was changed forever. Knowing you, having you as part of my life, is the greatest blessing I've ever had."

Through his sobs, Tommy just said, "Me, too."

Steve drew in a deep breath and held his son at arms' length. He smiled. "I'm happy for you, Tommy. You'll do fine. And I'm not that far away. We'll see each other soon— Thanksgiving for sure. And who knows, maybe I'll just pop over some weekend just to say hi." Tommy nodded, still too emotional to say anything else.

"You okay?" he asked. Another nod. With that, Steve gave his son one more robust hug, then turned and left.

On the flight home, Steve remembered so many things they had shared, good times, and tough times. He smiled to himself. His son had jumped off his own diving board, spring boarding into his life as an adult. He was ready. He knew how to swim, he knew how to float, he even knew how to grab a surfboard and really move. Steve had no qualms about Tommy. And more warmth filled him as he thought about the song Tommy sang earlier that day, one of the boy's favorites (well, not boy anymore, young man— his voice finally had started to change, but he still sounded good). "Day is Done"

And if you take my hand my son
All will be well when the day is done.
And if you take my hand my son
All will be well when the day is done.
Day is done, Day is done
Day is done, Day is done

The "day" started seven years ago when Steve found a small boy curled up sound asleep in his office early one morning. The day had plenty of ups and downs, moments of pain and anguish, and joys and pleasures. The day was done, all was well. Steve's eyes misted over.

He boarded his plane, the flight was nearly empty. Steve was lost in his thoughts. *Thanks to Tommy, I have discovered bonding, healing, a father/son love, even God more intimately.* Reflecting on the words to the song, he suddenly saw them in a bit of a different light:

And if you take My Hand my son

His Hand. He had indeed taken His Hand— God's Hand. Steve realized that Hand was always outstretched, waiting for you or me to take it.

And if you take My Hand my son
All will be well when the day is done.

The tune played in his head the rest of the trip home. Steve was happy, life was good. He was ready for another "day".

It was a short flight, and before long they were deplaning in Honolulu. As he exited the walkway, he was surprised, and grateful, to see Marco waiting for him. "What are you doing here?"

"It's what friends are for."

Steve nodded minutely, slung his arm over Marco's shoulders. They walked silently to the car. The top was down on the mustang. Marco chose to drive a while instead of taking Steve straight home. Waiting at a red light before the entrance to the Coast highway, Marco reached over, and touched Steve's arm. Steve looked at him and smiled. He was grateful for such a good friend. And in his deep baritone, he sang

> And if you take My Hand my son
> All will be well when the day is done.
> And if you take My Hand my son
> All will be well when the day is done.
> Day is done, Day is done
> Day is done, Day is done

The End

Take His hand!

ABOUT THE AUTHOR

Seven children (all adults but the last, my nine year-old) and six grandchildren occupy a fair amount of my time, along with other family and friends. The big garden is getting smaller each year as the birdies fly from the nest. I also enjoy website building and marketing and working with my husband and his business. But writing is the most fun, by far! ☺

Fun Fact: The one time I have been to Hawaii was in December 2011 when my husband and I went there to celebrate our 35th wedding anniversary and I also finished the Honolulu Marathon — my first and only marathon. It was a wonderful trip, I'm very glad I did the marathon (I walked it), and have no plans to do another!

BOOK CLUB AND MORE

When I first wrote this story, I didn't have this intention in mind, but I have come to realize that this novel (and really all fiction books) can change the world. If you read it and in some small way it helps you to better understand yourself or another, better relate to someone, if it teaches you how to deal with painful emotions or move on in life despite hardships, tehn in a tiny way I am changing the world. One person at a time, in one small way. That is powerful!

And so, for those interested, we have started an on-line book club/discussion group with the primary purpose of sharing how my novels and bits in them have affected you; and to consider the lessons the characters experience and how we might apply it to our own lives. This fits it with changing the world! You can get the link at KathySztymanski@bevcomm.net

I am also compiling a customer base/list. This is for the purpose of letting you know about future books (I have two more mostly done in this "series", plus ideas for more!) I won't sell or give your name to others, and I won't send you dozens of emails (you'll get very few). As an added incentive to get on my list, I will send you FREE a short story about Steve. Simply email me and ask for your free short story. KathySzymanski@bevcomm.com

Made in the USA
Charleston, SC
31 March 2013